LONG RIVER

LONG RIVER

A NOVEL BY
JOSEPH BRUCHAC

Fulcrum Publishing
Golden, Colorado

Library of Congress Cataloging-in-Publication Data
Bruchac, Joseph.
    Long River : a novel / by Joseph Bruchac.
        p.   cm.
    Sequel to : Dawn land.
    ISBN 1-55591-213-3
    1. Indians of North America—New York (State)—Adirondack
Mountains Region—Fiction. 2. Man, Prehistoric—New York (State)—
Adirondack Mountains Region—Fiction. 3. Adirondack Mountains
Region (N.Y.)—History—Fiction. 4. Abenaki Indians—Fiction.
I. Title.
PS3552.R794L66   1995
813' .52—dc20   94-36962
                                                                      CIP

Printed in the United States of America

0   9   8   7   6   5   4   3   2   1

Fulcrum Publishing
350 Indiana Street, Suite 350
Golden, CO 80401-5093
(800) 992-2908

Ktsi oleoneh wli dogo wãngan.
Great thanks to all my relations.

CIRCLES

That shape of clay
my fingers found,
an ancient being
formed in stone
between the layers
of long ago.

Further down the river
where a stream
circles into a cove
an owl waits
on an overhanging branch.

Eagles circle
above the Long River.

—Joseph Bruchac

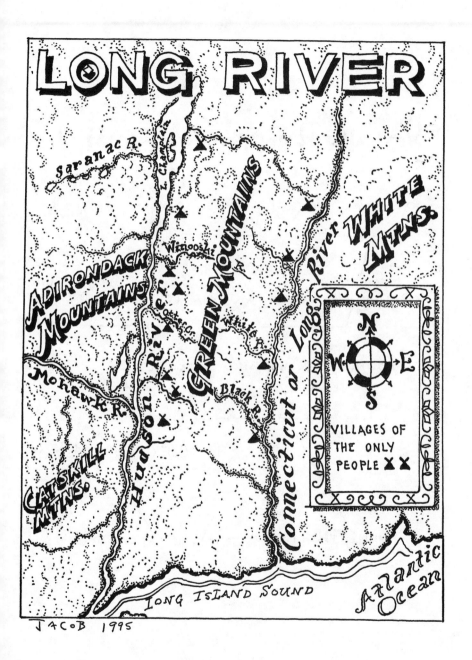

LONG RIVER

Saranac R.

L. Champlain

ADIRONDACK MOUNTAINS

Mohawk R.

CATSKILL MTNS.

Hudson River

Winooski R.

Otter Cr.

GREEN MOUNTAINS

White R.

Black R.

Connecticut or Long River

WHITE MTNS.

N
W E
S

VILLAGES OF THE ONLY PEOPLE ▲▲

LONG ISLAND SOUND

Atlantic Ocean

JACOB 1995

YOUNG HUNTER'S FAMILY

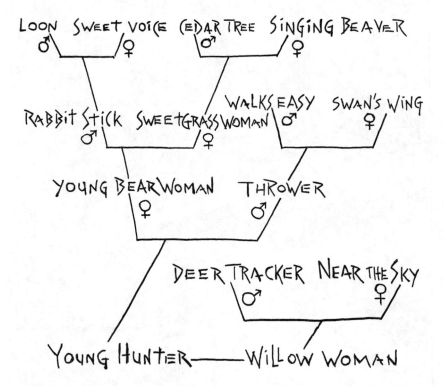

CONTENTS

ABOUT THIS BOOK

Long River, *Kwanitewk,* the name used by the Western Abenaki people of New England to refer to the river at the center of their lands, is the same name found on contemporary maps— even though it is now spelled Connecticut. Then, as now, it flows to the sea and carries with it the memories of many seasons past.

The *Abenaki,* the "Only People," of this story are part of the great Algonquin family of peoples that includes the Chippewa, the Cree, and the Menominee—to name only a few of those Native nations that share similar languages and traditions. The story told in this novel is, like its predecessor *Dawn Land,* a mixture of retellings of Abenaki oral traditions and the dreams that came to me in the course of shaping the tale. Although it is meant to stand on its own, it is also very much a sequel, continuing to tell the story of characters (both dogs and humans) who first appeared in the earlier book. The geography of the novel is that of the area European-Americans call Vermont, but to my Abenaki people it is *Ndakinna,* "Our Land." (That name "Our Land" does not mean that it is a land which the Abenaki people "own" in the European sense. It means more than that: it means that this is the land which shaped us, the land to which we will always be connected, the land which we must care for and respect. And because we human beings are part of the land, it means further that we must care for and respect each other.)

The time when the story takes place is, in European terms, very long ago. To the Abenaki, the "Dawn Land People," it is only yesterday. It is a time not too long after the great mountains of ice, the glaciers, have left the land—eight to ten thousand years ago. And because, in Native time, it is not that long ago, there are many similarities to be found between the way the Only People talk and think and behave and the way American Indian people behave and think and talk today. Human history, on this continent and in general, is much longer than we think if we think only in European terms.

Dawn Land, the first novel in what has now shaped itself toward being at least a trilogy, began with a dream. I woke one morning with the picture fresh in my mind of a young man sitting in front of a sweat lodge, preparing himself spiritually to do something for his people. I sat up in bed and said his name: Young Hunter. Then I got up and began to write—not because I knew his story, but because I wanted to find out what his story was. At each point where I was uncertain which way to go I took my direction from one of two sources—the extensive oral traditions of the Abenaki people (which I have now spent more than three decades only partially learning) and the dreams that came to me many nights during the writing process.

When I finished writing that novel in 1990, I thought I was done with it—until the night two years later when another dream tapped me on the shoulder and I found myself watching Rabbit Stick, the grandfather of Young Hunter, wade into the Connecticut River. So the writing of this sequel began.

Some of the most important characters in this story are not human beings, and I feel I should say a few words about them, especially the dogs. The dogs in this book and its predecessor are very much like the dogs it has been my privilege to spend much of my life with—intelligent, dignified, foolish beings who often make us humans feel unworthy of their devotion at one moment and exasperated beyond belief with them the next. The dogs are also drawn from the dogs in our traditional stories—animals who were given the choice by Gluskabe, our culture hero (one story tells us), to either live with the people and give their lives to them and help them or to be as independent from humans as the mountain lion or the bear. We all know which choice the dogs made and continue to make.

Then there is the Walking Hill. There are numerous stories in the oral traditions of all the Algonquin peoples, not just the Abenaki, of great beasts covered with hair, stiff-legged and with gigantic teeth. In some tales they are called the "stiff-legged bear," in others something like the "walking hill." The fossil record tells us that human beings and mammoths, the extinct shaggy-haired elephants of this continent, were in contact and conflict with each other in the period during and after the most recent ice age. I believe that our stories are a living memory of those times—which may not be as far in the past as some assume. My descriptions of the behavior of the Walking Hill come from many years of reading about elephant behavior, including recent studies that recognize that elephants are more intelligent than previously credited. (I have had a lifetime fascination with natural history and spent three years at Cornell University majoring in Wildlife Conservation before switching my major to English.) My knowledge also comes from a small amount of personal contact with elephants and the elephant lore of indigenous peoples, some during the three years I spent living in West Africa as a volunteer teacher.

Then there are those two interesting beings: *Mikumwesu,* the "Little People,"and the Ancient Ones. Abenaki legends are full of stories about both little people and giants. Both the little ones and the giant beings are very powerful and, depending on various circumstances, can be either benevolent or extremely dangerous. However, unlike the Walking Hill, which our stories tell us have all died, the little people and the giants have never left our land, even though they can be more elusive than the swirling mists that form on the surface of a river at dawn. I have been collecting contemporary stories for a long time from contemporary American Indian people about their experiences with the big people (sometimes called Sasquatch or Bigfoot) and the little ones.

Some of the understandings I've gained from them also went into this novel.

As was the case with *Dawn Land*, I have many people to thank for their assistance along the way. My wife, Carol, first of all, for being my first and best helper and critic with everything. *Everything.* I would like to acknowledge Sally Antrobus, who edited this work as well as *Dawn Land.* Such elders as Cecile Wawanolet of Odanak and Stephen Laurent, who has kept watch over our ancestral lands in the White Mountains of New Hampshire, have continued to help me hear the Abenaki language and see the old stories. Then there are my two sons, who have helped me remember that time of life which Young Hunter embodies. Like him, they know and love to read the messages written in the natural world. Jim, my older son, works with both young people and adults with his Ndakinna Wilderness Project, which has the aim of helping people in this day work toward a better tomorrow by learning the old respect for the earth through traditional survival skills. Jesse, his younger brother, a songwriter (in Abenaki) and a member of a traditional drumming group at our Vermont Abenaki community of Mississquoi, has also been working on a curriculum to teach Abenaki language in the schools.

Seeing how my sons' lives have been shaped in good ways by being raised with the old stories is one of the strongest reasons why I have continued as a storyteller and a writer, continued even in those times—not too many seasons ago—when it seemed no one was interested in listening to the stories Native people have been given: stories to help us all remember, stories of caring, stories that survive against all odds, stories of life.

Listen. Observe. Remember. Share. That is what my elders taught me. That is what I continue to do. That is why I offer you this story, this journey along the Long River. *Wlipamkaani.* Travel well.

LONG RIVER

CHAPTER ONE
THE LONG RIVER

The old man looked down the river. Though late-staying ice still edged the banks, glittering with the yellow light of the morning sun, each snowy crystal holding a bit of the Day Walker's brightness, the river was flowing now with the strength of the season of new life. It pulsed with that new life toward the Great Waters.

"*Kwanitewk*," he said, bending one knee so that he could cup the water in his heartside hand and hold it up to the rising sun, "I have come to speak to you. I have come to tell you what I have seen."

Rabbit Stick drank that first handful of light from the dawn. Then he waded into the icy river and stood, thigh-deep. The current parted around him the way it might divide around the brown trunk of an old cedar whose roots had been loosened by the high waters after a long winter, so that it would slip, still standing, into the Long River, into Kwanitewk.

But this old cedar, Rabbit Stick thought, *can walk out of the river after he is through freezing his lower parts off.* Then his thoughts grew, and he found himself, even as he gathered the right words to speak, remembering his own grandfather wading into this same river at this same season. Like Rabbit Stick and the others of the Only People, his grandfather and his whole village had moved their wigwoms to their spring fishing site not far from the place of the Salmon People, the villages coming together to join in the fishing for the great spring runs of salmon and shad coming up the Long River. Two days' walk upstream and more springs ago than he cared to number, yet this same river and this same season. Loon had been the old man's name.

Rabbit Stick saw it clearly in his mind. His father's father, Loon, had stood in the water of the Long River wearing a basswood headband decorated with red shapes—birds mostly. Then Loon had begun to talk to the water, telling it all of the important and special events of his life, those things he felt should be remembered, carried by the river's flow, kept by Kwanitewk. Deeply impressed, Rabbit Stick, then only five winters old, had sat on a cedar log near the water, listening to every word his grandfather spoke, determined to remember all that was said.

Loon's wife, Rabbit Stick's grandmother, had stood there, too. She was worried that her husband would lose his footing and perhaps drown. Kwanitewk sometimes took people at this time of the year, especially if they offered themselves this way. She was even a little afraid that Loon was ready to be taken. He had told her the night before how tired he was of having to work to loosen his limbs up each morning as if they were stiff pieces of rawhide. But her fear did not quiet her sense of humor. If anything, fear sharpened its edge.

"You did not mention," Loon's wife had called to him, "that even at your age you can still eat more than anyone else in our whole village."

"Quiet!" Loon said. "I don't want the river to remember that!"

But the river had remembered it. Rabbit Stick smiled, knowing that Kwanitewk had held that memory all of those years just to carry it down to him as he stood gathering his words for prayer this morning.

It was that way with the river and with the other powerful things that were part of Ktsi Nwaskw's great creation surrounding the Only People. One of the jobs of the river was to hold the memories that would keep the people from becoming too self-important. To remind the people that they must not forget how to laugh, even when they are ready to pray. A green stick floated up to Rabbit Stick's leg and he picked it up from the river. It had on it the bud of one leaf and sitting on that bud was a big ant.

Rabbit Stick shook his head and smiled again. Now the river was giving him back his own name. He waded out of the water and placed the stick carefully up in the dry grass so that the big ant could crawl out and sit in the sun. Big Ant had been his own childhood name, the name he was called by before he became known as the One Who Throws the Rabbit Stick. He had been only six winters old when he slept very late one morning. But when he woke, he had shouted and then come hurtling out of his parents' lodge, running very fast.

"What is wrong?" people had asked him.

He had stood for a long time without speaking, looking back into the lodge, but staying a safe distance from it. He was trying to see what had frightened him. He looked for so long that people understood: whatever it was, it had been in a dream.

Finally he spoke. "An ant was on my chest," he said.

Someone laughed.

"You do not understand," he said. "It was a BIG ANT."

And that had been his name from then on until he became a young man and a new name found him.

5

CHAPTER TWO
THE PATH

The path was not a familiar one, yet it seemed to the broad-shouldered young man as if many of his people had traveled it before him. It was not a broad path. It was one of those ways through the forest to be seen only by a person who knew how to look for it. Those who walked carelessly or were unsure of their destination would stray off it easily. Yet he could see it well.

The path rose, going steeply uphill now. There was snow around, one of those heavy snows that can come in the last moons before the Day Walker stays longest in the sky on his journey. This snow was strange, though. It was not just falling to the ground, but swirling around him in patterns, great flakes holding light and sparkling in the dark sky. But even though he was climbing now, even though this strange storm was all around him, he walked faster.

There was a single set of prints in the new snow, the prints made by the mokasin feet of a very large man, mokasins whose pattern showed the man to be one of the Only People. Mokasins like those his grandmother had made for him before he set out on this journey, though he could no longer quite remember when that had been. He thought he could just make out the figure of a tall person ahead of him, reaching the top of the hill and then disappearing over it without pausing.

If he ran, he could catch up to the man ahead. He knew that tall figure. It was another of the Dawn Land People, the one-eyed man who had once been known as Weasel Tail. Young Hunter remembered how Weasel Tail had earned a new name—Holds the Stone. Weasel Tail had been taken by the Ancient Ones, those gray cannibal giants who hunted with fire. They had used him as their dog when they hunted the human beings. But two winters past, Holds the Stone had shown that he was still a human being when he had stood up with no other weapon than a rock, stood bravely against the Hunter, a great black animal that served the Ancient Ones.

That terrible creature would have killed Holds the Stone had not Young Hunter's dog Pabetciman saved his life. Holds the Stone had joined with Young Hunter then. The two of them had faced the Ancient Ones and won a great victory. Young Hunter shook his head. What was it that he was not remembering? Something else had happened then on top of that cliff in the place of many hills far to the west. But for some reason, Young Hunter could not make the picture of it appear in his mind.

But Young Hunter knew that he had not seen Holds the Stone since then. There were many things he had to tell him. So many good things had happened in the seasons since their victory. He would catch up to him, embrace him, joke with him, and tell him everything! He would reach the top of the hill and go right over it to reach his friend. Holds the Stone could not be far away on the other side. But Young Hunter took only a few more strides before something stepped across the path in front of him, blocking his way. It growled fiercely at him. Seeing the bared white fangs, he stepped quickly back. But as soon as he did so, he saw that it was his dog.

"I know you. Step aside now," Young Hunter said.

That look of embarrassment which a dog can show so clearly came into Pabetciman's eyes. But the dog did not move.

"Pabesis," Young Hunter said, "come here."

But Pabetciman did not move. Instead, the dog spread his legs, standing firm on the path above him, blocking his master's way on the trail. Young Hunter had not noticed how narrow this trail had become. It ran right along the crest of a long ridge of white stones almost as sharp as the edge of a flint spear. They were so high that when he looked down to either side, all he could see were the sparkling lights of the stars. Young Hunter knew that if he tried to step around the dog he would fall.

He reached into the pack made of woven basswood strips which was slung over his shoulder and took out a tiny animal, the size of a squirrel. He blew on it with his warm breath, and then, as it grew larger and continued to grow, he placed it on the ground. When it ceased to grow, it was a dog twice the size of Pabetciman.

"Danowa," he said, "make your brother move."

But instead of doing as Young Hunter said, Danowa stood shoulder to shoulder with the other dog, helping to block the way.

Young Hunter reached again into his pouch and took out another small animal. He breathed on it and placed it on the ground to watch it grow into a dog larger than a great bear.

"Agwedjiman," he said, "you are their leader. Make them do as I tell them."

But Agwedjiman, too, stood with his brothers, his legs spread to prevent Young Hunter from going farther up the hill. The great dog looked at his master and there was such a look of knowing in his eyes that Young Hunter realized there was something his dogs knew which he was, it seemed, not yet ready to know. Then he remembered the tall figure he had been following.

"My friends," Young Hunter said, speaking firmly to his dogs, "I know you want to protect me. But I must follow that person. I need to see his face. You can come with me to protect me, but do not stop me from going over that hilltop."

The dogs looked back at him, and Young Hunter saw now that there was in the eyes of Pabetciman, standing there almost on the hilltop, such a look of sadness that Young Hunter felt sorry he had spoken to them in such a hard way. And there was something he needed to remember about Pabetciman. But he could no more remember what that was than he could remember when or why he had started to climb this hill. He went down on one knee and reached out his hand. Pabetciman stepped forward, placing his head under Young Hunter's hand in that old way he had always done when he was trying to get his master to pet him while Young Hunter's thoughts were elsewhere. For one moment, as the dog approached, Young Hunter saw that this great animal, so fierce to his enemies, was only a little puppy. He wanted to pick the puppy up, press his cheek again into that soft belly and smell the familiar scent, a scent that Young Hunter now realized he had not smelled for many moons.

But with that realization came another, and Pabetciman slipped back from his touch. Then, looking back over his shoulder so that his eyes were holding Young Hunter's, Pabetciman went over the hill. Young Hunter tried to follow, but Agwedjiman and Danowa were pressing forward now, pushing him back down the hill. He struggled to get past them. His eyes blurred with tears. He remembered now. He remembered the long journey he had taken with his three dogs. He remembered how Pabetciman had sacrificed himself fighting that great black beast which was hungry for human flesh.

"Pabesis," he called.

Then he sat up. The first light of dawn was coming in through the open door of their wigwom, open because the night had been so warm. A dog lay across the doorway, guarding their lodge: Danowa. Another dog's paws were on his chest: Agwedjiman. The big dog, smaller than he had been on the hill yet still larger than the other dogs, whimpered in the questioning way that showed his concern. Soft hands held Young Hunter's face.

9

"*Nezanawbam,*" Willow Woman said. "My husband. You have dreamed."

"Pabesis," Young Hunter said. "He is gone."

Willow Woman shook her head. "He is not gone far. There," she said, pointing with her lips to the door of the lodge, "I just put him out so that he would not disgrace himself again by turning our bed into a pond." She poked Young Hunter in his side with her hand. "But I knew when I married you that it would mean living in a wolf pack! I will call him."

She clapped her hands. Danowa stood and stepped aside from the lodge door as a gangly young dog, whimpering with joy, came leaping inside. The youngster tripped over his own huge paws as he tumbled onto the sleeping platform with them, whining, kissing their faces, and, as puppies are prone to do, turning their bed into a pond in his excitement.

CHAPTER THREE
A CIRCLE

Young Hunter leaned back against the outside of the lodge. Willow Woman and his grandmother had gone for a walk together, to visit some of the places where they would be gathering plants together after the passage of another moon. The trees were a misty green now with that blurred look trees have before their buds fully open into flower. It was one of Young Hunter's favorite times of the year, yet he was troubled. Not by one thing, but by many things.

He knew he should not be troubled. Things were going so well for the Only People, so well that no one even seemed to think about the fact that they were going well. No one seemed to think about how threatened the lives of the Only People had been only two winters before when Young Hunter had made his journey. Did they even remember that he had been sent out by the deep-seeing ones to face the danger that had threatened to destroy the human beings? The people had welcomed him home when he returned, but apart from their happiness at seeing him safe, no one had acted as if anything particularly unusual had happened. Everyone had listened closely as he told them of finding the gray giants who hunted with fire and were at war with all living things. But then, just as a group of children do when a nighttime story is ended, they had nodded and gone about their business. As if it had

11

happened nowhere except in the story Young Hunter had told them.

Sometimes Young Hunter even found himself wondering if it had only been a walking dream. Had the Ancient Ones really existed? Had his small spears struck and killed that great black beast? Had that tall, one-eyed man truly been the one once named Weasel Tail, and had Young Hunter himself ever really held that weapon which the deep-seeing people had given to him? He remembered the Long Thrower, the way it bent to send its small spears flying through the air farther than anything a human could normally throw. But it had been lost in the landslide that had buried the gray giants. And the deep-seeing ones, Bear Talker and Medicine Plant, had told him on his return to the Only People that the secret of the Long Thrower must again be kept from all others. It could live only in his memory. It was too dangerous for human beings to have such a powerful weapon.

All Young Hunter had to show for his adventure were the scars that he had gained on that journey and the tales he had to tell. Sometimes, it was only when he placed the scars on his hands on the long scar across Danowa's back and belly—the scar made when the long claws of the great black beast had slashed—that he felt as if it had all truly happened. His grandparents had listened closely to his stories and so, too, had Willow Woman. He knew that they believed him. But although Bear Talker and Medicine Plant had been the ones to send him on that journey, the way they had listened to his tale had been strange. They had seemed more interested in looking at each other that day when he made the journey to Medicine Plant's lonely lodge—no longer so lonely since Bear Talker had gone to move in with her.

"Boy," Bear Talker had growled, "I will call for you when there is need to do so. Now you can go. We are busy."

Medicine Plant had been less brusque, but it had been clear to Young Hunter that there were other things on her mind than his stories. It was as if they both had already been there and seen it all. True, Medicine Plant had placed one of her hands on his shoulder when he spoke of the death of Pabetciman, and Bear Talker had nodded twice when Young Hunter told of the way Holds the Stone had thrown away his own life to protect the people of the generations to come. But they had hardly responded when he told them of the shaking of the land and the loss of the Long Thrower. In some ways, they were like older children who had heard a story so many times that they knew what would happen even before the storyteller spoke it and were more interested now in watching the shapes made by the fire in the lodge.

Yet when Young Hunter had stood to leave, Bear Talker had shot up to his own feet like an otter coming out of a pond and embraced him, saying more in that embrace than words could speak. And Medicine Plant had joined in that embrace, her left hand on his head, her right hand on his chest. "*Wlipamkaani*," she said to him. "Travel well." Then she had smiled. "And do not forget to look for the fox." But when Young Hunter looked back the first time, he had seen that his leaving had not broken the embrace and that the two deep-seers were not watching his departure as they held each other closely. He had gone down the hill in confusion. And though his eyes searched the undergrowth by the trail for the flash of red fur, he did not see the fox that was Medicine Plant's guardian spirit.

That visit to see the two deep-seeing people had been two winters ago, just after he had finally returned to the land of the Only People after more moons of walking than it seemed he had taken to reach the place among the hills where it had all ended. Since then he had not spoken to either Medicine Plant or Bear Talker, and—until the past night—his dreams had been ordinary ones. He had thought of traveling again to Medicine Plant's lodge. Bear Talker was still there, having now been with the deep-seeing woman longer than with any of the several women he had married before.

But Young Hunter had heard stories from his brother-cousins Red Hawk and Blue Hawk that made him decide against traveling just now to Medicine Plant's lodge. When the two brothers had come to visit Young Hunter from the Salmon People village four seasons ago, they had told him how the people stayed even farther away from the lodge of the deep-seeing ones now. It seemed that Medicine Plant and Bear Talker fought each other constantly.

"Though no one has courage enough … " Blue Hawk said.

"To climb up to that hilltop and watch … " Red Hawk continued.

"Everyone knows what happens up there," Blue Hawk said.

"They battle each other with their medicine power … "

"They tear up great trees … "

"They make the earth shake as they change themselves into whirlwinds … "

"Or huge animals … "

Blue Hawk paused for breath. "It was never safe to go to that lonely lodge before, but … "

"It is doubly dangerous now," Red Hawk finished. Then he laughed.

"It is also true … " said Blue Hawk.

"That they seem well suited for each other," said Red Hawk.

"And Medicine Plant is expecting … " Blue Hawk added.

"A baby," Blue Hawk finished.

It all made Young Hunter feel as if he had waded into a familiar stream that had been suddenly transformed into a whirlpool like the one below the big salmon-catching falls on the Onion Land River. As a small boy, he dove into that water because he liked the way it looked. But when he came to the surface, he found himself watching the once-ordinary trees and land around him turn into a pattern that repeated again and again, making him weaker and dizzier each time it whirled past him. He would have been in that whirlpool still had not Rabbit Stick jumped in and pulled him out.

He had even—three seasons ago now—made a journey back to the place among the hills, retracing his steps to that spot where he had fought the great battle against the gray giants. But, after crossing the lake near the Guardian's Rock, he found it all changed. It was not just that there was no longer the palpable sense of danger and fear around him. It was as if his adventure had happened in another land than this, in another person's life than his own. As if the things that had happened there had either happened long long ago in an old story or were yet to occur and would only come to be in the time of his great-great-great-grandchildren.

He had not been alone on his second journey. His uncle, Fire Keeper, the sagamon of their village, had agreed that companions should go with him. Many volunteered, but he ended up going with his best friend Sparrow and with his two brother-cousins, Red Hawk and Blue Hawk. Like Young Hunter, his friends were not yet married; Sparrow especially was fickle and flitted from one young woman to another like that bird which was his namesake—and so it was easy for them to make such a journey. But before the four young men had reached the edge of the village, another, smaller figure with a pack on her back had joined them. When he saw the determined look in Willow Girl's eyes, Young Hunter had not even thought of telling her that only men were tough enough to make this journey. Everyone knew that Willow Girl was as good with a spear as most men. She was better than all the men at bringing down ducks or geese with the two stones tied to either end of a twined cord. In fact, Willow Girl was so quick and strong that in the ball games the men played in the summer against the women, she was not only the one who scored the most goals, but also the one who sent the most players on the other team limping back to their lodges.

Young Hunter knew that it had been a mistake for him to mention the Long Lodge woman known as Redbird, whom he had found in the forest after her escape from the gray giants. As soon as he had begun telling of how she had led him to her village and how he had been made a guest in her lodge, he felt as if the path beneath his feet had turned into a marsh and he was sinking deeper with each step. All the people in his village had been gathered around and listening to his long tale, but as soon as he mentioned Redbird, the feeling in the air had changed. Willow Girl had moved forward so close that she was looking right into his eyes as he talked, and he could feel her breath on his face. The harder she looked at Young Hunter, the older and less attractive Redbird became as he continued to tell his story. So when Willow Girl joined them, Young Hunter had only nodded to her and continued. At least he knew that Willow Girl believed his journey had really happened. The way the others of the Only People treated him now, it was as if he had gone no farther than the village of the Salmon People, stayed two seasons, and returned home to share stories from long ago.

The truth, though, was deeper than that. Young Hunter, though he had done great things, was still a young man. He did not yet grasp that everyone knew well what Young Hunter had done. Everyone admired him for it. They admired him so much that they carefully avoided burdening him with praise. People took special care to not treat him any differently than they had before, even though the stories he had shared about his great journey were now told in every lodge around the fires in winter. To be a hero was like being a sagamon. One did not choose to do it; one did it because it was what one had to do, because it chose you. Now that he had returned, he was part of the village circle again, and it was important for him to feel that he was at the same height as everyone else, not taller or more visible than others. On the other hand, people who tried to elevate themselves above others would be quickly teased back to the earth again.

The trip Young Hunter had taken with his friends to that land of his great adventures had been a good journey. It had also not been a good journey. Agwedjiman and Danowa stayed by his side, hardly ever scouting ahead. They sensed no great danger. The land and the path were the same and yet they were different. He located the places where he had sheltered before, and Sparrow and Red Hawk and Blue Hawk and Willow Girl spent pleasant nights around fires at each of his camps, talking as young people talk. He found the place where the big fire had burned and the place where the bighead herd had been driven by that fire to their deaths over the cliff, yet he could not locate the rock crevice and the cave that had saved him and his dogs from the fire that threatened to burn them. After more than a moon of walking, they found the path that led up between the cliffs, and they clambered carefully over the rock slide that had buried the gray giants and Holds the Stone.

Yet things were different than they had been in the Moon When Snow Comes. The leaves of the trees concealed things, and he could not find the place where they had buried the black creature. Perhaps the big animals and birds had eaten it and its bones had been chewed up by the little mice. Young Hunter had seen it happen before. He remembered how, as a child, he had found a deer that had been caught in deep snow and had starved. The melting snow had disclosed what was left of its body, and Young Hunter had come back each day to see how it disappeared, piece by piece, until all that was left was a scatter of stiff white hairs; then, one night after a hard wind, even those were gone.

Stranger still was that the village of the Long Lodge People was gone. There was little sign that a village had ever been there—except for one or two places where it appeared fires might have burned. Even the tall poles that had been lashed together to make the wall around the village had vanished. Perhaps those people had gone back to the western lands they came from? Or had he only dreamed them?

17

Young Hunter was confused. But his friends were not. They were excited, even Willow Girl, about traveling so far and seeing such new places. They did not question Young Hunter's story. Such things happened to people who traveled far, and if magic had erased all traces of the gray giants and the village of the strange people, it did not make the others doubt the truth of Young Hunter's words. It also did not prevent them from teasing their friend.

And so Young Hunter began to doubt—to doubt so much that he did not notice Agwedjiman and Danowa hold back as the young people made their way down from the pass between the hills. The people were out of sight down the trail when the two dogs turned their heads toward the north and the hair stood up on their backs. They growled and slowly backed away, turning to run after Young Hunter and his friends only when that menace they sensed in the cave opening above them did not attack or follow.

Young Hunter's head was down as he went down the trail, and Willow Girl, sensing his uncertainty, put her arm around him as he walked. That made it better. And from then on, every step he took seemed better still. He looked at her and realized how, even though they had been traveling out from the village for more than a moon, he had not looked enough at her.

"Walking with you," she said, "makes me feel as if I am walking in the story you told. I can see it all."

Young Hunter nodded, realizing how lucky he was. Red Hawk and Blue Hawk and Sparrow were some distance off, racing each other to the bottom of the hill. As always, Sparrow was far ahead, and, as always, Red Hawk and Blue Hawk were refusing to admit defeat. Young Hunter stopped walking so suddenly that he turned his ankle on a loose stone and began to fall. Willow Girl grabbed his arm and did not let go, even though she fell with him. They rolled only a few paces before a birch tree root stopped them when Young Hunter's head hit it. The pain was as sharp as the point of a flint knife, but Willow

Girl's hand was suddenly there, touching his head, making the pain go away. He looked up at her, so close to him that she was all he could see. He put both his arms around her.

"*Nizwiakw*," he said. "My wife."

"*Nezanawbam*," she answered. "My husband."

Danowa and Agwedjiman were standing on either side of them now, whimpering and urging them to get up and continue down the hill. Young Hunter and Willow Woman barely saw the dogs as they rose. They felt as if their feet were not touching the earth as they stood there.

When they returned to the village of the Only People, their formal marriage ceremony would take place. They would speak their hearts to each other in the sight of all of the Only People. The elders gathered in the circle around them would give them advice. The marriage necklace would be looped about both their necks, tying them together in the eyes of all the people. But Young Hunter and Willow Woman—for she would be Willow Girl no longer—knew that here on this slope their married life together had truly begun and their hearts were joined forever.

A redbird was singing from the branch of the birch tree that leaned above the trail, but though they appreciated its song, they hardly noticed it. There was singing enough in their hearts. They did not notice that Red Hawk and Blue Hawk and Sparrow had come back to look for them and were sitting, carefully looking up at the tops of the trees, waiting at a respectful distance with broad smiles on all of their faces. And they did not notice on the trunk of that birch tree arching above their heads the scars that had been made, seven seasons gone, by the great claws of the terrible black animal.

CHAPTER FOUR
PABESIS

Young Hunter touched Willow Woman on her shoulder as he left the lodge. She was getting ready to go to the maple trees. The flow of syrup was almost over now, but she had to check the bark bowls that had been placed at the bases of the trees, just below the hollow elderberry twig that was positioned at the tip of each tree like a giant spear point that had been cut carefully into the tree's bark to channel the dripping sweet water of the tree. The fires would be banked again to heat the stones which, when dropped into the big dugout canoe filled with sap, would boil the sap down until all that was left was syrup, thick and sweet.

"I am going to walk by the river," he said.

Willow Woman nodded. She understood that he not only needed to walk, he needed to walk without her. But not alone.

"Take your baby with you," she said. "If he goes with me to the maples, he will either drink the sap or chew up the bowls again."

Young Hunter smiled and bent to one knee.

"Pabesis," he called.

Before Young Hunter could stand up, the puppy burst out from a puppy snooze behind the sunny side of the lodge. Paws struck Young Hunter's chest, followed by a furry flank as the pup tried to leap up and roll on him at one and the same time. Young Hunter fell back with the dog in his arms. He rolled once and came back up to his feet, snow and twigs and dry leaves caught in his hair, but the dog held in his arms. Pabesis squirmed and threw his head back to lick Young Hunter's face, banging his hard skull against Young Hunter's nose. Young Hunter dropped him, and the dog fell with a yelp that echoed the sound Young Hunter himself had made.

Young Hunter carefully put his hand up to his nose. A little blood dripped from it.

"He will kill us all," Young Hunter said.

Willow Woman held a handful of clean snow against Young Hunter's nose as Pabesis licked their feet and then rolled onto his back, whimpering apologetically.

"You are the one who adopted him," she said.

Young Hunter said nothing. Complaining about Pabesis was one of the games they played together. Although neither of them ever shouted at or said a hard word directly to the young dog, they both adored and spoiled it, giving it the tenderest scraps of food while Danoa and Agwedjiman sat in dignified silence, like disapproving uncles too polite to tell young people they were rearing their little one wrongly.

Young Hunter saw in his mind the day when he had found Pabesis. Five moons ago, as he walked along the high banks of the Long River above the falls where the rocks speak, he had seen something moving in a clump of brush that was caught in the current and flowing down the swift stream. At first he thought it was a muskrat, but the color was wrong and he saw that it was struggling. He ran down to the edge of the stream and saw it was a puppy. Although tangled in the floating brush and struggling to stay above water, it was not whining with fear as some would. Instead it was fighting, as if its little body held a warrior's heart.

Young Hunter did not pause. He went into the river, wading and then swimming until he reached the small island of brush. For a moment, he thought the little one was gone, but then he saw it there, its nose just above the water, on the other side of the tangle. The current was turning them as he fought with the brush, his feet briefly touching the stone of the riverbed, but it was deepening again so that he could not touch the bottom. Young Hunter grabbed the main branch in both hands and broke it, separating the little brush island in two. He reached through the brush and pulled the little dog up. As he grasped its limp body, he felt how hunger-thin it was and he saw the open wound on its hip. But it was not drowned. It lifted its head, coughing out water. Suddenly, its eyes held his with a look that he could have sworn showed both recognition and joy. It whimpered and tried to lick his face. A name came to Young Hunter's lips, but before he could speak it, he realized how far the current had taken them both. They were at the edge of the falls. He grabbed at a rock to stop them before they entered the place where the current swept down into a roaring curtain of foam and spray, but the water-smooth stone was too slick to grasp. He held the little dog against his broad chest, protecting it with his arms, and took one last breath before the whole world around them exploded into white mist.

Much later that day, when the last light of the sun was only a faint glow through the trees, Young Hunter had limped into his grandparents' lodge where Sweetgrass Woman, Rabbit Stick, and Willow Woman were waiting, finishing off the last of a stew that Young Hunter knew well from its aroma. It was beaver tail, one of his favorites. His hands behind his back, he looked at them all, one by one.

"Grandson," Sweetgrass Woman said, smiling as she spoke, "we did not think you were going to return. Otherwise we would have saved some of this stew."

"Grandmother!" Willow Woman said. "Do not tease him. Can't you see he has injured himself?" She knelt and placed her hands carefully on Young Hunter's swollen knee.

"It is only a bruise ... ," Young Hunter began, but he did not finish his words. For the puppy he held behind his back chose that moment to whimper. Willow Woman straightened up and grabbed Young Hunter's shoulders to turn him around.

"Show me what you have! Ah, a little one."

And then the three of them, his grandparents and his wife, left him standing there, forgotten, as they petted the head and tickled the soft belly of the little dog that snuggled contentedly in Willow Woman's arms. It was a while before they noticed Young Hunter again, trying to bend his stiff leg and sit in his usual place. But even then, they only noticed him because, when he found the bowl filled with beaver tail stew that Sweetgrass Woman had hidden for him behind his basswood pack, the little dog lurched out of Willow Woman's grasp and leaped into his lap, upsetting the stew onto the floor of the lodge, where the puppy quickly began to gulp it down.

"Your little one is hungry," Rabbit Stick said. "Have you thought of calling him Big Mouth?"

Young Hunter rubbed his knee where the little dog had struck it with a hard head in running for the beaver stew, all of which had now disappeared, a small bulging belly the only remaining evidence of what had once been Young Hunter's dinner.

"*Nda*," Young Hunter said. "He already knows his name. His name is Little Ask Him. Pabesis."

At the sound of that name, the small dog came and placed his head gently in his master's lap, sighed, rolled onto his back, and began to snore.

CHAPTER FIVE
CLAY

As he walked toward the river, Young Hunter listened to the things the birds were saying. The little many-colored singers had returned from the Always Summer Land, and their thin sweet voices could be heard from the tops of the tall trees. Pabesis, too, was listening to the birds. Every now and then, the young dog would become so interested in their songs that he would leap up, as if trying to fly himself, to get closer or even join them. Young Hunter had to keep a close eye on Pabesis, for when the dog became too engrossed in something around him—a squirrel, a dry leaf moving in the wind—he might trot right into Young Hunter's legs, tripping him or cracking his hard head against Young Hunter's knee from the front or the side.

It had always been a challenge to walk with Pabesis. When he was a puppy, it was because he would come up from behind, growling and biting at first one and then the other of Young Hunter's mokasins, flattening himself out and leaping to attack from one side and then the other, jumping forward and then back at just the right angle for his head to hit Young Hunter on the capping bone of his knee.

Now that he was larger, approaching the size he would be when he was full grown, Pabesis seldom played that particular game anymore. Now, though, Young Hunter had to be even more careful of that hard head, for when it was lifted up it might strike him considerably higher than on his knee. Yet Young Hunter felt a great fondness for this new child of theirs, as Willow Woman called the puppy. In the five moons since he had rescued the pup from the rushing waters, he had become increasingly convinced that some part of his old friend Pabetciman had been reborn within this awkward animal.

Young Hunter remembered how Bear Talker had explained it to him many seasons before when he had come to the deep-seeing man, carrying the squirrel that his well-thrown stone had brought down from a beech tree. Holding its limp body had troubled the boy, who could not understand why it could no longer move. "Go ask Bear Talker," Rabbit Stick had said, after his own explanations had clearly not answered the questions held in his grandson's eyes.

"The animal people are like us." Bear Talker had said. "Our bodies and theirs carry life and are made from the earth. Those bodies go back into the earth. Then we have the breath-spirit that enables our bodies to move. That comes from Ktsi Nwaskw and is carried by the wind. It goes back into the wind when our bodies return to the earth. So, when we hunt an animal, we do not harm that part of it. That returns to the Owner Creator." Bear Talker had squinted his eyes then and looked closely at Young Hunter, to see if the boy understood and was still listening. Then the deep-seeing man had growled deep in his throat and continued. "There is more than that. There is also a life-spirit. That life-spirit is different and new for every being that is born. So none of us are exactly the same. No bear is exactly like any other bear. No human is exactly like any other human. When the body dies and the breath leaves, that spirit steps free. It does not die but goes to the Owner Creator."

Bear Talker had leaned close then and whispered his next words, for his wife of two seasons, Little Mink, was standing outside near the door of the lodge and eavesdropping on her husband's words. Some said the only reason she had married the deep-seeing man was to steal his secrets, and the village agreed that this marriage, like Bear Talker's last one, would not last long.

"Sometimes, when we sleep, that life-spirit leaves our body and goes walking about, seeing things. That is all I will say now about it," Bear Talker had whispered. Then he sat straight again and was quiet for so long that Little Mink grew bored and drifted away. Young Hunter, however, did not move. The boy knew that there was more to be said. At last Bear Talker looked down at him approvingly, took a breath, and continued. "I know the question you wish to ask. What of those who have memories of places they never saw and of people long dead? Why is it that sometimes when you do something for the first time you feel you have done it before? It is because, sometimes, that life-spirit of one who died comes back to join with the spirit of a new one and be reborn."

Although Young Hunter felt that some part of the young dog's spirit was that of the first Pabetciman, he had no idea where Pabesis had come from, though it was clear that there was a good deal of wolf in the youngster's background—as had been true with the first Pabetciman and his brothers Danowa and Agwedjiman. The river was so long and the little dog so stubborn and tough that it could have been floating for days, caught in that small moving brush island, before Young Hunter had found it. It had certainly been skinny enough for that to be so.

Perhaps it had only fallen into the river while trying to imitate a fish or walk on the surface like one of the water insects. But Young Hunter doubted the story was so simple. There was that wound on the little dog's hip, as if it had been pierced by the point of a giant spear. And there was the feeling Young Hunter had, that feeling of knowing beneath the surface of things which still came to him now and then. He knew, somehow, that the human people and dog people to whom Pabesis had belonged had suffered some great tragedy and that only this little one had survived. The Long River had saved him, carrying him away from a death that had tried to claim him.

Young Hunter stopped, knelt, and put his arm around Pabesis. For once, the young dog sat calmly and looked up into Young Hunter's face. He did so in the exact way that the first Pabetciman had always done many seasons ago. Young Hunter stroked his dog's chest.

"We all know who you are, brother," Young Hunter said. "You are Pabetciman. You are Little Ask Him. That is why Agwesis and Danowa accepted you as soon as they saw you. That is why they trust you to walk alone with me. They know that you need time and space to grow again. But how much do you remember?"

Pabesis whined, and the look in his eyes changed back to that of an eager and overly excitable puppy. He had caught sight of a squirrel; he tore free from Young Hunter's arms, his big feet moving like a whirlwind as he tore up leaf mold and scattered twigs, pursuing his elusive quarry which, in a rather unhurried way, simply went up the trunk of a massive oak. Unable to stop in time, Pabesis ran headfirst into the tree. It sounded like a rock striking a wooden bowl. The dog sat down and looked up into the tree, unhurt but clearly displeased that the squirrel had chosen this unfair way of ending a game barely begun.

Young Hunter shook his head. Then again, it was not just that Agwedjiman and Danowa trusted Pabesis to walk alone with him; it was that the young dog could not control himself around them. Pabesis was always leaping up, kissing their faces, batting at them with his paws to get them to play, rolling on his back in front of them. At times all three would play like puppies, but more often than not the look in the eyes of the two older dogs and their curled lips showed that they were not amused. Then, rather than growling or snapping at the young one, they would both quietly vanish into the forest, leaving Young Hunter alone to take on the responsibility of teaching proper behavior to this pesky young one.

"Pabesis," Young Hunter said, as the dog ran back to his side and Young Hunter put out both hands to stop him short of a collision, "you are growing, and in a few more moons you will be almost as large as Agwedjiman. But right now you are like clay that is still being shaped, clay that is not yet dry. I will continue to think good thoughts for you, and your uncles will help to shape you as you should be shaped."

Pabesis looked up, intelligence glowing briefly in his eyes. Then, picking up his ears as if he heard something, he whirled and leaped to run up the hill toward the river which was just over the next rise. As he sprang away, his feet tangled for a moment with Young Hunter's. Young Hunter found himself sprawled on his back, listening to the heavy feet of the dog pounding off into the distance. He lay there for a moment, remembering that the word *Pabesis* not only might mean Little Pabetciman. Said in another way, it might also mean half-wit.

"Then again," Young Hunter said to the sky, "this young one may destroy us all first."

Bear Talker had explained it again to Young Hunter soon after he had returned from his great journey. Young Hunter had just finished speaking of the death of Holds the Stone. They had sat in silence for a long time, looking into the fire in Bear Talker's lodge, a fire that burned with colors like no other fire in the village of the Only People.

"When we end this life," the deep-seeing man said, "our life-spirits walk from this earth. They walk the trail into the sky. That trail is a very narrow one, and it is like climbing a snowy hill."

Bear Talker had spoken in such a way that Young Hunter sensed his words were not words passed down from elder teachers, but from memory, memory of walking that way and returning.

"At one place, there is a deep gorge. There is a river far below, but you cannot see it. You can only hear it. A log is stretched across that gorge and you must cross there to continue up the Sky Trail. Each man and each woman must cross that log, but the log is unsteady and may roll and throw you from it as you cross. That is when your dogs help you. The dogs that were your companions while you walked this earth will be there on that trail ahead of you, and they will hold the log firmly with their teeth so that you can cross. But if you starve your dogs and if you beat them, they will not hold the log firmly."

Bear Talker growled then and shook his head as a bear does, startling Young Hunter.

"That is when I turned around and walked back," Bear Talker said. "And ever since then I have treated all dogs with greater respect." He reached out and struck Young Hunter in the chest with the palm of his hand. It thumped like a deep drum and reverberated through Young Hunter's body like a drumbeat.

"You, though," Bear Talker said, "you will have so many faithful dogs waiting to help you that you will not even be able to see the log!"

As they had spoken further, Young Hunter had begun to ask the same question that he knew many others had asked before him and yet others would surely ask again in the generations to come. It was the question he had not asked that day when he was a small child and had come to Bear Talker carrying the dead squirrel.

"But what about those who ... "

"Come back?" Bear Talker said. "You know about this body we leave behind," he added, thumping himself on the chest and making an even deeper drum sound than when he had struck Young Hunter. "You know that this goes back into the earth, back to feed the roots of the trees. You know, too, how the life-spirit can leave a body. That life-spirit is the one which walks to the Sky Land, or turns around and decides not to make that journey. You know this; you've seen this and felt it. Do not deny it. Your feet have traveled too far for you to say you haven't. You know there is a bone-spirit, too, which remains in the earth for a long time. That is why we make the fire over a grave or bury people in the earth under their wigwoms and then burn the lodge to the ground. So that bone-spirit will be peaceful and not move around. That bone-spirit can make it hard for those who are still breathwalking. And that is not all, either, Nephew."

Young Hunter nodded, but he was divided again. He was listening to himself listen, standing apart from himself and watching, understanding and not at all certain what it was he understood.

"There is the body, there is the bone-spirit, there is the spirit that can leave the body and return or continue to the Sky Land, and then there is a fourth one. And that one may return in the shape of a new one, may carry some of the memories from that earlier life."

And so, Young Hunter thought, as he lay there brushing himself off, *so it is with Pabesis.* He leaned his head back to look toward the crest of the hill above the Long River. *He remembers some, but not all. He is new and old at the same time and so his brothers have accepted him. Even if they lose patience with him because he is shaped but not yet shaped, like clay that can hold a useful form when hands press and shape it in the right way.*

Young Hunter rolled over. His face was exactly level with a small rotted beech log. On it a line of ants, wakened early from their winter sleep by the warmth of the sun, were moving steadily, feeling everything around them with great care, looking in every direction. One very big ant was far in front of the others.

Young Hunter heard a familiar voice cry out, followed by the sound of splashing water. He jumped up and ran to the hilltop to look down at the Long River just below. He saw the reason why his grandfather, Rabbit Stick, had shouted so loudly. There was clay smeared on the old man's face and water streaming from his long gray hair as he pulled himself up the bank out of the icy river. Pabesis was frolicking in the shallow water around him. The young dog had greeted Young Hunter's grandfather in his usual way.

CHAPTER SIX
THE WALKING HILL

He stood for a long time among the gray, moss-covered trees without moving, looking across the marshy land of the river's headwaters, far upstream from the village of the Only People. He was gray himself, blending into the trees despite his huge size. His thick, matted hair hung about him like the moss that coated the trees. His legs were like trees as he stood there, and he appeared to be rooted to the earth. Yet his small eyes were watchful, and the redness in them was like the pain he felt in his jaw where the thing was still lodged. A bird settled on his neck. He flapped his great ears and then rippled his skin, shaking the bird free. Such birds had once been welcome to ride his back and shoulders, picking free the larvae of the botflies that sometimes laid their eggs deep into his thick skin. But no bird could work free that sharp tooth which had flown through the air at the end of a stick and buried itself so deep that, though the stick broke off when he rubbed it against the side of a cliff, the stone tooth only went deeper and the wound did not heal.

He still ate. He still had all his strength. But all that was peaceful and contented was gone from his awareness, replaced by a red wash of something that had only come and gone quickly before, had only come and gone when he defended his cows and his calf. But the two cows and calf had both died in the great wind that had swirled across the land, uprooting trees.

He shook his head once as the pictures came to him, and as he did so he raised his trunk and made the high, piercing distress call that he had made that other day. He saw again the wind as it came through the trees, breaking the trees. The cows and the calf were not far from him, but he could not reach them. The wind pushed him away from them and lifted them, despite their size, twisted them, struck them against the stones, and dropped them. And then, as suddenly as it had come, the killing wind was gone. Though he remained by their sides for long days, pushing them, trying to get them to rise, bringing them sweet roots and grass and the tender tips of branches to try to coax them back to life, they did not move. At last he stood for a long time without moving, speaking to them with all of the sounds that he and the others had used to speak to each other. Some of those sounds were so deep that they could be heard from far, far away, so deep that a human ear could not hear them. But there was no response. There was only the small sound of the wind rippling his thick hair. Then, like a walking hill, he had begun to move. He walked south, away from the wind, the wind at his back. He came to the place where the Long River began. He began to walk down along its bank. He did not know where he was going, and as he walked, the heaviness of grief made his steps slow and shuffling.

When Walking Hill came to the first village near the river, he had circled it. He had not encountered this new village before. He did not know the beings that were there, but he avoided them. Despite his great size, he carried in his blood a remembered caution, and there was something about their strong scent that was familiar and unpleasing to him. But the small beings saw his tracks and followed. Many of them. They circled in front of Walking Hill and waited at a place where the cliffs were close to the river. They were upwind from him and, half-blind in his grieving, he had not seen them until it was too late. They had leaped out from behind the big stones, making loud sounds. And then the sticks with their sharp points had flown through the air to strike him. Most had merely pricked him, glanced off his thick hair and skin. But one point, sharper than others, thrown with more strength and skill from an atlatl, had gone into his open mouth.

Walking Hill had bellowed then with pain-anger and charged at them. His anger-cry was so frightening that some of the small beings did not move, but stood there staring at him. He killed them, grabbing them with his long snakelike trunk, crushing them under his feet, kneeling to press them into the earth with his broad forehead, throwing them high with his tusks. Two escaped but he had their scent, and he began to hunt them. Patiently, without stopping. The first one was caught later that day when the sun was in the midst of the sky. It climbed a tree, but the tree bent and then broke as Walking Hill leaned his weight against it. Beneath the broken tree that small creature died, lifted up and then struck again and again against the reddening earth.

The last one was faster and found its way back to the village by the river. Walking Hill followed and waited in the gray trees. Waited until the darkness was everywhere except in the small, red fire-eyes glowing out of the little piles of brush and bark where the small beings huddled together. In the mind of Walking Hill, those beings and the pain in his neck and the whirlwind that had killed the two cows and the calf were blended together as one memory now. If he could just wipe out all that he saw before him, perhaps the pain would be gone, perhaps things would be as they had been before and he would hear again the familiar sounds of the others speaking to themselves and to him as they dug roots from the marshy land and stripped branches from the trees. He stood there, the pain-anger red in his eyes, thinking those thoughts. The thoughts were simple and clear. The night passed. Soon it would be dawn.

But before the dawn could come, Walking Hill had gone into the village. He had entered as swiftly as the whirlwind that had killed his own small family, as swiftly as the small stick with its sharp stone point that had flown through the air. He flattened one of the piles of brush and bark and then another. The small beings were making loud noises again, and Walking Hill knew those noises to be fear noises. Even smaller beings, four-legged ones, were around his feet, biting and snarling. He swiped them away with his trunk, tossed them up. A very small four-legged one was thrown so far that it fell into the river and was carried away downstream by the current. Walking Hill spun and bellowed, stomped and struck. Another pile of brush and another and another. There were many here, but Walking Hill was faster than the small beings and they were confused in the darkness. Now the fire was eating the small piles of brush in which the little beings had been hiding. Only the voices of the fire and the river could be heard now, those and his own heavy breathing. No more loud noises from the small beings.

All that had happened two seasons ago. Walking Hill saw it in his mind again, saw himself as he backed away from the fires. In his memory, once again, he circled the piles of brush and sticks, nudging at the many silent bodies of the small beings. Light snow beginning to fall, he had turned and walked away, walked his pain back toward the north, toward the marshy places in the high lands where the Long River began.

But the pain had not allowed him to stay there. The mud that he rolled in had not drawn out the pain. He was thinner now than he had been then, for the pain grew sharper when he ate. And the pain brought to him again the pictures of the two cows and the calf, pictures of the village crushed beneath his feet. Gradually, there came a knowing. He knew that he must follow the river. He must find more of those villages of the ones who had thrown this pain.

CHAPTER SEVEN
FIRE

Young Hunter reached out his hand to pull Rabbit Stick up the last part of the slippery slope beside the Long River. His grandfather used one hand to hold his hair out in a long, wet rope. He slicked most of the wet clay from it with his other hand. Then he wound it back around his head. The hair would dry in place, the remaining clay holding it firm—almost like a cap. Men sometimes used wet clay to do their hair that way on purpose, but falling face first into the Long River's cold water was not the preferred way to coat one's hair with clay.

Both of them looked at Pabesis. The dog looked up at them, innocence in his eyes. They continued to look at him. Pabesis turned and busily began sniffing at the trail of a nonexistent squirrel. Young Hunter and Rabbit Stick could not stop themselves from smiling. Pabesis was proof, it seemed, of the old story that dogs had not only once been people but also understood human beings better than humans understood themselves. And though dogs sometimes seemed even more intelligent than the humans they chose to live with, a dog could always do as Pabesis had just done—conveniently wipe that look of intelligence out of his eyes and go back to being just a dog again, one with no idea that he had done anything wrong.

Rabbit Stick looked around for a dry place to sit. The Day Traveler was striking the western bank of the river now, having

36

lifted above the trees. He sat on the sun-bathed exposed roots of a leaning cedar, leaned back, and began to rub his hands along the trunk.

Young Hunter watched his grandfather carefully gather the cedar bark tinder as they sat there in the warm morning sunlight, neither of them speaking. The dry bark was loose, and as Rabbit Stick peeled it free, he rubbed it between his palms to release the fibers, which he then wrapped around his heartside hand. When he had enough, he placed that roll of cedar fibers into his pouch to add to his tinder bundle. Few things burned as well as cedar when one was starting a fire with a hand drill. Then he started making another tinder bundle, pointing with his lips toward the place on the bank where they had made fires before.

Young Hunter understood. He took out the fire-making tools from the bag he had slung over his shoulder. He had not brought with him a smoldering piece of punk inside a clam shell as he always did when he went out on long journeys. But he had carried his fire-making kit with him. He had already decided to make a fire by the river's edge, to burn some cedar on the coals and try to think more clearly as he did so. To make such a fire, a fire to help clear one's mind, it was important to make it fresh, not from a coal brought from another hearth. Bringing out his hand drill and positioning it in the groove in his cedar fireboard made him think of the story of how people had come to have fire.

Long ago, fire had been owned by an old woman and her two daughters who lived in a cave near the Long River where it flowed between the mountains. The other people, who lived in the valley downstream, were cold and freezing because they had no fire. But that old woman and her daughters were selfish and kept the fire for themselves. And they were powerful, too. They killed anyone who tried to take fire from them. The bones of those who had tried to steal fire were scattered all around outside the mouth of that cave.

But the people needed fire, for the winter was a long and cold one. The great mountains of ice were still there on the land, and without fire no one would survive. There was no Oldest Talker then among the people, no one with the deep knowledge they needed. It seemed all would have to die.

The Only People gathered together in a circle, trying to keep warm. The sagamon looked around the circle and asked the question again, "Who will go and try to bring back fire?"

No one answered, but a small boy sitting behind his mother felt something tug at his robe. He turned to look. A fox stood there. No one else seemed to see that fox.

"I will help you," the fox said, "but first you have to tell them that you will go and get fire."

"I will go," the boy said.

Everyone turned to look at him. They were surprised, but even his parents did not try to tell him not to go. They all knew they would die if someone did not succeed.

So the boy set out through the snow. As soon as he left the village, the fox joined him and ran by his side. But the snow was deep, and the boy began to lose heart.

"Look at the grouse," the fox said. "See the feathers it is wearing around its toes? You must make your feet like those of the grouse."

Then the fox showed the boy how to bend and weave together branches. He showed him how to make the *ogema*, the snowshoe, from the supple branches of *ogewakw*, the snowshoe tree, the ash. Now the boy could walk on top of the snow. He walked and walked toward the mountain, which was a long way away. After he had walked halfway through the day, he found himself growing tired, and he slowed his steps.

"I can go no farther," he said to the fox. "I must stop here."

"You must not stop," said the fox. "You will grow cold and freeze if you stop here."

"But I am too tired to walk farther," the boy said.

Then the fox began to nip at the boy's heels. The boy jumped, but the fox continued to nip at his feet.

"Stop!" the boy shouted.

But the fox would not stop. He stayed close behind the boy, snarling and nipping at him until the boy began to run. He ran that way all through the rest of the day until they came to the end of the valley where the Long River flowed.

The boy and the fox stopped at the edge of the forest to look up. There near the river was the cave in which the old woman and her daughters lived. As the boy looked out from the forest at that cave, he thought at first the ground in front of the cave was covered with very white snow. Then he saw that it was not snow. What he saw were bones, the bones of the people who had tried to steal fire and been killed by the old woman and her daughters.

"How can I get into their cave?" the boy said. "All those who tried before were killed."

"It will be easy," said the fox. "Take these four dry sticks. Hide them in your shirt."

The boy did as the fox said. As soon as he had hidden those sticks in his shirt, the fox leaped high in the air over the boy's head. When the fox landed on the other side, he seemed much larger than he had been before and very frightening looking. The boy could not understand why until he looked at his hands. They were gone and in their place were rabbit feet. The fox had changed him into a rabbit.

"Now," the fox said, "run fast or I will eat you."

The boy ran, trying to escape. But the fox was close behind him and getting closer. At last, in despair, he jumped into the Long River. The strong current swept him downstream, past the cave. But before he was swept farther down the river, hands reached down and pulled him out. It was the younger of the old woman's two daughters, who had gone down to the Long River as she did every evening to get water.

"Mother," she shouted, "I have found a little rabbit. It is half-drowned. Let me bring it up to the fire and dry it."

"Do so, Daughter," the old woman called back, "but watch out for thieves. I sense that someone is close who wishes to steal our fire."

Soon the boy who had been changed by the fox into a rabbit was warm and dry by the fire, held in the arms of the younger daughter. He pretended to fall asleep.

"Put down your new pet," the mother said. "It is time for us to go to sleep."

Then the mother and the two sisters prepared themselves for the night, making their beds up around the fire to guard it.

The rabbit boy waited until all three were sound asleep. Then he crept out and jumped over the fire. At that, he became a human being again. He pulled out the four sticks and lit one of them from the fire. As soon as he did so, the blazing fire went out and only his small stick still burned. Holding that stick tightly, he jumped over the younger daughter and began to run. But as he hit the ground, the sound of his feet woke the firekeepers.

"A thief!" the mother screamed. "Catch him."

The boy ran with the firekeepers close behind. He took the first stick and used it to light the second. Then he threw what was left of the first stick over his shoulder. The firekeepers grabbed at it, but it fell into the snow and went out.

On the boy ran, but the firekeepers again began to catch up with him. He lit the third stick and threw the remains of the second one over his shoulder. Again the firekeepers tried to grab it, but it burned out before they could reach it. Now the boy could barely run, but the fox came up to him as he lit the fourth stick.

"I will take it," said the fox. Then the fox grabbed the stick and the firekeepers ran after him, ignoring the boy. The stick burned down, making fox's mouth turn black—as all foxes' mouths are today—but fox held on tight as the smoke came from between his teeth. ...

Young Hunter smiled. He lifted the drill stick that he had been twirling. The smoke curling up from its point was thick, and he could see a small coal glowing in the groove in the board. With his flint knife he edged the coal into the tinder, folding the tinder about it carefully. He lifted the bundle up and began to blow through it softly. The smoke wreathed his hands and then turned into flame. He placed it under the pile of dry sticks shaped like a wigwom that Rabbit Stick had readied for him, and they watched the fire grow.

He felt as if he were the boy in that old story. It was just the way he had felt the first time Rabbit Stick had told him that story long ago. He remembered how the story ended. The fox had not made it back to the village of the Only People. But before the firekeepers could catch him, he had thrown that fire into a cedar tree, hiding it there. The firekeepers had tried to pull the fire from the tree, but it would not come out for them. At last, they had given up in despair and gone back to their cave. But the fox brought the boy to the cedar tree. He showed the boy how to draw the fire from the wood of the cedar tree with a hand drill also made of cedar. Rabbit Stick had shown him how to use the hand drill as he told the story, making a fire that had burst into life just as the tale ended.

Young Hunter looked across the small fire at Rabbit Stick. Rabbit Stick had taken his clay pipe from his pouch and filled it with the smoking herb, but he had not yet lit it. Instead he was looking at his grandson. Young Hunter knew from the smile on his grandfather's face that the old man had been remembering that same story, too. Indeed, Young Hunter found himself wondering if Rabbit Stick had learned that story from one of his own grandfathers. And as he looked at Rabbit Stick, he saw for the first time not the old man, but a boy. He saw a boy whose face was thinner but much like his own, a boy of long, long ago. He shook his head. He was deep-seeing again, and, as with his dream the night before, he was afraid of what this meant. He had not felt this way since the days before

41

the two Oldest Talkers had sent him on that long journey to the west.

I do not want to take such a journey again, Young Hunter thought. Yet another part of himself was saying the opposite. He stared into the fire and held out his hands to it.

Rabbit Stick cleared his throat. It startled Young Hunter, and he looked across the fire at the old man, who no longer looked like that young boy of ancient times who was guided and helped by the fox. Then Young Hunter realized that he was still holding his wooden fire drill, holding it right over the fire so that it was now burning and the fire of it was almost to his fingers! He dropped the fire drill and shook his hand.

"Grandson," Rabbit Stick said, "there are better ways to carry fire."

Young Hunter laughed. Then he sighed. "I have dreamed again," he said.

"That is why we are here at the Long River, Grandson," Rabbit Stick said. He took a small stick from the fire and used it to light his pipe. He breathed out a long plume of blue smoke and shook his head. "I have dreamed, too."

CHAPTER EIGHT
A MESSAGE

Bear Talker breathed hard as he came up the hill. His knee ached because he had just tripped over a tree root, but he paid no attention to it. He wished again that it were possible for deep-seeing people to do those things for themselves that they could do for others. He understood why Ktsi Nwaskw had made it that way. That way the power a deep-seeing person had been given would be used for others, and there would be no temptation to use it for one's own self. But it seemed as if in this one case, surely in this case, he would not just be using the power for his own benefit. He would be using it for her and for the small one coming.

Apparently, though, as always, Ktsi Nwaskw was wiser than he was. As much as he might be able to see for others, Bear Talker could discern neither the reason nor the solution for this trouble that had come to them. And whatever medicine might be needed now, he was not the one who could do it.

He thought of how easy it would have been if he could have left his body behind and traveled, like a star across the night sky, to carry the message as swiftly over the hills as the light of the Day Traveler at dawn crosses the land. But to do that kind of travel, one's mind had to be focused and clear. His mind was not clear now, but twisted with worry. The very presence of her pain, a pain he felt like a fist in his own belly, was enough to keep him inside his body.

As Bear Talker hurried up the hill, the final hill before he would look down on the Maple Sugaring Moon village of the Only People, he wished that he had the ability to run swiftly like Sparrow or Young Hunter. She had said that he would be swift enough, but the worry in his heart was not lessened by her words or by the touch of her hand on his face as she spoke them. He had felt her hurting too clearly for those words to help. He was only thankful that the Maple Sugaring Moon village of the Only People was closer than the village they would have occupied had it been the Moon of Frost. Then he would have been running and gasping for breath for a full day and a night, not just for the time it took for the Day Traveler to rise from a hand's width above the horizon to the middle of the sky.

He could smell the sweet steam from the last of the maple sap being cooked into syrup in the grove of trees near the edge of the village. Normally, he would have gone straight to that scent, for the good taste of maple syrup was second only to that of honey. As a small fat child, back when his name had been Slow Bird, he had always been the first to taste the syrup when one of the elders dripped it onto a mound of white snow scooped up in a rolled cone of birch bark. But there was no room for the memories of sweet tastes in his mind now. All that he could hold in his thinking was the urgency of delivering his message.

He passed people now as he ran. Some tried to greet him, but most simply stood in surprise at the sight of a deep-seeing person stumbling by with such lack of dignity. He paid no attention to them, heading for the familiar lodge set up at the village's western edge, recognizing it by the markings on its birch bark covering. That bark covering had been rolled from the outside of the lodge and carried from the winter village to this spring village closer to the Long River to be placed over the framework of new poles. He caught his foot on a stick as he reached the door of the lodge, and he went rolling in, losing whatever dignity he might still have had. But to his despair, as he raised himself up on his elbows, he saw that the lodge was empty. He lifted his hands up and pounded the earth twice in frustration.

"Slow Bird," said a voice from behind him, outside the lodge. "Do not beat the earth. It is not our Mother's fault that your feet have forgotten how to walk."

Bear Talker turned toward the door on his hands and knees, looking as confused as a just-wakened bear about to leave its den in late winter. A tall, strong old woman with her hair in long gray braids stood there, looking down at him. She held in her hand a large piece of fresh elm bark that had been scraped of its rough outer covering. It was ready to fold and sew with spruce root or sinew to make into a basket or a bowl. Bear Talker looked up into the woman's eyes, trying to find the breath to speak. She was the one he had come to find.

"Sweetgrass Woman," Bear Talker said, gasping as he choked out his words, "you must come with me."

"What is wrong?" asked Young Hunter's grandmother. The joking tone was gone from her voice now.

Bear Talker tried to stand, but it seemed as if his legs were connected to the earth, like those of the One Who Shaped Himself just after he sat up from the dust sprinkled by the Owner Creator.

Sweetgrass Woman knelt by him and placed her hands on his shoulder. "Just speak," she said.

"It is Medicine Plant," Bear Talker gasped. "I think she is dying."

CHAPTER NINE
SWEETGRASS WOMAN'S WORK

The big dog sat quietly at the base of a great cedar tree at the top of the hill. Below him, next to the flow of the big river, Young Hunter and Rabbit Stick were talking. Though he was more than a spear's throw away from them, the big dog could hear every word they spoke clearly. And he could see clearly in all directions for a long way, see if anything that might bring danger was approaching. There was no need for him to come closer. The young dog was rolling now next to Young Hunter, who reached out one hand and began to scratch Little Pabetciman's stomach. And though Agwedjiman, too, loved the feel of Young Hunter's strong hands, he did not leave his self-appointed sentinel place.

It was not that he was jealous of Pabesis. Though the young dog had quickly claimed much of Young Hunter's attention, Agwedjiman knew that Pabesis had filled an empty place for that young man who was his friend and master. And in the way that dogs have of seeing beyond the visible things that humans sense, Agwedjiman sensed beneath the exuberant clumsiness of Pabesis the presence of an older and more familiar spirit. True, it was a trial to have one's ears constantly being chewed and paws flopping in one's face, but it was not just to avoid the constant invitations to play he would have to endure if he came down the hill that Agwedjiman stayed on the hilltop, keeping watch.

46

Again, much as before, something was coming. It was not the same danger as had entered the lands of the Only People two winters ago, but it was old and powerful. And it was coming from more than one direction. Agwedjiman lifted his head and sniffed the wind that blew from the west. There was no trace of the scent of those dangers, not yet, but they would come.

"Breathe deeply and then speak clearly," Sweetgrass Woman said.

Bear Talker pushed himself up from the woven cattail rush mats on the floor of the lodge. He noticed that his hands were shaking.

Sweetgrass Woman saw it as well. She took the deep-seeing man's hands between her own and held them firmly. "Be calm. Tell me."

"Medicine Plant is trying ... she is trying to give birth to our child," said a voice that Bear Talker hardly recognized as his own. "But the child, the child is stubborn. The child will not come."

"How long has it been?"

"She began to try to bring the child forth yesterday. She began when the Day Traveler was just beginning to show himself. But the child is too stubborn. Medicine Plant is strong, but she is growing very weak now. At first she would rise and walk and then come back and hold on to the birthing pole. Now she can no longer rise. I asked her what I should do. She told me that she would die unless you came to her before the end of this day."

"Has the child turned its back to the world?"

Bear Talker nodded. "Uh-hunh," he said.

Sweetgrass Woman gathered together the things that many winters of midwifing had taught her she would need. She said nothing more as she did so, though she was already beginning to hum softly the song she used when a child about

47

to be born turned the wrong way, facing back away from new life, too stubborn to leave its mother.

"Child," she sang, "this world is good to see. Child," she sang, "we want you to show us your face."

She placed on the mat the herbs she would use, the sinew string, the fish bladder filled with bear grease that she would use to make her hands supple and slippery, the sharpest of the slate knives with a blade the shape of the Night Traveler when half her face is hidden in the sky. She motioned with her hand, and Bear Talker backed out of the lodge, out of her way. She looked carefully at the items spread before her. All of her helpers were there. She named them, asked them to help her, then bundled them together, placed them in her basket, stood up, and went out the door.

Bear Talker stood there, rubbing a large bruise on his knee, his face that of a lost child. She reached out both her hands and took hold of him by his shoulders. "You know this is my kind of work. I will do all that can be done to help."

Then Sweetgrass Woman moved him aside as she picked up a sharpened stick and made marks on the large piece of elm bark. The shapes—a bear, a woman with a plant in her hand and a child in her belly, the sign for difficulty, and an arrow pointing in the direction she had taken—would tell the story clearly to Rabbit Stick and Young Hunter when they returned from the river, and to Willow Woman when she came back from gathering birch bark. Such clear talking shapes were often used to leave messages. Sweetgrass Woman's family would see the bark and know that she had gone to help Medicine Plant with a difficult birth. They would probably all follow. Not that it would do any good. Whatever was going to happen would have happened long before they got there. She wedged the piece of message bark in between the bark layers covering the lodge so that it stuck out at face level in the middle of the door opening. She thought of telling someone else in the village where she was going, but the nearest lodge was more than a spear's throw away and the shortest trail to reach Medicine Plant did not run through the village. The message bark would be enough.

"Slow Bird," she said, "I am older now, but I have not forgotten how to run. Come behind me at the best speed you can."

Then she turned and ran, almost as swiftly as that young girl who had always beaten him in their races when he was a small fat boy. But, for the first time, Bear Talker felt neither envy nor regret about the speed that had been given to Sweetgrass Woman and that even now, as a grandmother, she still had. His heart only urged her to run even faster as he ran behind, keeping up as best he could.

CHAPTER TEN
DREAMS

Rabbit Stick nodded his head. Young Hunter had spoken clearly and well. It was plain to him now that both of their dreams, so similar in so many ways, had been true ones. Both of them had felt something begin, and both of their dreams had told them that trouble was coming.

Their dreams were not the kind of deceitful dreams a person would sometimes have, dreams sent by those who wished to lead that person astray or cause that person harm. Nor the kind of dreams young people who wished to have powerful dreams sometimes convinced themselves they had dreamt, when in fact those were only their own thoughts and wishes and not messages from Ktsi Nwaskw.

Rabbit Stick remembered well what had happened to that one called Mole. It had happened when Young Hunter and Mole, who were born in the same moon, were both thirteen winters old. Mole did not like the name people called him. His eyes were weak, for some reason. It was not easy for him to see things far away, and he always squinted so that his eyes seemed as small as those of the little one who burrows beneath the earth.

Bear Talker had tried to reason with the boy. The name Mole could be a powerful name. The Little Burrowing One sees beneath the surface of things and goes deep into the earth, just as a far-seeing person goes. Ktsi Nwaskw had plainly intended Mole to be one of those who pay close attention to the things near at hand, to learn from them what others might overlook. Then, while Young Hunter and the other children gathered around them listened, Bear Talker told Mole the story of a boy called Sees Close.

Sees Close lived long ago and could not see things clearly when they were far away. So he kept his eyes on the ground and was always looking closely at things. It was in the days when there were many of the Ancient Ones, those beings that hunted and killed the people. There were seven of those particular Ancient Ones. They were giants with long arms, and they were always hungry for human flesh. The Long Arms lived in the forest near the village of Sees Close. Nothing seemed able to kill those monsters. When the people struck them with their spears, even when the spears went into the monsters' chests, the Long Arms would just pull out the spears and laugh.

One day, Sees Close was walking along looking at the earth. He saw that a big rock had fallen down and covered the hole of a mole. With great effort he moved the rock aside. As soon as he did so, the mole came right out and spoke to him.

"You have helped me," the mole said. "So I will help you. I know those Long Arm monsters have been hurting your people for a long time now. I will show you how to destroy them. Come down here to me."

As the mole said that, Sees Close began to shrink. Soon he was very small, so small that the tiny mole looked bigger than a bear.

"Climb on my back," the mole said.

Sees Close climbed onto the mole's back. It crawled into its tunnel and began to carry him under the earth. They went right under the feet of the monsters no one could kill and came out at the base of a big oak tree. All around that oak tree were Long Arm monsters, guarding the tree. But the monsters did not see the mole or Sees Close because they were so small.

"See this tree?" the mole said. "Look up into its branches and tell me what you see there."

Sees Close squinted up. There in the tree, not far overhead, were the hearts of the Long Arm monsters. That was why no one could kill them. They had hidden their hearts in this tree.

Sees Close began to climb the tree. It was hard to do because he was so small, but he finally reached the branch where the hearts hung. Then he said what the mole had told him to say.

"Large again, large again," Sees Close said.

When he said that, he became the same size he had been before he rode on the mole's back. Then he began to grab the hearts of the monsters and squeeze them. Each time he squeezed one of those hearts a Long Arm monster screamed and died.

"Someone is killing us," they screamed. "Someone is in the tree with our hearts."

The Long Arm monsters ran to the tree and started to climb it, but Sees Close began squeezing their hearts even more quickly, and, one by one, the Long Arm monsters fell dead. The last one was just about to reach Sees Close and grab him when the brave boy squeezed the last heart and killed it. Then, having saved his people, Sees Close climbed down the big oak tree while Little Burrowing One sang a victory song.

Bear Talker was a great storyteller. Even though the children were sometimes afraid of him because of the way he could speak with the deep ones under the earth and because of the way he sometimes growled like a bear and even grew long sharp teeth like a bear's, they always gathered around him whenever he indicated he was going to tell a story. And on the day when he told the story of Sees Close and Little Burrowing One, it seemed that every boy and girl was there and that every one of them looked at Mole in a different way when that story was done.

Most of the children, like Young Hunter, understood. That story was meant to give Mole pride in himself. But Mole did not like the story. Even while Bear Talker was telling the tale, Mole kept squinting off into the distance, trying to make out the shape of a hawk that had landed in a cedar tree beyond Bear Talker's lodge.

Young Hunter walked beside him as they returned to the village, Mole kicking at the snow which was ankle-deep in the path.

"It was a good story," Young Hunter said.

"It was a foolish story," Mole said. "Who would want to go under the earth? I would rather fly like the hawk."

Four sunrises later, Mole announced to his parents, who also were not happy with the nickname their son had carried for more than a handful of winters, that he had dreamed. A powerful dream. The dream had told him, he said, to dress himself in white buckskin and climb to the top of the hill. A hawk would come to him there, and he would have the name of the hawk from that time on.

When he told his story to the elder men in the village, those who were always told the powerful dreams that people had to see if those dreams meant good or ill for the Only People, Rabbit Stick and Bear Talker turned and looked at each other. Both had the same sad look on their faces. They knew Mole's dream was a lie. Mole's parents, though, were proud of that false dream, and it was not the place of other elders to correct them and their son. Mole's parents dressed him in the white buckskin, and he walked off alone proudly toward the hill.

But Mole did not make it to the top. With his bad vision fixed on the highest place, he missed his footing on the narrow trail as he climbed up through the snow. He fell a long way. His head struck a stone and he was killed. His eyes were wide open when the people found him. They carried him back to the lodge of his parents and dug the hole to bury him there inside the lodge, where the earth was kept thawed by the central fire.

So Mole did not go to the hill with the hawk but went instead under the earth. He was wrapped in elm bark and buried in a sitting position, his eyes still open, still dressed in the white buckskin clothing of his false dream.

Young Hunter was now holding the leather pouch he always carried around his waist. He had untied it while Rabbit Stick was remembering. As he held the pouch in his heartside hand, he reached over to place his other hand on his grandfather's shoulder. Rabbit Stick looked again at his grandson. The last two winters had been good to the young man. He had grown a full hand taller and no longer was shorter than the erect old man. The wisdom he had gained on his long and dangerous journey when he walked out to face the Ancient Ones was held there in the place behind his eyes.

Rabbit Stick could see that wisdom, and it made his heart good. But Rabbit Stick also could see the uncertainty that was there once again in the young man's eyes. Despite the training his grandson had been given by Bear Talker, so that his gift of deep sight might someday be used even more effectively to serve the Only People, that uncertainty had returned. But that was not surprising. One did not become a deep-seer overnight. Even if the medicine teachings he carried were powerful, Young Hunter was still a young man—and a young man just married and not ready to leave the side of his wife.

Rabbit Stick reached out and put his arm around Young Hunter. Young Hunter leaned his head against his grandfather's shoulder in exactly the same way he had done when a very small boy.

"Grandson," Rabbit Stick said, saying it as he had said it so many winters ago when Young Hunter had come to them after the death of his parents. "Grandson," he said, patting the strong young man's back, "remember this. You are not alone."

CHAPTER ELEVEN
THE BLANKET TREE

It had happened the evening before Rabbit Stick went to the river. It had begun when the light of the Day Traveler was fading. A gray stone shaped almost like a large sitting man rested at the edge of the clearing. The clearing was a two-day walk for a normal human being toward the sunset from the village of the Only People. It was a clearing among the mountains on the other side of the Long River.

A deer emerged from the forest and stepped hesitantly toward the gray stone. It scented something unfamiliar, yet so unfamiliar that she did not feel the urge to run that the scent of a wolf or long-tailed cat would have sent pulsing through her blood. The deer was a young one, a year-old doe. She lifted one foot slowly to step closer to the gray stone, aware that this stone was different. But, like all deer, she was curious to know more.

Another cautious step, another, but not cautious enough. Suddenly, the gray stone stirred to life. A great hand struck out at the young doe, which would never have a fawn. Neck bones and breath were crushed with that blow. The doe lay dead at the feet of the last Ancient One, the only survivor of that dawn when the earth had shaken and the cave in the hills had collapsed on its brothers.

Darkness was now walking across the clearing. The Ancient One looked around to see that there were no other eyes there to watch it before it stood, reaching down with one great hand to pick up the doe and carry her body back into the forest, back to the place where it had chosen to hide, a place of many caves in a hill, a place under a great slanted stone where it could eat and not be seen. It would eat without fire, for it was alone and feared being discovered by the small dangerous one whose strength had been great enough to destroy all of its people.

It had followed that small one for two winters now, watching always from a distance, careful to leave no tracks or trace of itself to be seen, careful to hide at night deep in the caves. It did not try to touch the small dangerous one's mind. It only followed, watching and waiting. Though why it watched and what it waited for, even the last of the Ancient Ones did not fully know.

The last of the Ancient Ones had found many caves in which to hide. There was even one very close to the Long River, close to the place where Young Hunter and Rabbit Stick would sit and talk of their dreams. When the light had faded again from the sky and the last of the Ancient Ones had finished eating, it would go again to that cave.

Willow Woman walked among the birch trees. Her eyes looked carefully for a tree whose bark would be just right for the basket she wished to fashion, but her mind was elsewhere. Her mind was dreamwalking far ahead of her, to that time when she would not walk alone to gather bark but with a child by her side. A child of hers, a child of Young Hunter's. As she imagined the things she would teach that child, her lips moved silently with the words she would speak.

"We call these trees *maskwamozi*. They are the blanket trees, these birches. We always ask their permission before we take part of their bark, because that is the blanket that keeps them warm. And when we take a part of their blanket, never too much, we take care not to cut too deep. And in exchange for that blanket we always give something in return."

Willow Woman nodded, still walking. That would be good to say. But if the child were anything like Young Hunter, then that child would surely not just listen. There would be questions.

"How did we learn to take the blanket from the tree?" the child would surely ask.

Willow Woman stopped and leaned back against a very large birch. She saw herself looking down at that child and answering.

"Why do we take the blankets from the birch? That is because, a long time ago, a child was caught in a late spring snowstorm when she was out walking in the forest. The Only People looked hard for her, but the storm was too strong. Everyone in the village was sure she had frozen. But when they found her the next day, she was alive, wrapped in birch bark at the base of one of the trees. That tree had taken pity and stripped off its bark to give that child a blanket. The people thanked that tree, and from then on they knew they could use its bark in many ways."

Willow Woman put her hand up to her chin and looked at the birch tree she had been leaning against. The story she had begun to tell her child, a child yet to breathwalk, a child who still lived only in her mind, was a good one. But it was not a story that any of the Only People had told Willow Woman. That story had just come to her. It was as if the big birch tree itself, one of those generous birch trees, had given her the story.

Willow Woman put down the spear she had been carrying in her other hand and reached into her pouch to take out some of the smoking herb. She placed it at the base of the large birch.

"*Wliwini,* Grandmother," she said to the tree. "I thank you for this special gift. I will listen to that story carefully in my heart, and when I tell it one day to our first child, I will remember it was your gift."

She grasped the spear again, having placed it on the ground so that it was touching her foot. Then she straightened and looked beyond the large birch up the hill. There were other trees there to look over and see if they would give their bark as freely as this grandmother birch tree had given her that story. Though blanket trees always healed when their bark was taken in the right way, not cut too deep with the sharp-edged flint knife, Willow Woman knew that the trees were sacrificing a part of themselves each time such a gift was given. That was why no tree had more than one dark-barked ring about it to show where part of its blanket had been stripped in some past season.

But as she walked, she heard a cry. It was coming from the other side of the hill. *Danger,* the cry said, again and again. *Danger! Danger! Danger!* She began to run, not away from that cry, but toward it. It was the cry of a little one in desperate trouble.

CHAPTER TWELVE
IN THE GREAT PINE

Walking Hill stood by the base of the great pine, a tree that towered over all the others in the forest, so large that even the great animal seemed small next to it. His eyes were closed, yet as he leaned against the tree, Walking Hill did not sleep. The constant throbbing in his jaw, just behind the huge right tusk, made sleeping no easy thing at any time. And now, knowing that the little upright one he had pursued and almost caught had climbed the few low stubs of the great tree's dead branches to find refuge above, Walking Hill would not sleep. He would wait until the small one grew unwary and descended or until it became so weak and tired that it fell from its perch. Walking Hill could still smell the blood of the small one. It had been wounded when Walking Hill destroyed its village in the valley below, next to the Long River. Before it reached this tree, it had left the blood scent behind it, and Walking Hill had come up from the valley like a whirlwind, breaking down the trees and brush until he came to this tree, too large for him to break. Looking up, he had seen the motion of the small one perched there on the branch above. Eyes closed, Walking Hill waited. Patient, alert.

Young Hunter held the stone shape he had taken from his pouch in his hand, the hand closest to his heart. It seemed to grow warmer in his hand as he held it, and he pressed it against the center of his forehead. He still felt his grandfather's hand on his shoulder, but he felt something else as well. He felt rough bark against his cheek and smelled the familiar scent of pine. And there was another scent, too, the musky smell of an animal. But it was no animal he had ever smelled before. It was below him, below the tree in which he sat and did not sit, the tree that filled his awake dreaming. He moved and felt the weakness of the dead branch beneath him. It might give way from his weight were it not for the fact that he clung so tightly with both outstretched arms to the great trunk of the pine.

Young Hunter took a deep breath and felt in himself a fear that was not his own. He focused his eyes, wholly in the awake dream now. His eyes did not want to focus. It was as if they were the eyes of a much older man, one whose vision was no longer so keen, one in whose eyes the world looked as blurred as if seeing underwater. He blinked, squinted, and saw the left hand of the person whose life he was sharing. It was not his own hand. This hand was, indeed, the hand of an older person and it was terribly wounded. It was only half a hand. The small finger and its closest older brother were gone, and the hand still bled. As the blood flowed from that hand, the strength also flowed out.

Now the one whose eyes Young Hunter shared turned his head to look down, down at something that was not far below, no more than three spear lengths. It stirred and looked up, a huge animal with dark fur. It was not easy to see it clearly because of the blurred vision of this man, but Young Hunter could see that the two fang teeth were even longer than those of the great black beast that had served the Ancient Ones, although these teeth curved up. Great glistening spears, these teeth.

The one whose body Young Hunter shared was very weak indeed. Young Hunter felt the weakness and tried to counter it with his own strength. He wished for strength to come into this wounded man's arms, but it did not. There was nothing he could do. The huge animal beneath the tree moved back a few steps. Then, with surprising speed, it charged forward and struck the tree with its head. Despite its great size, the tree trembled. The wounded man's grasp slipped further. Yet, as the branch beneath him made a cracking sound and his body weakened, Young Hunter felt the fear lessen in this one whose vision he borrowed. Then the wounded man spoke.

Young Hunter heard and spoke with him as he did so. It took Young Hunter the space of two breaths to understand the words that had been spoken. Though this wounded man spoke the language of human beings, the true tongue of the Dawn Land, the language shared by the people of the thirteen villages of which Young Hunter's Only People were one, he spoke it differently. His words were said almost as if with a mouthful of food, not in the way of the Thirteen Villages. Yet it was their language, not that of the smaller people to the south or of the painted people farther to the east, not the strange talk of the Long Lodge People to the west. He remembered his grandfather saying that there were more of the Dawn Land People to the north and that they were good enough people, even if they could not speak the real language all that well.

"*Nidoba*," the northern man said. "Brother-friend. I feel you with me. I welcome you, *m'teowlin*, deep-seeing person. I feel you try to help me. Thank you for coming to share my body. I know you have tried, but you cannot give me your strength. For your help, let me give you my name. I am *Ktsi Azeban*, Big Raccoon. But I have climbed my last tree."

The wounded man paused, took a breath, and laughed. "You cannot help me, but you have helped. The great beast, the hill that walks, followed me, even as I hoped it would. I left the trail of my blood so that it would follow. It did not see the others of my people come out from the place where they were hiding below the riverbank and float down the Long River in

61

our big dugout. You gave me the strength to hold on here long enough for them to float farther, far enough perhaps to be safe for a while."

Big Raccoon swayed back, and it seemed that he was about to fall, but he pulled himself back again close to the trunk. There was more that he had to say.

"My friend whom I cannot see," Big Raccoon said, "there is one more thing for which I must thank you. You have reminded me that my spirit can leave my body. Life is a very sweet thing, as sweet as the taste of ripe berries, but I remember now that all real human beings one day must let it go. I can go to my dying without being afraid."

Then Big Raccoon took an even deeper breath. Young Hunter understood. He was filling his lungs with the taste of the air, breathing in the goodness of the life all around them. Young Hunter felt the man move his lips into a smile.

"*Nidoba*," Big Raccoon said again, and as he spoke his wounded hand slipped from its hold on the rough bark of the pine, "help my people."

The limb beneath them broke and Big Raccoon fell. He fell back and down but Young Hunter did not fall with him. His vision separated from the wounded old man who fell. He saw something long and supple, like a huge snake, lift up from between the glistening white teeth of the great animal. Then there was a great flash of light. Then there was darkness.

Young Hunter opened his eyes. He lay on his back. The great pine was gone. His grandfather leaned over him. There were cedar boughs above them. He heard the cool voice of the nearby waters of the Long River.

"Bear Talker told us it would be this way, Grandson," Rabbit Stick said. His grandfather's voice was calm, yet it shook slightly. "Still, though he told us not to worry, I am glad to see you back in your body. *Wlipamkaani?* Did you travel well?"

Young Hunter lifted his left hand. All the fingers were there. It was again the hand of a young man, unwounded, unmarked by the stains of age. It still held the stone shape he had found between the layers of clay in the bed of the Long River. He had carried it for several seasons now in his pouch. He lifted it up and looked at it. It was like the shape of a stiff-legged bear, yet with a long, long nose. He touched it with the fingers of his right hand, knowing it now. He sat up and looked up the Long River, in the direction of the Always Winter Land. His last thought to Big Raccoon had been a promise. He would try to help the old man's people.

There was moisture in his eyes as Young Hunter held out the stone shape so that Rabbit Stick could see it. "I have seen this one, Grandfather," he said. "All of the Ancient Ones that hunt our people have still not gone from this world."

CHAPTER THIRTEEN
THE LONG-TAIL

As Willow Woman ran through the brush, following the trail made by the deer, she did not go headlong without looking, the way a frightened rabbit might run. She ran like a fox, like an animal wise from living both as hunted and hunter. When still a young girl, Willow Woman had been taught as much by her father about hunting as had any of the boys.

Her father, Deer Tracker, had always been one of the finest hunters among the Only People. That was one of the reasons—though, as her mother often said (looking toward her husband in a way that always seemed to make him look intently at whatever work he was doing to escape his wife's gaze), not the only reason—that Willow Woman's mother, whose name was Near the Sky, had chosen to marry him. Near the Sky was herself known as a woman who could handle a spear. She was the woman who killed a bear with her spear when it attacked a party of women gathering berries one summer.

Not having a son to learn his ways had simply strengthened Deer Tracker's determination to make his daughter that much more aware of the way of the hunter.

"We are like the wolf," he said to his daughter. "We are not like the deer or the rabbit. Our eyes are in the front of our head so that we can follow the tracks, so we can be hunters. The rabbit and deer have their eyes on the side of their heads so that they can better watch for the ones who hunt them. And we are the ones who hunt them. We are the wolves."

So when Willow Woman ran, she ran as a hunter runs. She kept the point of her spear ahead of her, her other hand held up and out to push aside the branches of the small maples and beech trees that grew thickly here. But though she ran with care, she also went quickly. The cries of the little one were urgent.

There was a stony place ahead, an exposed ledge of blue rock that made a natural clearing. It was not one of those clearings the Only People would make here and there in the forest, knowing such places to be needed by the animal and plant people. Some tall beech trees grew at the farther edge of that clearing, and it was from below those trees that the cries came.

Willow Woman stopped running before entering that clearing. Her eyes had swept across and taken in the scene before her. She understood the story of all that she saw, understood it as well as if it had been spoken to her by the voice of a storyteller. She saw the black feathers flecked with blood around the base of the beech tree in which the nest had been torn apart. She had seen that nest before, watched the wide black wings of the crows as they worked, readying the nest for the young ones who would come in the season of the long days. But one of the big night-eyed ones had come in the darkness, the deep darkness of a cloudy night when the Night Traveler and the *awatawesu*, the little distant ones far above, had not shown their bright faces. Only one of those crows had survived. Though it called in the remembered voice of the little one it had been, it was large enough to be in its second cycle of seasons. Clearly it had stayed with its parents as the young ones sometimes did, helping them ready their nest before leaving to find its own way. Although it would not have gone far. The crow people were like the Only People. They loved their families, and they would often gather together with many of their relatives, chanting and talking.

But from this small family, only the little one had survived. The parents it called for would not hear it. Their lives had ended in the talons and the sharp beak of the great owl. And so, too, would the life of this little one, it seemed. Its wing was injured and it could not fly. Only a leap away from it a long-tail crouched. The tip of the panther's tail switched back and forth slowly. Willow Woman knew the meaning of that, too, knew why it crouched even lower still. Soon, very soon, it would spring. Like the wolf people and the human people, the panther people were hunters and stalkers. This one was about to finish its hunt.

The long-tail, despite its sharp senses, had not noticed her, even though she was just a short spear cast away. Willow Woman understood why. It was not just that the wind was in her face, carrying her scent away from the long-tail. Nor was it just that the small sounds of her careful running had been covered by the little one's cries. Another panther might still have heard her. But not this one. It was too young. Clearly, from its carelessness, it was too young and foolish to be on its own. Normally, a long-tail stayed with its mother through two full winters.

Willow Woman remembered her father, Deer Tracker, explaining this to her one winter as he showed her the tracks of two panthers in the snow—one large and one smaller. After that younger animal's second winter, another litter would be born, and the two-wintered one would have to leave its mother. But the last few winters had been easy ones. The acorns and beech trees had produced so many nuts that despite all that the squirrel people and the Only People gathered, there had been enough to make the deer people become very, very fat. That fat and mild weather with little snow had meant that few of the deer people died in the cold season. Many young ones had been born in each of the last few springs, so many that the long-tails, which fed on the deer, themselves grew fat. The wolf people and the Dawn Land People also relied on the deer, but there were so many deer now that even the many hunters had scarcely lessened the numbers of the herds.

So it was that with easy winters and much food, the long-tail mothers were now having a litter each year. It was that way with all the different peoples. When times were good and the balance allowed it, both human and animal people would grow more numerous. However, for the long-tail young ones it meant that they might be sent out on their own before they were truly ready. They would have to care for themselves too early not to be foolish. Often, such bold and foolish young ones had not learned yet to respect the human people. This made them dangerous.

Though the winter-old long-tail Willow Woman saw in that clearing weighed no more than she did herself, she knew the strength in its limbs was many times greater than her own. Sometimes, in fact, young people or elders were injured or even killed by such a long-tail with no fear of the human people. But when the little one cried one more time for help, Willow Woman did not hesitate. She crouched, scooped up a stone the size of her fist with her free hand and hurled it sidearm. It hit right in front of the long-tail's nose, striking sparks from the rocky ledge.

The panther leaped up and back, its hindquarters high above its head, twisting itself in midair so that it landed facing back toward Willow Woman. It crouched, opened its mouth, and bared its teeth, hissing more loudly than a great snake. Its long tail switched back and forth faster now, and its eyes were filled with the anger that comes with fear.

Willow Woman stood still. She knew that if she ran or even moved back quickly, it would attack her. Slowly, she began to draw herself up, standing taller. Her mother had taught her to do this if one had to face a long-tail. When facing a bear, one must bow and make one's self smaller, for bears demand respect. But a long-tail will attack that which is littler.

"Be tall, do not crouch," Near the Sky had said.

As Willow Woman stood taller, the little black one at the base of the tree continued calling. But its call was different now. No longer was it the baby's fear cry for help. In spite of the danger she was facing, Willow Woman smiled. The little black one, seeing that it now had a defender, was taunting the long-tail.

Willow Woman held out her spear, the point toward the panther. If it leaped, she would catch it on that spear, grounding the spear's base on the stony ledge beneath her feet. But she had no wish and no need for the long-tail's death.

"Speak simply and clearly to the animal people," so her mother had always said.

"*Kita, pihtolo,*" Willow Woman said. She kept her voice soft, but firm. "Listen, long-tail! This small black one is not your food. *Mzakas* is too small and tough. Go and find *madegwas.* I saw *madegwas* in the meadow below this hill. Go and find the rabbit. Rabbit is your food. Follow the trail of *nolka.* I saw *nolka* just down there, in the thicket. Deer is your food. The small black one is not your food. *Mzakas* is my child."

The long-tail moved one foot backward and then another. As it did so, Willow Woman moved forward and to the side, holding out her spear so that it now was between the long-tail and young crow. The long-tail looked directly into Willow Woman's eyes. The fear-anger was gone from it, washed away by the softness of Willow Woman's firm, clear voice, washed away like a swirl of dark silt carried downstream by the cleansing waters of a flowing brook.

"Hunt well, *pihtolo,*" Willow Woman said.

The young mountain lion turned away and leapt. One leap and it was across the ledge. Another leap and it was gone, vanished into the brush and the small trees.

"*Kah-gah!*" The small black one said. It hopped toward Willow Woman, its little eyes brightly focused on her face.

Willow Woman bent one knee, leaning her spear back against her shoulder as she held out her hand to her new child.

CHAPTER FOURTEEN
LOOKS BACKWARD

As Sweetgrass Woman ran, she thought of the times when breech births had happened before. Such a stubborn birth was no easy thing if a midwife was not immediately at hand. The child might become so caught that it and its mother might not survive. The birthing cord might become tangled around the child's neck and choke the baby or be twisted so tight that its mother's life could no longer flow into its body. Birth was always like dawn. It promised new life, but there was also the possibility of danger and even death each time the Day Traveler showed his bright face.

Sweetgrass Woman was one of those to whom the gift of helping others bring new life into the world had been given. It was not only in the strength and the gentleness of her hands, but also in her knowing spirit that the gift showed itself. Though the village might call her She Who Has to Know Everything behind her back, that wish to know of all the things others did and said among the Only People was a part of her gift of knowing what was going to happen before it would happen. Not with everything, of course. Mostly, Sweetgrass Woman was able to predict the exact moment to be there to help with births.

It was Sweetgrass Woman who would appear, a braid of sweetgrass in her hand, at the door of a lodge just at the time when a mother-to-be was ready to send for help. Her instinct had never failed her with this. She knew when she was needed, when the knowledge she had been given to hold was needed to bring a healthy child to its first breath. She would know how to make the mother relax and lose her fear. With her strong hands she would straighten the child's path, then help it enter life in the proper way.

It bothered her now that she had not known when Medicine Plant would need her. *Why is this so?* part of her mind asked, even as another part went through memories of other births when the child had turned its back to the waking world, when the child had tried to choose to remain in that deep sleep before tasting the air. No other first-time mother among any of the real human beings had held as many winters as Medicine Plant. Medicine Plant was not an old woman; other women of her age gave birth to healthy children. But never their first child after so many winters. Would her body be strong enough; would it remember what to do?

Each person is given original memories from the Owner Creator. Sweetgrass Woman knew that to be so. Those memories are clear at birth, but for most people those older rememberings fade, their place taken by new memories that are needed more for this lifetime. If a woman did not have children by a certain age, her body might go past that time of remembering what to do. And then a late, first birth would be hard, perhaps too hard.

"Soon I will find out how strong the birthing memory is in Medicine Plant," she said aloud.

Sweetgrass Woman began to climb the long hill that rose up above the Long River. She was still running. She had left far behind even the sound of Bear Talker's stumbling feet. *But why,* she thought again, *why have I not been aware of this birth that was coming?*

And then the answer came to her. It came to her so strongly that it frightened her and she almost stopped running.

"It is because of the child," she said aloud. "This child does not wish to be born. It wishes so strongly to stay with its mother that its spirit has reached out and closed the eyes of my knowing."

Sweetgrass Woman shook her head, but did not stop as she climbed. It was so steep now that she could not run, but her walk uphill was swift. It was not a common thing for two such as Bear Talker and Medicine Plant—deep-seeing people—to marry each other. But even when such marriages did happen—perhaps once in a dozen lifetimes—never would children come of that marriage. With such parents as his—and Sweetgrass Woman sensed now with great certainty that this stubborn child not wishing to be born was surely a boy—it was no wonder that he was already refusing to cooperate. No wonder, either, that he was able to put doubts into her mind, she realized.

Sweetgrass Woman chuckled. *When this one is finally born,* she thought, *I will have earned the right to name him. And I know what that name will be.*

As she thought this, a stone gave way beneath her feet and she fell to one knee. She grasped hold of a blueberry bush as she slipped further and pulled herself back from the edge over which she had almost tumbled.

"Little boy," she said, "Looks Backward, your trick did not work. I have not fallen and I will not fall."

Even as she said those words, a stone the size of her head came rolling down the slope toward her, and she had to throw herself to the ground to avoid it. Her knee ached as she stood up, but it held her weight. She had not dropped the thick sweetgrass braid in her left hand, and the pack was still firmly over her shoulder. She looked at the path ahead of her.

"If I continue this way," she said, "what other tricks will you try to play on me? Do you not know that I am a grandmother?" Then Sweetgrass Woman sighed and turned her back to the trail. "You are too powerful for me," she said. "I am turning back to my lodge."

She put the sweetgrass into her pouch and pushed back her braids. She wiped her hands on her deerskin dress and carefully looked up out of the corner of one eye. A redtail hawk circled overhead and then disappeared back up the face of the hill in the direction of Medicine Plant's lodge.

Good, she thought. Then, swiftly and silently, Sweetgrass Woman slipped off the trail and began to climb up the slope, pulling herself up by grasping the roots of the small trees. She climbed with her mind calm, thinking no thoughts so that the powerful little one would not sense her approach.

When she pulled herself up over the last ridge, Sweetgrass Woman saw the lodge of Medicine Plant below her, on the downward slope. The Long River was a thin piece of silver light trailing through the valley below like the dew-moistened strand of a spider's web glittering with the light of the Day Traveler as he neared the end of his day's journey.

"Looks Backward," she said loudly, as she walked toward the lodge. She panted as she spoke, but her voice was calm and strong. "Give up your stubborn wish. I am Sweetgrass Woman and no baby has ever defeated me."

CHAPTER FIFTEEN
THE BIRTHING LODGE

Down on the slope below Medicine Plant's lodge, Bear Talker could run no farther. It was not only that he was so tired that he could taste his own blood in the back of his throat, nor was it that his knee throbbed like another heart where he had struck it on the log. It was the storm. He had not felt it coming, but now, as suddenly as a partridge opening its wings and bursting up through the trees, it was here.

The storm that now swept down from the hilltop was not one of which the sky had spoken. There had been no slow coming of the strong wind. There had been no motion of clouds across the sky from the sunrise way or the sunset direction, gradually showing the faces of the Thunder Beings, the Grandfathers in the Sky. Nothing in the Sky Land or in the smell and feel of the air had told Bear Talker this storm was arising. And Bear Talker was one who, since his earliest childhood, had always felt the coming of storms.

Even Two Sticks had shown something like respect for the boy's way of knowing the breath of the winds. Two Sticks, Bear Talker's father, had been a man too lazy even to build a fire for himself in his lodge when the water in the drinking pots froze solid and cracked open the clay. Two Sticks' face had reflected his narrow way of seeing the world. His face was so thin and sharp that people would joke that he needed no stone hatchet but could cut wood with his nose. It was a double joke, for everyone knew that Two Sticks would never be seen carrying anything that could be used for real work. His face was also almost like that of one of the little underwater people, and everyone knew that they had no fires in their lodges, there under the waters of the Long River.

After his mother died when he had known only enough winters to be able to talk, Bear Talker had had to keep the fire in their poorly built lodge. He tried to make as large a fire as possible, but it was not easy. Other grown-ups would sometimes bring wood to help the boy, although they were careful not to let Two Sticks see them and to never bring more wood than it seemed possible for a small boy to gather. Lazy as he was, Two Sticks also had a kind of pride-anger twisting in his head. If he thought anyone had helped his son, then he would speak the kind of mean words that always brought pain to the small child's round face. Two Sticks would do almost nothing for himself, and yet he also wanted no one's help apart from the work he forced upon his son.

That was why he had eventually built his lodge far on the western edge of the village—so that no one could interfere with his lazy way of doing things. People had tried. One day when Two Sticks was out picking berries—not into a bark basket, but eating them as he picked them—some men and women from the village had come to his lodge and replaced the rotten bark shingles at its base where the wind always blew in on Bear Talker's small back. When Two Sticks had returned, his face and hands red from the juice of berries—but not a single berry in those skinny hands to share with his son—he had not spoken a word. He had simply loaded the few possessions they had into his small son's arms and then shoved the child ahead of him along the trail to the river. A few young boys followed, keeping out of sight, and were surprised to see the energy with which Two Sticks built his new wigwom in the clearing on a certain small rise, even though the birch bark with which he covered it was half-rotten and curling.

Two Sticks had been given his name as a small child when he showed himself too lazy to carry anything heavier than two tiny sticks when asked by his parents to bring firewood into their lodge. Usually such a name was replaced later in life when a person did something more noteworthy. But Two Sticks never did anything that justified his being called a new name by the Only People. If Two Sticks saw anyone bringing so much as a small stick toward his lodge—perhaps because he so resented that name of his which he could never lose—he would turn his back until that person went away. Yet, lazy as he was, he was not too lazy to carry such sticks brought by others for his son's fires to the high nearby bank of the Long River. Then he would drop them in and watch, with whatever satisfaction he felt in his narrow spirit, as they floated away downstream. On cold mornings, when the small fire (a fire as big as a small boy could make it without an elder's help) had burned out as it always did, Two Sticks would simply cover his head with the only warm robe in the lodge. Then his small son would work to blow the embers of the fire from the night before back into life.

Yet if Bear Talker should mention in an offhand way his feeling that a strong wind and rain were about to arrive, Two Sticks would quickly be up and looking anxiously at the sky. Even Two Sticks listened with interest when his strange child said that the Thunder Beings, his Sky Grandfathers, were coming to speak to them. When Medicine Plant came and claimed the boy as her apprentice, Two Sticks had sighed with relief. It had seemed to him that more and more often, the boy had been foreseeing the coming of thunderstorms. He felt that the boy's absence might mean lightning would strike at his very doorstep less often and the wind's harsh breath would have fewer chances to tear apart the covering of his wigwom. Things would change if that troublesome boy were gone. In a way, Two Sticks was right. Only three moons after Bear Talker's departure from his father's lodge, an immense storm came sweeping up the Long River. So many bolts of lightning were thrown by the Thunder Grandfathers that all of the Only People stayed inside with the doors of their lodges tied tight.

It seemed to the man who was sagamon in those days, a very tall and straight old man named Little Pine, that the storm and the explosions of thunder had been strongest in the direction where that disagreeable man's wigwom was placed on the rise by the Long River. People had long said that, in fact, the rise was the wrong place for anyone to make a lodge. It was a spot where the little underwater people were said to have danced before Two Sticks had claimed it for his homesite.

Little Pine and several other respected men and women went to that spot as soon as the storm was over. Where Two Sticks' lodge had stood, nothing was left but a blackened circle on the ground. Lightning struck there. The dry sticks and rotten bark had burned to ashes, and the ashes had blown away. There was no sign of Two Sticks to be seen.

Bear Talker had a special relationship with the Sky Grandfathers. Yet this storm had come unforeseen, come from the west as suddenly as a panther leaping from an overhanging branch onto the back of a deer. Bear Talker tried to lean into the wind as he climbed up the hill, but its direction kept changing and he found himself growing confused about whether he was going up or down, even though his eyes told him that he was still climbing.

He looked overhead and what he saw made him gasp. It was as if there were an eye above him. The sky directly overhead was as clear as the surface of a morning pond, yet there was darkness all around that strange blue circle. Yet, awesome as it was, it made Bear Talker grow calm. He had seen this before. Not above him, but below him as he descended in his shaking lodge to the place where the old voices called to him. He knew now that this was something that could not be understood, and so he understood it.

He stopped trying to climb. He could see the familiar arched shape of Medicine Plant's wigwom there ahead of him. The place where it stood was high above him, yet it was easy to see, for the storm was circling that place. The clouds moved over it in two great circles. Bear Talker knew that he was meant to stay where he stood. Sweetgrass Woman was up there in that lodge now. She was with Medicine Plant. There was no need for him to be there.

"Ah!" Bear Talker said it aloud, a sound half-word and half-rueful laugh. Indeed there was no need for his help. When those two women were together, what could they not defeat? Bear Talker knew this all too well from the long years he had known both of them—and from the love he held in his heart for both women. It was a love that Sweetgrass Woman had always understood so well that she would never miss any chance to tease him or to remind him of all the faults he had shown as a small boy. And as a grown man. He did not envy Rabbit Stick. Yet who had he, Bear Talker, chosen to live with now but a woman so strong that the very Thunder Beings circled her lodge?

Bear Talker sat down on the wet stones. He was still breathing hard and his leg ached. He chose a smooth stone carefully and then held it against the bruised knee, feeling the pain lessen. His heart felt full, so full that he knew it was being touched by the breath of a new one. In that lodge on the hill, his new son was drawing his first breath. He looked up again. The sky was clearing, the circle widening. And as it did so, a rainbow appeared—the sky putting on its bright colored coat, arcing like the roof of a great wigwom from horizon to horizon.

The lodge held the familiar human smells of birth along with the gentle scent of the burning sweetgrass that Sweetgrass

Woman held in her left hand as she walked about the lodge. The boy was crying. No, not crying. It seemed as if, young as he was, he were trying to speak and became impatient that his throat and tongue would not shape the words held in his ancient memory. Sweetgrass Woman looked into the child's face, and the child stopped crying to look back at her. Those eyes were the eyes of Bear Talker; the chin and the shape of the head—those clearly belonged to this little one's mother. Yet this child was very much himself, and that look in his eyes—was it a look of challenge?

"Looks Backward," Sweetgrass Woman said, "it is good that you have a strong mother. With parents such as yours, you are going to need much guidance."

"That is not so," Medicine Plant said.

Sweetgrass Woman turned slowly to look at her. She waited, but Medicine Plant said nothing further. "I do not understand," Sweetgrass Woman said at last.

Medicine Plant's voice was calm. It held none of the exhaustion or elation that Sweetgrass Woman had heard so often in the voices of those women whose little ones had chosen to make them new mothers. Her voice seemed to be coming from a distant place, yet it was a voice that held in it a caring for the little one which Sweetgrass Woman did understand.

"This strong child," Medicine Plant said, "this gift that the Owner Creator has given, is not a gift that I can hold. This one will help the people in a special way, but he will do so without me. I must give him away."

Medicine Plant looked at the face of Sweetgrass Woman. The shock there almost made the deep-seeing woman laugh, for she knew that it was a shock that would soon be replaced with the delight of having such strange news to spread to everyone in the village. The child reached up and placed a hand in her face, and then Medicine Plant did laugh.

"But I will not give him away to strangers," Medicine Plant said.

78

CHAPTER SIXTEEN
WALKING INTO THE STORY

As they passed through the village, Young Hunter found himself once again walking as one divided. Danowa and Agwedjiman ranged ahead of them, one of them in sight while the other swung off the trail to see what lay ahead. They sensed the way Young Hunter felt and so were more watchful than they knew they needed to be, as if to reassure him. They were there as his brother-helpers when he needed them. But Young Hunter did not notice it in the place where his mind spoke within him. His hand was on the back of Pabesis, the dog's shoulder touching his thigh now and then, but though the big young dog kept glancing up as he walked close to Young Hunter, Young Hunter did not return that look.

It was as if his thinking circled over his own head, the way the little hungry ones do. Much as you may swat at them, they do not grow discouraged until your hand chances to catch them. And where they bite, if they find a place where the bear grease salve is not thick enough, that good-smelling salve which everyone wears at the season when the little hungry ones swarm, their bite leaves a welt. That was how it was with his divided thinking. He was here and not here. He found himself back in the awake dream again, the great beast below him, reaching for him as he fell. Yet he was Young Hunter, not Big Raccoon, not the one whose death he had shared.

His grandfather's hand remained on his shoulder, guiding him as he walked, yet he was feeling so confused by his thoughts that he hardly felt that strong hand. Why did these things come to him? Why was he not done with all of this?

After Young Hunter returned from his great journey alone, Medicine Plant and Bear Talker had allowed him to live his own life. They had not taken him away to train him as a deep-seeing person—as he had feared they would do. Instead, they had allowed him to return to his family. The two *m'teowlins* had welcomed him but then paid more attention to each other than to him. In a way, his relief had been mixed with disappointment. Was that all he was to them, a thing to be used? Was he like a firestick that has grown too short to twirl and so can be left by the trailside? A bit of the smoking herb might be placed with that firestick. Some words of thanks might be spoken, of course, but it was still abandoned because it was no longer useful.

Young Hunter petted the back of Pabesis with his heartside hand as he continued to walk. He was grateful that he had been able to do as he wished, though it had been a long time before he had stopped feeling uncertain in those early days after returning from the west. For more than two seasons he walked the way a person going to check his traps walks when he knows that there is ice under the snow which holds him and that the ice might be thin. Young Hunter did not want to break through and fall into deep water.

Then, as nothing unusual happened, nothing more than each day's round, he slipped back into the old comforting cycle of village ways. He woke with the Day Traveler's light to see to what each season bade the Only People to do. He went out to strip bark from trees to repair the lodge and to drink the sweet sap of the spring trees. As season followed season he picked berries, caught fish, followed the tracks of the moose in the snow of winter. By the time four full seasons had passed, it seemed as if he had never left. It was as if the story of his great journey, of his battle with the monsters, was only a winter tale he had learned from some wise and strong elder.

Now and then, when he found himself telling his story— not just to the many children who would always be at his feet whenever he sat by a fire, but also to his friends and to the elders who came, until all of the elders of the Thirteen Villages had heard with their own ears the tale as it was carried on Young Hunter's own breath—it seemed to him he was telling a story about a young man who had lived long ago. He told the story but no longer thought of it as his own, even though he told it well.

He told it so well that Fire Keeper had nodded and given him the gift of a beautiful clay pipe when he first listened to Young Hunter tell of the great journey. This young man was clearly becoming *ktsi ndatlogit*, a great story remembered.

By then, Young Hunter was no longer in the story. He was walking around the story. The story had its own life now. Its tracks went beyond his own. And it was with both relief and a kind of sadness that he watched the tracks of the great story lead away over the hills, leaving him behind. But he did not feel that sadness those times when Willow Girl was sitting beside him, poking him hard with an elbow when he paused too long in his telling, and teasing him afterwards that he had not told her everything about that old woman he rescued. And, indeed, Young Hunter had not told her all.

"What was her name?" Willow Girl asked. "Red Nose?" Then she had looked so intently into Young Hunter's eyes that he had seen what was to be between them and his heart had pounded like a lifting partridge's wings.

Two seasons after his return, in the Moon of Ripe Raspberries, Willow Girl's mother had come to see Sweetgrass Woman. She came to talk of many things and of one thing. Sweetgrass Woman was more than ready. In fact, she almost asked the other, younger woman what had taken her and her daughter so long. Did they not know that every marriageable young woman in the Thirteen Villages wanted her mother to come to Sweetgrass Woman to arrange a wedding with her grandson?

In fact, Willow Girl was very much aware of it. If Young Hunter had been more aware of what was going on about him in the villages, he might have heard of those times when Willow Girl confronted one of her potential rivals. He might even have seen, had he gone down to the river one warm day two moons earlier in the Strawberry Moon, the spectacle of Willow Girl covered with mud and sitting on the back of one particularly persistent young woman named Sings Sweet. Although Young Hunter had been oblivious to it, Sings Sweet had been sitting by the young man's side almost as often as Willow Girl had been, on evenings when he was asked to tell his tale. And Willow Girl had not been pleased to see Sings Sweet offer Young Hunter strawberries from her birch basket earlier that day.

"They are sweet, are they not?" Sings Sweet had said to Young Hunter. "Would you like to share them with me?"

Willow Girl had asked her the same question about the mud into which she pushed her rival's face.

"Is this mud not sweet?" Willow Girl asked. "Would you not like to share it?"

"My daughter and I wish to marry your grandson."

That was what Willow Girl's mother, Near the Sky, said.

It was the right way to ask the question, and it pleased Sweetgrass Woman to hear it said in the old, formal way. So many of the women of Near the Sky's generation no longer cared about doing things the right way. It was clear where Willow Girl had gotten her good manners. And though she knew already what the answer to that question would be, she continued in the same way that Near the Sky had begun.

"There is much to talk about," Sweetgrass Woman replied. "Tell me about your daughter so that I will know what sort of young woman is going to come to my lodge."

When the day had come, when the elders of several other villages and a great many teasing children had assembled, a very serious Young Hunter and a very pleased Willow Girl stood up before the gathered people. They spoke their faith to each other and then were joined by the long marriage cord, placed by Medicine Plant around the necks of the two young people. Fire Keeper, Young Hunter's uncle and the sagamon of the Only People, had stood at the sunrise edge of the circle, his hands raised in blessing. Facing him, on the sunset side, skinnier but no less straight, was Big Story, sagamon of the Salmon People village. His hands, too, were raised to the sky, to bring a blessing down on these two fine young ones.

That day was in Young Hunter's vision now. It briefly took his walking thoughts away from the story that was again beginning to force its way into his life, to take over his life, to make him walk with it. Young Hunter lifted his heartside hand from Pabesis' back to the medicine bag at his waist. He felt within it the stone, no longer so comforting to the touch. *Why did the Little People leave this for me to find in the clay of the Long River?* he thought. He saw himself once more in that day when he had reached down and pulled the long-nosed stone shape from between the layers of clay at the river's edge. He felt like a very small child who wanted to cry.

Why have I been chosen again to be part of a story, he thought. *Am I strong enough, sure enough of foot to walk that kind of path once more?*

Suddenly, something was under his feet. He heard and felt the sharp yelp of Pabesis just as the dog's foot was pulled out from beneath his own. Rabbit Stick grabbed at his arm but missed and barely kept himself from falling too as the earth of the trail's edge gave way. Young Hunter went sprawling and rolled off the trail head over heels, down the slope, right into a tangle of blackberry bushes.

"Grandson," Rabbit Stick called, "are you hurt?"

Young Hunter sat up. But before he could speak, Pabesis was on his chest, a heavy, wriggling weight, a huge tongue licking his face as the gawky young dog tried both to apologize and take his master's mind off this latest indignity.

Young Hunter carefully disentangled himself from the dog, the berry bushes, and the crumbling dead branch of a trailside sumac that had ended up wedged under his belt. He said nothing as he crawled back up the trail to his grandfather, who pulled him back up and then gently picked several thorny, dry blackberry canes from Young Hunter's long hair.

Young Hunter looked around for the one who had tripped him, uncertain whether he was going to scold the dog or laugh about what had happened. But Pabesis had vanished.

"He has gone up the trail," Rabbit Stick said. "From the look on his face, he is determined to scout ahead for danger." Rabbit Stick paused and then reached over to carefully pull free yet another blackberry cane that had become caught under his grandson's loincloth. "It is certain," he said, "that we are safer when he does so."

"Grandfather," Young Hunter said, "it is not easy to walk into a story."

CHAPTER SEVENTEEN
ANGRY FACE

The others who had escaped from the Bear People village tried to stop her.

"It may be following along the riverbank," they said. "Do not pull us in to shore."

But when she looked at them from her place in the front of the boat, they became silent. All that could be heard was the water of the river, washing over the stones, lapping against the side of the dugout, swirling about the poles of the three men who steered it. Her scarred face was enough to silence anyone, even when it was not clouded with the kind of anger that darkened it now. The long scar across her face, angled from her forehead down to the swollen corner of her lip, was almost as red as if it were still a line of blood. The scar was not smooth. It was puckered and twisted, as though the skin were being held between someone's fingers and twisted. And it was stiff, so stiff that it made it hard for Angry Face to say anything that was not harsh. There were very few people who dared to look at her face, for it seemed as if there was no way to look at her without deepening the anger that always lived there.

Now, though, her face was more than angry. Her face was a storm cloud. She stared in turn into the eyes of each of the seven other adults in the dugout canoe. One after another, each quickly turned away. She did not look into the faces of the children. The five children all kept their faces turned away from her. It was nothing new. It had always been that way with the children. Although she did not know it, in the other villages of the Dawn Land People the parents would have told their children not to tease in such a cruel way. But in the village of the People of the Bear, where the luck always seemed to be bad, even many of the adults were not kind to each other. So she was used to the children being afraid of her, used to the ugly-face songs they sang after she passed and was far enough away that they thought she could not hear.

But her hearing was sharp. Her hearing had grown keener after that day when as a very small child she had fallen face first into the fire the older children had built, fallen and torn open the whole side of her face on a jagged and burning stick. There had been no one in their small bad-luck village who was a good healer. Perhaps there would have been no such scar if she had been taken down the river for a journey of many days, to the village where it was said there was a young woman among their cousin people, a young deep-seer named Medicine Plant, who could make such wounds heal so smoothly that no mark would be left. But her body had grown so hot that they had been afraid to move her, afraid she would die on the long trip. When her fever had ended and her face had healed, it had left that scar. It had also left her with hearing better than anyone else's, hearing as keen, it seemed, as that of the dogs. The old people tried to tell her it was a gift. But it was not a gift that had comforted the little girl she had then been, two handfuls of winters gone.

It was because of her hearing that she had survived and saved their lives. For she had heard something moving out in the forest before dawn. And a voice within her had told her to go quickly and silently down to the river. She had risen in her solitary lodge, slipped on her mokasins made of mooseskin, belted her knee-length robe of deerskin about her waist and fastened to it the bag made from the whole skin of a fisher. It had taken her only a few breaths to do this before slipping out the door. The voice within had told her to remove the stones from the big dugout so that it would float up to the surface and be ready for use. Angry Face was a tall young woman, stronger than most of the men in the village, and she had moved quickly. But she had not moved quickly enough. Again, just as she lifted the last stone from the dugout and it was floating in the shallows, she had heard that noise and seen what looked like a walking hill come out of the darkness, moving slowly toward the sleeping village. It came out of the trees just as the dawn was about to come. Her throat tightened with awe and terror as she saw it, for she saw that it was death. From where she stood on the riverbank, she saw it all.

Fools, she thought. *Why did I even bother to save you? If I had not dragged you and pushed you into this dugout, you would have stood there like trees rooted to the earth. If I had not kicked you until you crawled in, you would have died with all of the others. But I was the one who put the poles into your hands; I was the one who told you what to do when your limbs were frozen.*

"We will go to the opposite shore," she said. There was scorn for their fear in her voice as she spoke. "The legs of the great being may be long, but they are not long enough to jump over the Long River here where it is deep and swift."

No one answered her. They were still stunned by what had happened to their village. In less time than it took for the sun to rise a hand's width above the trees, all had been destroyed. The Walking Hill had gone through the village of the Bear People like an angry wind. The smoke from their burning lodges could still be seen rising above the trees two bends in the river behind them. Had it not been for their old man drawing the monster away from the village, surely all of them would have died there, for it had been herding them, like frightened deer, keeping them away from the river. It seemed determined that nothing would escape alive. It had killed all the dogs and flattened all the wigwoms with its huge feet. None of them would have been able to run to the river, to reach Angry Face where she stood waving her arms.

But the old man had crawled out of one of the trampled wigwoms. Although he was wounded, he had thought quickly. His eyes had touched the eyes of Angry Face. Even at that great distance, Angry Face had seen the old man recognize her. She had seen him nod and decide. And instead of running for the safety of the dugout, the old man had run back through the ruins of the village. He had climbed to the top of a big rock on the bluff above the Walking Hill. He had angered the great being even more by throwing stones at it and taunting it. When a stone struck hard against one of those great teeth, the monster bellowed and turned and saw him on top of the giant boulder.

He would have been safe had he stayed up there, but he had not. The great being was intelligent and would have gone back to kill the other people who were more vulnerable. So he had thrown more stones and then climbed down the other side of the rock, luring the Walking Hill to chase him, up the slope and into the big trees. The great being had followed, followed with such frightening speed that it was clear the old man would soon be caught.

Angry Face struck her hand against the side of the dugout, and the others in the canoe flinched. That old man, Big Raccoon, had been foolish to give up his life that way. He was the closest person their poor village had to a deep-seer, but he did little good with his pitiful knowledge of healing. He was a foolish old man. That was why she had never really liked him. Even when he had spoken to her in a gentle voice. Even when the old man had told her that a scarred face was not a bad thing as long as one's heart was not scarred. But if that were so, then why was the old man the only one in the village who would look at her without either fear or, even worse, pity in his eyes? No, she would not miss the old man, he was foolish and weak.

Angry Face turned her head so that the others in the boat could not see the tears in her eyes.

"Up there," she said in a voice as harsh as a raven's, pointing with her lips at an outcropping of white stone on the sunrise bank of the river. "Bring us in to shore there. Be quick about it or I'll break your foolish heads. You can climb the cliffs and hide up there."

They did as she said. But as they began up the cliff trail, Angry Face did not go with them. She turned her back on them, faced south, began to walk and then to run. And though she knew that at least some of them must have seen her leave them, and though she listened for a long time with her keen hearing as she ran, no one called her back.

CHAPTER EIGHTEEN
BRIGHT SKY

The Thunder Beings had spoken. The storm had ended, but the rainbow remained. Now it was no longer an arch across the sky, no longer the garment worn by the storm. Now it was a circle in the sky arch, a bright many-colored eye looking down at the land. Bear Talker sat by the edge of the fire pit just outside the closed door of the lodge. He spat into his cupped hands and then reached them down to lift some of the still-warm firesand, bringing it up to his nose. He had always loved the smell of such ashes, moist after a hard rain. He washed his hands and his arms and his face with the firesand, cleansing his touch and his seeing.

Although the rain no longer fell from the face of the sky, it did fall from the face of the deep-seeing man as he sat there. Tears made two lines through the gray of the firesand, from the corners of his eyes over his broad cheeks, and fell on his wide chest. There was a smile on his face and his heart was fuller than he could ever remember it being, for his keen ears, made keener by the cleansing of the storm and the firesand, heard the sweet sounds coming from within Medicine Plant's lodge. He heard the voices of two strong women singing a greeting song—voices gentler than the small wind that now touched his back, a wind answering that song. He heard, too, the voice that had not yet been given words answering them.

He heard the voice of his new son, his first son. And as the sunset wind washed over his back, he began to sing with them. He sang the name that the day had given the new one who had come to join those who walk with breath. Others might know this child by a different name, but for Bear Talker this would always be the name of his son—Bright Sky. Bright Sky.

"Bright Sky," he sang, "we welcome you on this new trail."

And because his heart was so full and because he, like Medicine Plant, now began to see what was to come, his tears continued to fall as he sang, sang that greeting song as old as the circle of breath, sang that song with sorrow and joy.

As the sky darkened, the Ancient One looked out of the cave. It felt safe when the day was dark, when the bright eye of the sky was not looking down upon it. It had been waiting for a long time and was hungry again, yet felt a tiredness it could not understand. Until the earth had shaken and swallowed all of its brothers, it had never been truly alone. In this loneliness in which it now lived there were things that it had never felt before. The Ancient One and its brothers had been separate from the other things around them before. They had been taller, stronger than all other things. Only the fire was given respect. That fire which they had always sent before them had killed everything. Even the grass had usually been shriveled and black under their feet as they walked.

But it was not so now. Alone, it did not make a fire. Alone, it did not walk the land without feeling strange. What it felt, in part, was fear, though it knew no name for this, no way of speaking this within its mind. And there was no longer the touch of the others' thoughts to soothe it when it felt that new fear, that new loneliness. And so it felt another way it had never felt before: it felt its own smallness.

The Ancient One looked at a small thing crawling along a stone at the edge of the cave. The tiny being humped its back and extended its body, then followed the arc of its own length.

A quick breath would dislodge it. A touch would kill it. Yet the Ancient One looked at it instead, not reaching out to touch it, nor moving its great gray hand when the little furred thing touched and then lifted itself onto that hand. The Ancient One watched, without moving, as it crossed the back of the great hand, reached the stone again, and then went along its way, vanishing into a crack in the stone.

The Ancient One stood. Darkness had come, a wind blowing. It would walk out now. It would look for the small one whose image was in its mind. Perhaps it would not just follow from a distance as it had done for so many seasons now. Perhaps this time it would come close enough. Close enough to touch. Close enough to ...

But its thought was broken by a great clap of thunder overhead. A bolt of lightning struck a tree below the cave mouth, and a dead branch blew free, twisting in the air like a broken-backed snake before it fell splintering to the earth.

The Ancient One moved back deeper into the cave, back to place its back against the cool moist wall. Back to think those thoughts without words and without the touch of another mind. It was alone. It was alone and no longer strong.

By the time they came to the edge of the village, the sky was bright again. For a while it had seemed as if a storm were coming. Dark clouds had suddenly formed in the center of the sky, and they had moved quickly to hover above the hilltops close to where Medicine Plant and Bear Talker had their lodge. The rumble of thunder had made it seem as if this storm would surely spread out and rain would be falling on them soon. But then, as suddenly as it had darkened, the sky had cleared, and not one but two rainbows had arced over the land. It was a good sign and it lifted their hearts as they walked.

Young Hunter began feeling like himself again, a single person in a single body walking a familiar trail. He glanced around and found that Pabesis was nowhere in sight. There was no chance of the dog running in between his legs and tripping him. They were at the other end of the village from their lodge. Now was the time. He poked his grandfather in the ribs.

"*Momanimmamawdzo!* You are one who moves slowly!" he said. Then he began to run.

For as long as he could remember, he and Rabbit Stick had done this. Unless some heavy matter weighed down their minds, they would race this way to see who would be first to touch the side of their wigwom. Young Hunter remembered how often he had won those races when he was very small, so small that his head barely reached his grandfather's waist. What was strange, though, was that the taller he grew, the faster his grandfather became. It amazed him, for a time, that his grandfather could have gotten so much faster as he grew older. At last, when he was the same height as his grandfather, the old man became so fast that he would beat his grandson to the lodge more often than not.

Now, though, as Young Hunter ran, he knew more than he had known as a little child and as a youth. He no longer found himself either amazed at his own speed or thinking of running so fast that he would leave the old man far behind and discourage him. He did not think of slowing in deference to his grandfather's age, either. Whenever, as a youth, he had even thought of slowing up to give his grandfather a chance, the old man had sped by him so quickly that he seemed more like a rabbit than a rabbit stick. Although he was old, Rabbit Stick's legs were still just a bit longer than his. So Young Hunter ran just as fast as he could, hoping that he had enough of a jump to win this time.

Other people in the village shouted and joked as they passed.

"Better hurry or your food will be cold!"

"Take pity on him this time and let him win."

"You're doing well. Soon you will be able to run as fast as my grandmother."

None of the comments were mean-hearted, but Young Hunter tried not to listen to them. If they made him laugh, he might lose his concentration and stumble. He could not afford to give up a step or his grandfather would be past him like a gust of wind.

The last few strides to the place where their lodge was always set up in the summer village were uphill. It was here that he usually lost. But today he speeded up as the trail rose and he touched the lodge pole first. He turned, his back against the lodge, and slid down into a sitting position, looking to see how far behind him Rabbit Stick was.

But the old man was not behind him. He was over to the side of the lodge, trying to coax Pabesis closer. The young dog had come ahead of them by another trail, and there was something in its mouth: a well-chewed piece of elm bark. The dog was playing that game of I-have-it-and-you-want-it which dogs love to play. Rabbit Stick would get just close enough and then the dog would crouch and leap aside, growling in delight.

Young Hunter realized then what he had noticed, or rather what he had not noticed. He had not smelled food cooking from within the lodge. He looked through the open door. The fire was out and neither Sweetgrass Woman nor Willow Woman was there.

CHAPTER NINETEEN
MESSAGES

"I have been thinking," Willow Woman said as she walked slowly back toward the village, "that perhaps you would like to be our child. Since your own family is gone, perhaps you would like us to adopt you?"

The little black one, which had been watching the trail ahead of them from its perch on the shoulder of Willow Woman as she walked, bent forward and swiveled its head to look up into her face.

Gannh-gannh-onh? it said.

"*Nda,*" Willow Woman said, "*ida yo* uh-hunh. Say yes."

Gannh-gah-onh, said the little black one, ruffling its neck feathers.

Willow Woman sat down. She leaned her spear against a large ash tree and placed the pile of peeled birch bark by the base. Then, crossing her legs, she reached up to take the little black one from her shoulder and seated it on her knees.

"I can see that you are going to be a stubborn child," she said. She held one finger in front of the bird's beak. It pecked gently at it, and she moved the finger back a bit.

"*Kita,*" Willow Woman said. "Listen! Repeat after me. *Ida ni mina.* Uh-hunh. Uh-hunh. Uh-hunh. Uh-hunh."

Gannh-uh, said the little black one.

Willow Woman nodded. "Now that you have agreed to be adopted, we can continue. I will teach you to speak like a real human being."

Although the trail he left behind as he pushed his way through the thick alders growing at the river's edge was so wide a track that it seemed it must have been made by the giant snake of the Waters in Between, he made little noise. Rain covered whatever sound there was. He moved as slowly and as certainly as the gray mist rolling up from the river. He was more than a day's journey south now, far beyond the marshy lands where the river began its flow and past the rapids that began just below the last village he had destroyed. The wavering line of the river had now deepened and straightened.

He had waded in that water until it was deep enough for him to roll. It was the way, long ago, his mother had taught him to rid himself of the small biting ones, to cleanse the matted dirt from his long hair. He came out onto the other bank, water streaming from him in small rivers, washing away the dirt, the pieces of burned wood, the blood. But not washing away the pain lodged there in his jaw, there where it could not be reached or lessened. In the haze of that pain, another image came to him. He could see his mother. He felt the touch of her body against his as she protected him in the shelter of her great legs, then like the trunks of giant trees to him. The taste, the sweetness of her milk came into his mouth and then was replaced by the high loud sounds of fear, by the redness of flames circling them, and by the stones of the high place to which they ran, ran half-blinded until the land was gone under their feet, as the edge of the cliff came and his mother fell down, down far below the ledge which caught him but did not catch her.

When the fire hunters had gone, he had made his way down to the base of that cliff, but she did not move. The light in the sky came and went many times, but still she did not move. At last, when the sight and sound of the birds pecking at her body—more than he could drive off though he ran around her again and again crying out with anger—when the sight and sound of them and the smell had become too much for his senses to bear, then he had begun to wander. Calling for his mother as he wandered. Again the light came and went as he wandered, and then he saw them. They were moving among the trees. Only a few of them. An old bull, two cows, two female calves of his own size. He almost ran from them, but they came and circled him, speaking sounds that soothed him, touching his back, caressing him with their long breath.

Walking Hill blew out a short, hard breath. The images vanished, but the pain stayed with him. It was a red pain, a pain that filled him with anger toward all things that were small and walked upright on their hind legs; toward their smell, which was melded with his long pain; toward the small hills of branches and bark and skins that were their nests. There were no more such nests in the land of the marshes behind him where the Long River began. The light and the dark had come again and again as he hunted down those few who escaped from their little circles around the hated fires that were as red as his anger-pain.

There were a few new small wounds on his chest and his sides. There the toothed sticks had struck him as the little upright ones tried to defend themselves from him. But his long gray hair was shaggy and heavy and armored him against their toothed sticks. None of them struck deep enough in his thick hide to cause great injury, and the stone teeth had come free when he rubbed against the trees. He was growing cleverer each time. His senses were stronger than theirs. He could hear better, smell farther than even the four-legged ones which lived with them and tried to trouble him as he attacked. He knew now how to draw the four-legged ones out, to corner and kill them so that their barking would not alert the upright ones to his coming. And when the dogs had been silenced, they could not let the upright ones know that their death was close.

He knew now to wait, to wait silently and barely moving before attacking. To watch until the light was about to return. He had learned not to try to kill all of them at once. Not to try to kill all of their fires. Then they would throw their long sharp teeth at him. Instead, he would crush a few of their nests, scatter some of their circles of fire. Then, as they screamed with fear and pain, he would blend back into the dark. Then he would wait again, wait and then attack from another direction.

Waiting. Walking Hill had grown very good at waiting. Waiting for the best opportunity. And it was best at this moment. Best to attack now, now in the grayness between the light and the dark. The eyes of the little upright ones were good in the time of light, better than his. When their eyes were of the least use, confused between seeing and dreaming, this was the moment he chose to come. First he would move as slowly as the looming gray mist coming up from the river. Then he would do as he already saw himself doing in the pictures he held behind his eyes. He would come slowly within sight of the fires and then rush as swiftly as the whirlwind. And feel his feet smashing their nests and their fires. And pull them from their lodges and throw them down. And crush their soft bodies and their cries of despair.

When Angry Face reached the village, it was too late. She had dreaded that it would be so. She had come as quickly as she could, but the twisting of the Long River on the dawnside bank along which she ran, and the rapids which she could not cross until she was across from the village, had made her journey less direct than it would have been on the other side. It was because of the rapids, so swift that no dugout could survive them, that she had been forced to continue on foot. For the great beast, whose legs were longer than her own, it would take much less than the two nights and two days she took. Her only hope was that it had not gone directly down the river.

Late morning of the second day she had looked downstream and seen the thick smoke drifting up. She knew then that, fast as she had journeyed, not sleeping but continuing to run as the Night Traveler looked down on her, the gray monster had come before her. She crossed at the place above the village where the river was shallow, climbed the trail up the hill and looked down onto the desolation of the village of those her people had called cousins, the village they called Below the Cliffs. Every wigwom was flattened. She walked down into the village. The bodies of the people showed no life, except for the many flies that clustered about the blackened wounds and the open eyes of the dead. She sat on a great stone, in the shadow of which the people had met to listen to stories or to speak of the things that had to be spoken of. Each time she had visited, it had been another season and so another discussion. Who would be the ones to be the drivers, and who would be the watchers on this deer hunt? Which of the older women would lead them this season when they went to the berry picking place? Where were the true boundaries of one family's hunting grounds when they quarreled with another family who had, they said, placed snares on a trail already claimed?

Angry Face had been to the Below the Cliffs People a handful of times. They had treated her better than those in what had once been her own village, although her own anger and shyness kept her from speaking to most of them. But there had been one woman in this village in particular, one who had invited her to come along when the women went out to pick berries the first time she had visited. That woman's name was Gray Braids. Although Angry Face saw that she was the elder who always seemed to be the one everyone turned to for her wise judgment at those councils below the great stone, she had not been too proud to greet and welcome Angry Face. She had even held onto the shoulder of the young woman with the scarred face and told her not to listen when some of the other girls made jokes. Like that girl who said that it was good to bring someone along whose face would frighten away any bears that might come close to them. Gray Braids had held Angry Face and not let her run away.

"I am your aunt," Gray Braids said. "You must stay in my lodge when you come here. You know my lodge is very empty now that my husband has walked the spirit trail. You tell me that your parents are dead. Clearly you need an aunt. My children are all grown and they are too busy to visit me. I have made a space for you just inside the door. If you do not come and stay with me, I will only have myself to talk to, and I have already heard all of my own stories."

Angry Face had smiled then, a smile that took the tension from the puckered line of flesh crossing her face. It let the light in her eyes shine in a way usually dimmed by her anger, an anger that anticipated what people would say and how they would look at her long before they saw her. So each time she had come to this place, she had stayed with Gray Braids. And each time, her adopted aunt had made her smile.

Despite the smoke and blood and scattered pieces of homes below her where a village had once been made in a careful circle, despite the fact that the place of the Below the Cliffs People was now like a beautiful spider web torn apart by a careless hand, she knew which lodge had been the lodge of Gray Braids. Half of that lodge was still burning in the fire that had been scattered against the dried birch bark of what had once been the tall cone shape of a beautiful wigwom. The other half had been torn away and hurled up into the branches of a hemlock tree, the early morning wind moving it slightly. Angry Face blinked her eyes to clear them, and she saw what she thought she had seen. She saw that not only Gray Braids' lodge, but also what remained of the old woman who had always spoken to her with such kindness had been hurled high into that tree.

By the time Rabbit Stick retrieved the piece of elm bark from Pabesis, it was so thoroughly chewed that it looked like an old piece of gristle. Because elm bark was tough, it had not been torn apart, but the markings on it had been well punctuated by the young dog's teeth.

Rabbit Stick unfolded the bark and smoothed it against the side of the lodge. He wiped his hands on his thighs and then studied the piece of bark closely. Young Hunter looked over his grandfather's shoulder. He had learned long ago from his grandparents the simple way of picture messaging. There was a more complicated kind of writing that only the deep-seeing ones used. Most people did not know that. Young Hunter only knew of it because both Bear Talker and Medicine Plant had begun to teach him that way of speaking with signs on bark.

For a time the two deep-seeing people had argued over which of them was the better one to teach him. Each had whispered to Young Hunter that the other did not know the proper way. Young Hunter smiled inside when he heard those whispers, for he knew both of his teachers had been taught the picture writing by Oldest Talker. Eventually their disagreement became an open argument.

"Stay outside the lodge, boy," Bear Talker had growled. "I must concentrate all of my attention on speaking to this stubborn woman."

Medicine Plant had said nothing, but the way she raised one eyebrow was enough to tell Young Hunter that he should not only leave, he should leave quickly. As he walked down the hill from Medicine Plant's lodge, he heard the loud sounds of their argument, and then, suddenly, there was silence.

Have they killed each other? he wondered. But he did not turn back to see. A wise person did not intrude upon such silence.

That was the last of his lessons. Both the deep-seeing people ceased their teaching of Young Hunter when they became so involved with each other that all of the rest of the world around them seemed to vanish from their eyes.

But the simple way of talking with pictures was easy to learn. It was used by all of the Dawn Land People as a means of leaving messages. Although there were other ways to leave messages—piling stones, tying small flexible branches in certain ways along the trails and at crossroads—this kind of messaging on bark was the most common. One would take something sharp—a stone, an antler, a stick, even a fingernail—and then draw the symbols on the inner side of a piece of newly peeled bark; elm or birch was the best. If no bark was available or it was a time of the year when bark could not easily be taken from the trees, one could take a burned stick and use the charcoal end to draw on the dry trunk of a dead tree. Those trees were called message trees. They were common throughout the watersheds of the Thirteen Villages.

"It is a message from your grandmother," Rabbit Stick said at last. "See, there is her sign in the lower corner."

"Uh-hunh, Grandfather. I see it. But what else does the message say?"

Rabbit Stick shook his head ruefully. "Our young friend there," he gestured with his chin at Pabesis, who sat at their feet, tongue lolling out, tail wagging at the attention he was being given, "has added too many of his own messages. It may say ... ," Rabbit Stick paused, holding the bark up to the light, "that your grandmother is in a cave on a mountain eating beaver tails. Or ... ," he paused again and turned the bark sideways, "it may say that many deer are going fishing for porcupines in the big lake. Then again, it may just be a map of the Sky Land."

Rabbit Stick started to throw the piece of bark down but stopped when Pabesis jumped up, ready to catch it. Instead, he folded it and placed it on top of the lodge, well out of reach.

"Whatever your grandmother wished to tell us, we must wait for her to return to let us know what it was. But one message we do not need to read. It has been given to us there," he said, looking at the cold hearth. "If we wish to eat before the Day Traveler leaves the sky, we will have to cook for ourselves."

"I am glad to hear that you are going to cook for us," said a voice from behind them.

They turned to look. Willow Woman had come up on them so quietly that neither of them had heard her. Young Hunter nodded with pride. His wife was becoming even better than he was at moving with silence. But she was holding her hands behind herself, and there was that look on her face. He knew that look. More often than not, it meant he had to prepare himself for something.

Willow Girl, her name not yet changed to that of a married woman, had worn such a look on her face five seasons before when they were sitting together by the river. Young Hunter had just finished telling her part of his story of his great journey, and his tongue had started to stumble as he told her more about Redbird. With each word he spoke, Redbird became older and uglier, but he knew the damage had been done. And there was nothing he could do but wait for whatever would happen. Willow Girl stood up, walked calmly to the river, and dug out a handful of wet clay. She carried it back up the bank to Young Hunter and then, before he could lift his hands to take it from her, dropped it into Young Hunter's lap.

"If you want someone to listen to your stories about another woman," she said, "then shape that person out of clay. As for me, I have other things to do."

And she had walked away, leaving Young Hunter sitting there, the clay drying in his lap. Though Young Hunter did not know it, she had not walked far but had stopped to peer out at him, barely controlling her laughter as he sat there puzzled about what to do and what to say the next time he was asked to tell about his great adventure.

"You want to see what surprise I have brought with me?" Willow Woman took a step forward.

103

Without knowing he was doing it, Young Hunter raised his hands up instinctively, as if to protect himself. But when Willow Woman brought her hands out from behind her back, he saw that her surprise was a young crow. It cocked its head to look straight at Young Hunter, and then it opened its beak.

Gwahhhh, gwahhh, it said.

Willow Woman smiled.

"Do you not hear our little one greeting you?" she said. "Are you not going to say *kuai kuai* back?"

CHAPTER TWENTY

TALKING

Willow Woman sat with the little black one on the sleeping bench Young Hunter had made three mornings before by
tying together small springy branches across a raised frame of
other peeled branches the thickness of a spear. He had used
willow, for willow peeled easily at this time of year. They had cut
away the branches they needed from the edge of the Long
River, where they were setting up spots for spearing fish or for
placing fish traps.

Young Hunter had liked the little black one as soon as he
saw it, but the young bird was obviously not yet so certain of
him. Young Hunter had quickly learned that when the little
black one was in doubt, it used its beak like a spear point.
Young Hunter was sucking now on the fleshy part of his
heartside hand where blood had been drawn by one particularly hard peck as he held out his hand the way Willow Woman
had told him to do. Willow Woman was busy teaching her new
child to talk like a human person. Already it could say not only
the greeting words, but also those for yes and no.

Certain of the birds were like that, able to speak the words
humans spoke and not reticent to do so. It was well known that
all the animals and birds of the dry land and the sky and all the
creatures who lived below the surface of the earth and in water
could speak. They were always speaking to each other. Often

they gathered together to tell stories about the doings of those strange ones, the human people. Everyone in the Dawn Land villages knew stories about people who had been adopted by various animal nations. When a human was adopted by animals, those animals would speak to their newly adopted relative freely, and their speech would seem just like human words.

It was usually different when animals came to live among the human people. Most animals either were unable to talk as humans do, or they simply refused to use human speech. When a person was alone, seeking assistance from a spirit helper, then an animal might come and talk to that person, but not in the midst of the village where others could hear. Perhaps it was because talking was more important to the animal people than to the humans. So they did less of it than did the humans and only spoke to their human friends on very special occasions.

But the birds were different. They loved to talk about anything and everything. They filled the days with their talking from the first breath of dawn, even before the Day Traveler showed his face, until the little stars opened their bright eyes in the Above Land.

Young Hunter recalled a crow that had lived in his uncle's house. Big Mouth was its name, and it was a gossip. Big Mouth would fly about the village from house to house. He only had a few human words, but he used them to good effect. He would sit unseen, perhaps perched deep in a cedar tree near someone's lodge watching what they were up to. Then, just at the moment when his victim was doing something private, Big Mouth would cry out, *Ki-ta, ki-ta, ki-ta. Look, look, look,* he would cry. *What you are doing I see. What you are doing I see.* Then he would fly away, laughing as crows laugh.

Some of the people just laughed with him. But others became very serious about Big Mouth spying on them. They would spend much time each day looking up and down and then make a great show of shaking the branches of the bushes and trees near their wigwoms to prevent Big Mouth from seeing the very important things they wished to do in private. Whenever they were surprised by the crow, they would shout threats and throw stones at the tree or bush in which Big Mouth had been sitting—though they would be very careful to throw those stones after the crow had flown safely away.

Big Mouth lived to be very old. When he was found one day in the corner of the lodge, sleeping that sleep from which no one wakes, many people were sad. Some of the saddest were those who had always searched around their houses to make sure he was not watching them. It was strange how many of those people were also the ones who, just accidentally, left scraps of food sitting out where Big Mouth could see the morsels and come to eat. Perhaps it was because their secrets were so small and uninteresting that Big Mouth was the only one they could always count on to care about what they did.

Talking. Young Hunter found himself thinking about it. He thought of how talking was the start of so many things. Many things began from talking. Perhaps that was why talking started as soon as things began. As soon as the One Who Shaped Himself sat up from the earth he began to talk.

And though it was not the season for telling that story, Young Hunter could hear it in his memory. He could hear his grandmother's voice talking to a grandson who had tried to wrestle against a boy a head taller than himself. He had been thrown and then held on his back in the snow like a squirrel in the claws of a hawk. Leaning back, eyes closed, he was again that angry-faced little boy asking Sweetgrass Woman why he was not able to be big and strong *now*. Why was it that he had to wait to grow? And the memory voice of his grandmother was as rich and patient as it had been back then.

"Grandson," Sweetgrass Woman said, "I cannot explain why it is that we have to wait to grow tall. I only know that Tabaldak has made everything to be this way. But I can tell you a story."

"Uh-hunh," Young Hunter said. "Tell the story. I am listening."

And Sweetgrass Woman had told the story of the One Who Shaped Himself from Something.

"*Kina.* Listen. Listen to this story of Odziozo."

Long ago, when Tabaldak, the Owner, had finished making things, some of the dust of creation was still on the Owner's hands. So Tabaldak began to brush that dust away. It sprinkled down upon the earth. Where it fell upon the earth, the earth began to move about. It began to shape itself. It shaped itself a torso. It shaped itself a head. It shaped itself shoulders, arms, and hands; it shaped itself hips. Then that earth which shaped itself sat up.

"*Awani gia?*" said Tabaldak. "Who are you?"

"*Odziozo nia,*" said that earth which shaped itself. "I am Odziozo. I am the One Gathering Himself Together."

"You are very wonderful," said Tabaldak.

"*Nda,*" said Odziozo. "No. You are the one who is wonderful. You are the one who sprinkled me."

Then Odziozo looked around. All around was the beauty of the newly created earth. And Odziozo became eager to get up and see it. But like a small child eager to run before it can even stand, Odziozo did not notice that he was not yet ready. He had not yet shaped legs and feet. He was still connected to the earth.

So Odziozo tried to stand. He pushed very hard to one side, but he did not move. He pushed harder and harder, so hard that the earth was pushed up into mountains. But still he could not stand. Then Odziozo pushed very hard to the other side. He pushed so hard that the earth rose up into mountains on that side, too. But still he could not stand.

Now Odziozo reached out his long arms. He reached all the way to the mountaintops to either side of him. Then he pulled, trying to pull himself up. His fingers gouged down the channels of the rivers. But still he could not stand.

Then Odziozo saw that Tabaldak was looking at him. Tabaldak looked at him with that look of patience a parent shows when a child does something wrong but that parent is determined to let the child learn through his own mistake. Odziozo looked at himself then. He saw that he was still connected to the earth. He did not have legs or feet yet.

Then Odziozo reached down. He shaped legs and feet for himself. Then he stood. And when he stood, he left behind him a great hole in the earth. The waters flowed in and made that hole into a big lake. It is *Petonbowk*, the Waters in Between.

Then Odziozo walked around. He walked around for a long time seeing many things. But when he was done, he returned to the beautiful lake and the beautiful mountains he had made. This was where he wished to stay. He changed himself into a great stone and sat down in the waters. He sits there to this day, watching over the mountains and the lake.

So the story goes.

Young Hunter had sat for a long time when the story ended. His small hands were on his own legs, and it seemed to his grandmother as if her little grandson were trying to make his legs longer by shaping them as Odziozo had done long ago. At last, the small boy nodded.

"I see, Grandmother," he said. "You must be prepared for things before you try to do them."

"That may be so," Sweetgrass Woman said. "If that is what that story told you, then that is what the story means. That story knows more than I do, though. I have heard it many times, and each time I hear it I learn more from it."

"Will you tell it to me again, then?"

"Yes, Grandson. I am certain that I will tell the story of the One Who Shaped Himself to you again."

Young Hunter stood up very slowly, almost as if standing for the first time on legs that had just been made. He walked to the door of the wigwom.

But before he could go through the door, Sweetgrass Woman's curiosity got the better of her. "You are going to wrestle again with the boy who beat you?" she asked.

"*Nda*, Grandmother. I am not yet ready. I am going to wrestle now with someone I know I can beat. I am going to wrestle with my grandfather."

Young Hunter opened his eyes and looked at himself. He had been so firmly in that memory place that it seemed magical to look at his hands and see, not the small hands of a five-winters-old boy, but the wide, strong hands of a young man. It was strange to look at his own long, heavily muscled arms and not see the stick-thin limbs of the child he knew that he still was—somewhere not that deep inside himself.

We grow as the trees do. That was what Bear Talker had explained to him. Each circle of seasons the trees grow new bark around the outside, like putting on a new coat without ever taking off the old one. So they grow larger and larger. But the small tree is there, right in the heart of the tallest pine. That is how we are. We are still the little child, under all those layers of growth. When we dream, sometimes that little child talks to us. And if we live long enough, that little child may even come out of us again, and we will talk again with the same voice we had when we were very young. That is a gift the Owner Creator gives some of us. To live as a child again for a time before we die.

Young Hunter remembered the old, old man named Otter Skin. He had been one of Young Hunter's favorite playmates among the big people, aside from his own grandfather, when he was small. But Otter Skin had been different from Rabbit Stick. For while Rabbit Stick would behave as a little child sometimes, take part in their games and try his hardest to do as well as his grandson, there would always come the time when Rabbit Stick would straighten up and become a grown person again, a person with important things to do which took him back into that world of the big people.

Otter Skin, though, had stayed with the little ones all the time, not just by playing with them and going everywhere with them, but in the way he talked and saw things as well. Just like Young Hunter and the other children, he was also worried, at times, about being caught by the big people when he was doing things big people might not like. For some reason, which Young Hunter could not understand back then, Otter Skin's mother was also his daughter. That was what he called her, his daughter. And she called him her father. Yet it was clear by the way they acted who was the parent. One had only to see her wipe the old man's face and then lead him home to help him change out of clothing made wet and dirty by sitting with the children up to his waist in a mud hole imitating the frogs. She was patient with him, and the two of them smiled a great deal when they were together.

Whenever she came to get him, Otter Skin would always ask the same question. "Daughter, have you been picking blackberries? Are there some ripe blackberries at home? I like to eat them very much."

Even when the ice had closed the eyes of the lakes and rivers and the snow was so deep that it was over Young Hunter's head, Otter Skin would always ask his daughter about the berries. Young Hunter understood why Otter Skin liked blackberries. He liked those berries himself. He liked them very much. He liked the sweetness on his lips and in his mouth and even the feel of the blackberries between his fingers as he picked them from the bushes. Their scent would reach his nose before the berries were in his mouth, and it seemed as if he could taste them with his fingertips. And after he had eaten those blackberries, his fingers would be red for a long time. When they were berry picking, he and the other children would paint their faces and their bodies with the juice of the berries, imitating the tattoos that some of the older people had.

Otter Skin had such real tattoos on his own face: four wavering lines on each cheekbone. Rabbit Stick had explained

111

to Young Hunter that those lines stood for the river. Otter Skin had been given that name because he used to be able to turn himself into an otter, swim great distances underwater, and catch big fish with his hands. But since he had become a child, he no longer went to the river much, and he did not seem to want to become an otter any longer. He just wanted to play with the small children. And ask if the berries were ripe.

Young Hunter understood why Otter Skin liked black-berries so much. But he could not understand why Otter Skin could not understand that those berries were only ripe in the summertime. So he asked his grandfather.

"Perhaps," Rabbit Stick said, "Otter Skin thinks that talking about the berries will make them appear. And he may be right. Have you noticed how his daughter keeps dried blackberries for him so that he can chew them or taste the drink made from their juice at almost any time of the year?"

Rabbit Stick paused for a moment and looked at his grandson before continuing. "And there is also this," Rabbit Stick said, "Otter Skin has almost finished the circle of his life. He is so old that the Owner Creator has allowed him to be a little child again, free from all the worries we big people have to carry with us. When Otter Skin was a young man, there was a hard time. There was a bad winter and game grew scarce. The game animals went away somewhere, perhaps into the earth, perhaps to the south, and the spring came very late. There was little rain, and even the berry bushes dried up and many of the plants the people gathered to eat were hard to find. The bark of the trees was tight and hard, and the ducks and the geese did not come back to our land. It seemed as if the great mountains of ice were getting ready to return. Some people began to die from hunger.

"That was when Otter Skin got his medicine. He went out from the village alone at the time when the blackberries should have been ripe. He was gone a long time. When he came back, he had those tattoos on his cheeks. He had learned how to become an otter, and he could catch fish now where no one else could catch them. Even though he was very young, he began to provide for the people. And although times became good again, he continued to work for the people all of his life. He remembered those hard seasons. He was very good at being a father and very good at being a grandfather. Some of the children that he plays with are the children of his children's children."

Rabbit Stick paused and looked at Young Hunter, as if there were more he thought of saying to his grandson. Then he went on, "But Otter Skin did not take much time for himself. When he was young the first time, he was always too busy helping the people to have the opportunity to play and to be able to pick berries or share in some of the things that taste sweet. So the Owner Creator has made his life full of playing and blackberries now that he is a child again."

Rabbit Stick paused once more, and Young Hunter saw that he was smiling even though his eyes seemed moist. He put his small hand on his grandfather's knee and patted it encouragingly. Rabbit Stick smiled down at him for a moment before again finding his voice.

"We are very blessed to have him among us and to listen to his voice talking about blackberries."

"My husband?" Young Hunter opened his eyes. He was no longer a little boy, holding a basket filled again with the biggest and ripest blackberries he could find, holding that basket up again to the old man who sat at the edge of the berry thicket. That old man whose tattooed face was stained red around his mouth, whose hair was long and white and tangled with leaves and twigs, and who took those berries from him with a smile as happy and innocent as that of a baby.

Willow Woman was leaning over him, her hands lightly on his shoulders. "My husband," she said, "our little black one has gone to sleep. He is perched inside our lodge with his head under his wing. The little stars are circling the sky, and our grandmother has not yet returned. Our grandfather is not worried about her, though; he is in his lodge next door. If you listen, you may hear him snoring."

Willow Woman straightened, and the firelight caught her eyes in a way that made Young Hunter remember other times together in their lodge. How fortunate he was to have married her.

Willow Woman shoved him. "Are you going to sleep again?" She placed her hands more firmly on his shoulders and shook him. "I have been talking to you, but it seems you are not here." Her voice became even more teasing. "Have you forgotten how to listen?"

Young Hunter looked at his hands. Perhaps it was only the reflection of the glow of the fire in the hearth, but it seemed, even though the season for blackberries was still three moons away, as if his fingers were stained red. He was certain that if he held them up to his mouth he would taste a familiar sweetness.

"*Nda*," Young Hunter said. "I have been listening."

"If that is so," Willow Woman said, and now her hands had moved from his shoulders, "then it is time for you to stop listening and do something else."

CHAPTER TWENTY-ONE
THE WHIRLPOOL

Before the first light of the Day Traveler, Young Hunter was awake. Willow Woman still slept, and the little black one, perched on one of the crosspieces at the top of the lodge, still had its head under its wing. There was no fire in the center of the lodge, so it was still very dark. He could not see any movement through the door leading to the older part of the lodge where his grandparents always slept. But he knew his grandmother had not returned in the night. Quiet though she might be, he would have sensed her presence. Instead, he sensed her absence. It troubled him.

When he and Willow Woman had married and she had moved out of the lodge of her parents, it had been decided that they would connect their lodge to that of his grandparents. So they had made the lodge of the old people longer by extending the roof poles. This was not the smaller lodge his grandparents had lived in before his great journey to the north and the west, the wigwom with a frame shaped like a rolled piece of bark, tapered so that it was pointed at the top. This was a newer lodge, one built after his return. It was shaped in an arc, like the sky dome above, like the houses the beaver and muskrat people make above the surface of ponds. But it was longer in shape, for there were two compartments now, one for each of the couples living there.

They had used some of the birch bark covering from the older wigwom. That bark lasted many seasons, and it was easy to roll up and store or carry to a new place when the season came to go where the hunting or fishing was good. Each compartment had its own hearth, and there were two smoke holes in the roof. But no smoke rose up from either hearth this morning. The night before had been too warm for a fire in the lodge. A small smudge fire burned outside the lodge door, though. Green cedar or leaves from certain other trees were placed on that smudge fire to produce enough smoke to keep away the biting ones, the *peguesak*, and their tinier cousins. But even without the smoke, the good-smelling bear grease that darkened their skin and shone on the limbs of all of the Dawn Land People was a good defense against those little ones that lived on the blood of the animal and human people.

Young Hunter moved quietly to the door between the two compartments and dipped his fingers into the bear grease kept in the small wooden bowl there. Rabbit Stick had made that bowl from a maple burl, hollowed out with burning coals and a scraping stone, long before Young Hunter was born. The outside of the bowl was rubbed so smooth by use that it reflected light whenever the fires burned. There were no fires now, but Young Hunter had no trouble finding it. He rubbed the clear oil between his hands and then massaged his forehead and his cheeks. It was this same bear grease that the older people like his grandparents rubbed into their knees and elbows when the cold made them grow stiff. Perhaps it would do the same for his stiff thinking, for the confusion he felt all around himself. He took out a bit more of the sweet oil and massaged it into his chest over his heart. He needed to see clearly there, too.

Then Young Hunter quietly went out of the lodge. He would let Willow Woman and his grandfather sleep, he thought. But he could not sleep himself without knowing for certain where Sweetgrass Woman had gone. Rabbit Stick and he had asked others in the village if they knew where his grandmother had gone. They had told about seeing Bear Talker running through the village in the direction of their lodge. He wished again that his grandfather and he had reached the lodge before Pabesis had chewed the message bark so thoroughly that they could gain no knowledge from it. He was sure that something big had happened. It was likely that Medicine Plant's time had finally come and she had sent Bear Talker to bring Sweetgrass Woman to help her with the birthing. That was probably it, but he was not certain. Perhaps it was that and it was more than that. Maybe it was more than one thing.

Young Hunter shook his head, almost expecting to hear a sound like stones inside a bone rattle as he did so. Everything that had seemed so simple, so easy, only a few dawns ago was growing hard again. It was not easy to be in the middle of things, with things happening all around you. So many that you were unable to look at one thing long enough to understand. Young Hunter felt as he had felt many winters ago when he had leaped into the whirlpool in the Long River at the base of the big falls. All the world seemed to be whirling about him, even though he knew that he was the one being spun into dizziness. A dizziness he knew he had to escape from or he would drown. Yet the center of the whirlpool—the water darker there—drew him toward it.

There was light now in the sky, the light that comes before the Day Traveler shows his face.

I will walk, Young Hunter thought. And he began to walk away from the lodge, away from the direction of the coming dawn. Soon the lodge was far behind him, yet the confused thoughts still swirled like leaves caught in a gust of wind. As he walked in the half-darkness, a shadowy, taller figure suddenly loomed up from the trail beside him. Young Hunter whirled, his hands held up to defend himself.

"Grandson," Rabbit Stick said, "are your ears so filled with your thinking that you cannot hear? I have been walking behind you since you left the lodge."

Young Hunter dropped his hands.

"My thoughts keep turning around in my head, Grandfather. I feel like everything is spinning around me. I feel as I felt when I was a child when I ... " Young Hunter paused.

"When you leaped into the whirlpool under the Great Falls?" Rabbit Stick said. "Do you think I did not know about that?"

The old man put his hand on Young Hunter's shoulder, a gesture of understanding and approval that always spoke more than any words could say.

"I was alone that day, Grandfather."

"*Nda*, Grandson. I was watching you. I had seen how afraid you were of that whirlpool when we fished there the day before. I saw how you sat thinking and thinking all that evening, and when you rose the next morning, with that look of determination on your face, I knew what you were going to do. Whenever something makes you afraid, you always lower your head and run toward it. That is one reason why the older boys were always very careful not to get you upset when you were little. They did not like getting hit in the stomach with your hard head!" Rabbit Stick chuckled. "I remember the first time you did that. You were three winters old, and I thought I would scare you. But when I jumped out from the corner of the lodge with a bearskin over my head, you ran at me yelling. You know where your head hit me!"

"So you followed me," Young Hunter said.

"Just as I followed you this morning. And your ears were as deaf to me then as they were this morning. I watched you from behind the big flat stone on the bank, just above the whirlpool. I had a long stick, and I was ready to use it to pull you out. But I waited." Rabbit Stick squeezed Young Hunter's shoulder again. "I was glad I waited. You found your own way out. Do you remember what you did?"

"I am not certain, Grandfather. All I know is that I kept trying to swim, and then I found myself on the shore a long way downstream."

Rabbit Stick said nothing. They walked farther. They were climbing the hill now toward the place where a flat shelf of rock jutted out from the hill and there was a clear view toward the first light of the new day. Farther up the slope and on the other side of the same long hill there were caves, but when they came to the crossroads of the paths they did not turn that way.

As they passed the trail toward the caves, Young Hunter felt a strange pull, as if something were reaching toward him farther down the trail, which led to those dark and hidden places where the light of the Day Traveler never reached. It was a familiar feeling, yet he could not tell why it was familiar. And that feeling was gone as quickly as the touch of a feather blown across his face by the wind and then whisked away before he could touch it. Young Hunter reached a hand up and brushed his cheek, as if wiping away a spider web.

And as Young Hunter did so, in the deepest of the caves on the other side of that hill, less than a look away from them, the last of the Ancient Ones moved back from the cave mouth where it had been waiting, where it had been calling with his mind, even though it knew that none of its people were left to answer its call.

Young Hunter and Rabbit Stick rounded the hill and climbed up to a place above the trail on a mossy ledge where the stone was blackened in a circle and there were a few coals remaining from other fires. The ledge faced in the dawn-coming direction. As Rabbit Stick began to place the dried branches he had carried with him up the slope into the shape of a small wigwom, Young Hunter climbed to the place farther up on the slope where they had stored the fireboard and firestick for starting a dawn fire.

When Rabbit Stick was done laying the bed for the fire, he stood back. Young Hunter knelt and took out some tinder from his pouch—dried cedar bark that he had rolled between his hands until it was as fluffy and dry as a bird's nest. He placed his firestick in the groove in the long fireboard and began to move it swiftly back and forth, scraping the dry surface down to push out a coal. He could have brought coals from the smudge fire in front of their wigwom, but it was better to start a new fire to greet a new day. Especially when coming to this high place to try to clear away the confusion.

It was a dry morning, no feel of rain coming in the air. The coal formed quickly and slid off the end of the groove into the nest of tinder. Young Hunter folded it into the cedar bark tinder, lifted it, and gently blew it into life. He cupped the flame in his hands and placed it under the little wigwom of dry sticks his grandfather had made. As the Day Traveler showed his face, the small fire burned brightly. The shadows lengthened and spread across the land. The first breeze of the morning touched their faces. All around them on the hill the small birds were flying up with their songs, greeting the new day.

A sharp whistle came from above them, and Young Hunter's gaze followed his grandfather's as they looked up. It was an eagle, coming down across the sky toward them, coming from the direction of the Always Winter Land. At this spot they would always see, in this moon when the grass began to run green, the many hawks flying their long sky trail from the direction of the summer land, but this great bird was coming from the opposite direction. The eagle whistled again and glided by them, so close that they felt the wind of its wings. Wings locked, it coasted down the slope of the mountain and was gone from sight, though they heard it cry—once, twice, three times, four times. Then there was silence. Even the songs of the small birds were no longer to be heard.

Rabbit Stick placed a handful of newly gathered cedar on the coals of the fire. Thick green smoke billowed up. Young

Hunter leaned down to reach out and wash his hands and face in the smoke. He was grateful for its touch. Not just for the way it would help clear his thoughts, but for its ability to clear away other things as well. Though the birds were silent now, the little hungry ones were not. Those small insects, the *peguesak*, those who love the moisture of human bodies, also always returned in this moon when everything was waking. Those *peguesak* had already found Young Hunter and Rabbit Stick. And though the bear grease gave protection where it was rubbed into skin, Young Hunter had forgotten to place any on his ears. Before the cedar had been dropped on the coals, he had reached one hand up to an itching earlobe and brought his finger away smeared with his own blood.

Rabbit Stick reached out and washed his hands and face in the cedar smoke, too. He leaned back against a flat stone that had been propped up from behind by two other rocks to form a backrest. He started to take the kind of deep breath he always took when he was about to say something meaningful. But instead of speaking, he coughed, having drawn in a mouthful of little swarming insects. With a rueful look on his face, he dropped more cedar onto the fire and swirled the smoke about him with his hands. Young Hunter kept his gaze on the stick with which he was carefully prodding the fire, his own lips tightly shut, even though he was making choking noises of his own as he tried not to laugh.

Gradually the little biting ones grew discouraged, and soon only a few remained. Rabbit Stick drew in another breath, a smaller and more cautious one this time, and then spoke.

"I remember what you did to escape from that whirl-pool," he said. "At first I thought you would not get out of it. You were facing into the center of it and it was drawing you deeper. I thought then that I would have to rescue you. But I didn't want to hurt your pride. So I waited a little more. And I was glad that I waited, for you did what you needed to do. Even though you may not have known it was the right thing, it

121

was what you did. And that is the way it is sometimes. Sometimes the Owner Creator puts the answers in us so deeply that we do not know that we already know them."

"What did I do, Grandfather?"

"You turned away from the center of the whirlpool. You saw which way was downstream and that was the way you swam. Then the Long River helped you. Its current helped pull you free and brought you to the shore."

CHAPTER TWENTY-TWO
SPARROW

"*Kuai, nidoba!* Hello, my friend!"

The familiar voice that broke the morning silence, as Young Hunter walked alone back toward the village, was that of his friend, Sparrow. Now that Young Hunter had joined the generation of the married men, he was technically Sparrow's elder, but there was no difference in the way he acted toward his old friend. Yet Sparrow himself felt a difference and wondered why it was that he had never found as fine a person as Willow Woman to share his life with. Not that she appealed to him. But still, if she had only had a younger sister and not four little brothers.

"Hello, my friend," Young Hunter called back, as Sparrow pushed through the slender branches of the young maples, their buds just beginning to break open into leaves. He came onto the trail where Young Hunter stood next to the great stone covered with markings which everyone said were placed there long ago by the Little People. Young Hunter clasped Sparrow's wrists in the firm handshake of a close friend. "You appear new to me," Young Hunter said. "It has been so long since I have seen you."

But Sparrow did not answer in the words that would have continued the long greeting that the Dawn People always loved to give to each other on the first meeting of each new day.

123

Often people would stand asking of each other's health, telling their friends at such length how glad they were to see them that the Day Traveler would move a full hand's width across the sky. Even if the two had just seen each other the night before, it was common to say such things as "It has been so long since we have talked" and "It has been so long since I've seen you that you appear new to me."

Young Hunter looked carefully at the other young man. Sparrow was not saying anything with his mouth, but his whole body proclaimed that he was almost bursting to speak. There was sweat on Sparrow's brow, and his hands were moving in that excited way they always moved after running some distance, almost as if they were wings trying to lift their owner into flight.

"Have you come to bring me a message?" Young Hunter said.

Sparrow smiled. Now he felt important again. Indeed he did have a message to deliver!

"I have seen Bear Talker," Sparrow said. "He wants you to come to him, to their lodge. Your grandmother is there."

"The baby has been born?"

"Uh-hunh," Sparrow said. "The baby was born last evening, during the storm. I ran into Bear Talker, limping down the trail to find you. Of course, when he saw me, he knew that his message would be carried much faster. So you must go there quickly and ... ," Sparrow paused, but he delivered his message faithfully, "you must bring Willow Woman with you."

"Can you come with us?" asked Young Hunter. He was already running as he spoke, back toward his lodge where he knew Willow Woman would be waiting for him and Rabbit Stick to return. Rabbit Stick, though, had stayed on the mountain ledge. His grandfather had said that he needed to see to something.

Sparrow ran easily next to his friend. Fast as Young Hunter was, Sparrow knew that his own quick feet could run circles around him. "I am not sure," Sparrow said. "It seems that I may have things to do. But ... do you really want me to come along?"

"*Nidoba,*" Young Hunter said, "there is no need to play like *Azeban,* the raccoon, with me, saying you do not want to do something in the hopes you will be asked to do it."

"I want to come with you," Sparrow answered.

Young Hunter smiled, seeing all that was going through Sparrow's mind, even when he tried to act indifferent. Unlike Red Hawk and Blue Hawk, Sparrow was not a person who could do anything without thinking or questioning, his mind talking with itself. Sometimes the play of emotions washed across his friend's face like a cloud crossing the sky, darkening the sun one moment and letting its light shine brightly the next.

Sparrow's thoughts were always flitting about like that little bird which gave him his name. Thinking so much and of so many things at once made it hard for him to make decisions. Sometimes it was even hard for him to take a single step, and he would stand for so long that people would look closely at his mokasins to see if roots had yet grown from them into the earth. Yet when he did move, it was with such speed that no one could match him.

All of that thinking and questioning. That was why Sparrow had never settled on a single young woman, why he always ran away from the young women who tried to choose him. Red Hawk and Blue Hawk were also not yet married, but everyone knew why that was so. It was because neither one wished to marry without the other one getting married at the same time. Sweetgrass Woman said that the young men might remain bachelors forever unless a set of female twins could be found to match them. But with Sparrow, it was not so easy to understand. It might be his always-changing mind—or it might be because of his father.

On the Hills was the father of Sparrow. He was called On the Hills because that was where his gaze was always focused, always somewhere beyond the place where he was. He had a way of climbing to the hilltops and looking beyond, looking out as far as he could. Some said, even though he was married and he and his wife had four children, that he was in love with Woman Who Walks Alone, that beautiful being told of in stories who lives in no village but sleeps in a cave with the wolves. On the Hills, some said, was looking for her. Perhaps he found her, for one day Sparrow's father walked out of the village, climbed a hilltop, and never came back down again.

Sparrow was the youngest of the four children, just old enough to walk when his father disappeared. His memories of his father were few. Perhaps those memories were not happy ones. Perhaps they combined with the angry stories Sparrow's mother told of her missing husband to make him afraid of marriage. Afraid that he, too, might be one who would walk away and not come back.

Sparrow and Young Hunter ran side by side, Sparrow allowing Young Hunter to be just half a pace ahead, for they were going to Young Hunter's home. Young Hunter knew that his friend could easily outdistance him. Sparrow could dart along a trail through the forest as swiftly as a chipmunk whisking along a branch. He would be there one breath and gone the next. And Sparrow's hands were as quick as his feet. Young Hunter had seen his friend snatch a wasp with one hand and then reach in with the other to grasp it by its wings so quickly that not only would he escape being stung, but the wasp would be held there, buzzing but unhurt.

When the young men of the villages gathered together for the big ball games in the late summer moons, Sparrow would always be among the first mentioned when the time came to choose sides. Although he never allowed them to stand him up as a leader, Sparrow always managed to be where the ball was. His stick would be darting in quick as a heron's beak. Almost no one was able to get past him without being hooked, tripped, robbed of the ball, and spun around to watch

Sparrow flying toward the goal stick. Had he been just a bit larger, no one would have been able to stand up to Sparrow in any of the sports the young men of the Thirteen Villages loved to play.

Weight and strength, though, were not on Sparrow's side. Tough and determined as he was, his quickness did not save him from being thrown hard to the ground. More than once he found himself limping or being carried to the lodge of Bear Talker. There the deep-seeing man would treat his scrapes and bruises and put his dislocated fingers back into line. Bear Talker spoke to the boy as he worked.

"Just because the sparrow is quicker than other birds does not mean he can knock the eagle out of the sky," he would say. He would growl as he spoke, trying to put pine pitch onto his words so that they would stick in the young man's head. But Sparrow's thoughts were always fluttering past the deep-seeing man's words.

As Young Hunter and Sparrow ran the hillside trail which was the shortest way back down the slope to the village, round stones went rolling off to the side from under their feet, making little avalanches, down the bare slope that fell off to one side. Their sound reminded Young Hunter of other stones that had fallen two winters before. In his mind he saw the determined face of the man who became Holds the Stone as he faced his own fear in the shape of the one-eyed leader of the Ancient Ones, those cannibal giants who tried to destroy all others that walked with breath. It had been more than one season since the face of that new man, that man who changed his own face and his own destiny to become human again after acting as the dog for the gray giants, had come into Young Hunter's mind. But since his dream of two nights before, that face had been at the edge of his thinking almost every waking moment. Seeing that face, he faltered as he ran, and Sparrow, unable to hold himself back any longer, sped ahead, leaping down the trail and disappearing into the trees below.

CHAPTER TWENTY-THREE
THE EDGE OF THE LAND

The shadows moving across the land as the Day Traveler began his journey had touched something in Rabbit Stick's mind. He had closed his eyes for a breath and felt himself carried by those shadows toward the sunset place, toward the edge of the land where earth and sky meet. Young Hunter had not noticed, even though Rabbit Stick thought surely his grandson must have been able to hear, how the old man's heartbeat had quickened as he felt himself drawn onto that journey. He had opened his eyes again, half-thinking he would see his feet no longer planted firmly on the earth but standing at the start of the trail of stars.

"I will remain here for a while," the old man said. Young Hunter had not noticed the hesitation in his grandfather's voice as he spoke. Rabbit Stick understood why it was hard for the young man to be as aware of his grandfather's moods as he usually was. The young man could feel himself being drawn again into that place where his walking breath and the old stories mingled together like the quick waters of a mountain brook suddenly joining the strong, deep flow of the great Long River. Young Hunter was awake dreaming, the excitement and uncertainty of it all filling him so fully that he was already looking far ahead, hardly seeing those things closest to him.

"You will stay here for a while, Grandfather?" Young Hunter repeated Rabbit Stick's words almost as he had done when he was a very small child and half of the words adults spoke usually had no clear meaning for him.

Rabbit Stick put his arms around his grandson and shook him gently. "Uh-hunh, Grandson. Have I not just said as much?" He let go of the broad-shouldered young man who could still look up at him with those same innocent eyes that had touched the old man's heart so deeply when Young Hunter was a questioning little boy. "Go on down the hill."

Young Hunter nodded, his face serious. It was not a morning for smiling, it seemed. He began to turn to walk away. But before he could take a step, Rabbit Stick grasped him by the shoulders.

Young Hunter looked into his grandfather's eyes. There was something different there. Young Hunter felt himself come fully awake for the first time that day at what he saw there. It was as if Rabbit Stick had seen something and was still seeing it. But he would wait for his grandfather to tell him. It was not polite to pry into the inner thoughts of your elders.

"Grandson," Rabbit Stick said, "on your way down the hill, do not forget to watch the earth beneath your feet as closely as you watch the tops of those distant ridges."

Rabbit Stick watched as Young Hunter made his way back down, angling from one side to the other down the slope, disappearing among the new green of the berry bushes, then appearing again, lost for a moment from sight in the contour of the hill, and then his head and shoulders visible for a few breaths before being swallowed again by the land. Rabbit Stick watched for a long time, until Young Hunter went around the great stone with the markings scratched into it at the head of the trail that led to the western entrance of their village. Then he turned his gaze toward the river.

From the hilltop where he stood, Rabbit Stick could see a small section of the Long River. It was like a length of sinew cord, sewn into the land. He could hear it speaking to him. He often heard the river speaking. He remembered how he had decided, as a young man, to walk to the place where that great flow began. That was what the river had been telling him to do. And he had said to himself that he would surely do so.

He had done that once with a smaller stream, a little brook flowing behind his parents' lodge with a voice like a friend gently talking in the night. He had climbed higher and higher as the stream grew smaller, as it chuckled through ravines and slid over wide ledges. But he had not found its source. He had not found the spring he imagined. Instead, the little stream had fanned out, like the fingers of an opened hand, and he had found it impossible to tell where any of those fingers truly ended. For the trickle of each had grown imperceptibly smaller and smaller until, as he followed one after another, he found himself on dry earth. It was as if that little stream were the breath of the mountain he had climbed. *I have learned something*, he said to himself then. But when he got back down to the lodge of his parents, he was no longer sure what he had learned. Perhaps only that it was never clear where anything began.

Somehow, one thing and then another had happened. He had grown taller. He had earned the name of a man. He had married the only really interesting girl in all of the Thirteen Villages. They had children and grandchildren. And Rabbit Stick had become an old man. Contented. He had followed more than one stream to the place where it began. But as he stood looking out at the sinew of the Long River, feeling its old voice call him once again, he realized he had never done what he had said he would do as a youth. He had never walked to the place where the Long River began.

"Are you disappointed with me, old friend?" he said. Then he listened, listened so intently that he began to hear his own heartbeat. It was calm and regular now, not racing as it had been for that moment. No, the Long River was not upset with him. But he knew what he needed to do. He needed to walk farther around this hill, take another trail and climb higher as the Day Traveler climbed up into the sky. There was a place there where he needed to stand, a place where he could see far up the Long River, far up along the trail that he now knew for certain his grandson would soon be walking. There was a place there where one could get a good long look out over the cliff, out over the edge of the land. A place right in front of the deep mouth of a cave.

From his vantage point on top of his cliff that leaned over the dead camp like the face of a grandfather, the Mikumwesu watched. It was the way of his people to watch. To watch and try not to interfere. His parents had taught him that once one started to interfere in the lives of the big people, there would be no end to it because the big people always needed a great deal of help. He had watched as that big woman with the angry face had gently taken down the body of the old one from the tree. He had felt her tears, but he had not moved. It was the way of his people to watch. It was hard not to interfere.

Those people of the Below the Cliffs camp had always remembered him. They had left food for him at the edge of their village by the mouth of the small ravine where he and his parents had lived their solitary life. He had never showed himself to them, not even to the little children as his parents had sometimes done while they still walked. Yet he had felt a fondness for the strange tall ones. Sometimes, after one of the tall ones had left the food, he had run ahead through the brush and placed something nice in the trail so the tall one would find it. That was surely not interfering.

Now all of them were dead. The big angry animal had killed them all. It had come in from the edge of the trees, come in the time just before the day fire returned to the Sky Land. It had driven them toward the swift river. They did not have the quick boats like those he and his parents knew how to make.

They had one dugout made of a burned-out basswood log. But they could not push it out into the stream quickly enough. Those who had not been killed on land by its heavy feet and the long snake of its nose had run to the river, hoping their boat would take them to safety in the water. But the big animal did not stop at the shore. It acted as if it had seen such a boat before and it knew what to do.

It followed them into the water, foam splashing high about it, and it thrust with its long teeth to impale one man. Then it turned and crushed their boat with one stamp of its foot, flipping one man and woman high into the air and piercing with the splinters of the shattered boat the chest of another man holding a tiny child. Another great foot came down. The water grew darker under it, and the man and tiny child were gone. There had been twelve full households in that camp—many handfuls of the big people, although some of the children had been almost as small as the Mikumwesu. Now there were none living there. Aside from the angry-faced woman who had come and gone, there was no one left to make the high sorrow sounds for them.

The Mikumwesu reached out yet again with his mind to touch the thoughts of the big angry animal and soothe it. It was not that far away, just over the slope behind him. He had spoken to it that way with his mind to keep it from coming back while the angry-faced woman was here, or she would surely have been dead also. Although its tracks led downstream, it had doubled back to wait. But he had, with the touch of his mind, softened the big animal's rage, turned its thoughts to finding food, and directed it away from the ruined landscape of the village below the cliff.

He had done something like this before when a bear had been close to several of the children of the tall strange people of the Below the Cliffs camp without their knowing and it had been about to charge them with its fear. But the Mikumwesu's thoughts had stopped the bear's fear, had convinced it to move back to the berry bushes away from the children, and they had passed on, unhurt and unknowing. It had made the Mikumwesu feel good to do this, almost as good as he had felt when his parents had still been living. He was as old now as they had been when he was born, and they had been very old in the way of their people when they had given him birth. They had lived even longer after that, but there had been a limit on their living, as there is on all things. Like the very ripe grapes that fall from the vine, their time had come. Together, both of them had ceased their breath as they slept. It was just as the three of them had dreamt it would happen, so Mikumwesu was not surprised when he woke to silence in their little cave, which had always before been filled with the sound of his mother's and father's breath. He did not make sorrow sounds as he had heard those tall strange people make when one of them died, no matter how old and full and ripe they were.

Mikumwesu had carried first his mother and then his father to the cliff place above the deep oak tangle and the rocks of their ravine where none of the tall people ever ventured. Using the ropes he and his parents had made of the fiber of the milkweeds, he had pulled their bodies, first his mother's and then his father's, up the cliff wall to the place they had prepared for themselves a long time before. He had tied them securely to the cedar branches up there where the birds and insects and winds would clean away the ripeness of their skin and sinew and flesh, and he had come back often to be sure that their bones were not taken.

Mikumwesu knew he would have to plan very carefully to be sure that he was well and strong enough when his dying time came to climb to this spot himself. He wished to have his bones rest with those of his parents, and he knew there would be no one to bring him to his final sleeping place except himself. He and his parents had not been able to find any more of their people, especially one who was like his mother and could join with him to bring more. His parents told him of how there had been more, so many winters gone. But when they crossed the ice mountains, his people had become divided. Only a few had come this way, down to this river valley. And there were no others that they had found after finding this good place. Their travel had been hard for them. They were people who did not travel, but rooted to a place the way the trees and the stones rooted. So they did not seek far for other little ones. They were content with each other and with watching the tall strange people. Watching and trying not to interfere. Though it was hard not to interfere.

The tall strange people were very amusing to watch. They talked so much and were always doing things that seemed to have no real purpose. It was hard to understand how people could be so tall and still be able to live like real human beings. But somehow the strange people did so. Many seasons passed and so, too, did more than one generation of the tall strange people. Mikumwesu and his parents waited, but no others of their people, no other little ones, came to find them.

Mikumwesu was alone. He wanted his bones to join the dust that his parents' bones would become, and so he knew that he would have to plan well to make sure he could do it. When his dream that he was about to be ripe came, he would go to the cliff place where the well-cleaned, beautiful painted bones of his parents were tied with milkweed twine to the standing stones. He would wait there without water and food, his face looking up at the sky fire as it passed over for as many times as it took for his ripeness to reach him.

He reached out with his thought to touch the big angry animal. But his thought could not reach it this time. It had tried to eat, and pain had filled it. Its mind was like a boiling pot, hot and swirling. Anger red as blood. Mikumwesu pulled his thought back, feeling the way he had felt when he was a tiny baby and had placed his finger against a stone made red by heat. He could do nothing now but watch. And he watched as

134

the big angry animal came again from the forest. It could smell the scent of the angry-faced woman, and that made it even angrier. It went back and forth in the camp, lifting those who were dead and throwing them down and hurling them up into the branches of the pine trees. Mikumwesu could see clearly that even killing all the tall people in the world would not be enough for the animal. At last, it followed the scent of the woman to the river, losing her trail at the place where she had crossed, wading through the ford. The big animal turned away from the camp and began walking, walking down the Long River.

Long after it was gone, Mikumwesu watched. Two times the Day Traveler rose, crossed the sky, and disappeared. Then, from a place inside him Mikumwesu had never heard speak before, a sound came. It was much like the sorrow sound of the tall people. It wailed from his throat. The sorrow sound was as sharp as the edge of the obsidian knife that was sheathed and belted to his waist. It called down a golden eagle from the sky to circle about the camp. It made the leaves tremble. It stopped the songs of the birds and the insects. And when he could make that sound no more, Mikumwesu looked back over his shoulder, back toward the place in the cliff where his parents waited for him.

I will be back, he thought, seeing the beauty of their painted bones in his mind. Then he climbed down the cliff and made his way to the hidden place among the rocks where no tall person ever walked. He lifted the bark and branches and disclosed his small boat, made of the bark of the birch tree, sewn together with spruce roots. He placed the paddle carved from a cedar branch at his feet and then lifted the leaf-light boat upside down onto his shoulders. When he picked up his paddle and stood, he looked like a big walking seedpod. He went straight to the Long River. With no hesitation, he flipped his boat into the water, climbed in, and allowed the quick current to carry him.

CHAPTER TWENTY-FOUR
THE NEW ONE

Willow Woman smiled as Sparrow burst out of the trees and came running through the village clearing. It was clear that his swift feet had left Young Hunter behind again. When the two raced, it was always Sparrow who won, yet her stubborn husband would never admit that such contests were futile. She could imagine the two of them still racing against each other when both were old and gray and had to use walking sticks to keep from falling. But her smile left her face as Sparrow came closer. There was something serious in the look in Sparrow's eyes.

Yet as he came to a stop in front of her, he did not speak. Perhaps he would have done so had not the little black one filled the air with sound; it squawked a combination of crow talk and human words as it came hopping through the lodge door at that exact moment and jumped up into Willow Woman's lap as she sat there.

Ka-awk, kwiak kwiak, ganh hanh, the little black one said.

Willow Woman gently held the crow's beak together so that it became silent. It looked up at her, a mixture of fondness and irritation glittering in its eyes.

"Sparrow," she said, "this is another of the bird people. He is my new child. He has told me that his name is Talk Talk."

Sparrow shook his head. There was too much to say and he had too few words to hold it all. So he spoke quickly.

"You and Young Hunter are to go now, to the lodge of Medicine Plant and Bear Talker."

He spoke it all as one quick word, the way the language of the Only People could be spoken, everything flowing together like drops of rain to make a stream.

Willow Woman stood. She could see her husband now, running swiftly as he entered the clearing. From somewhere, Agwedjiman and Danowa had found him, and one dog ran to either side. But Pabesis was nowhere in sight. Chasing moths again, perhaps. The little dog had become fascinated with moths and butterflies, the lazy way they flapped their wings to lift themselves just above his mouth as he jumped and snapped at them. The little wide-winged ones almost seemed to be teasing Pabesis, and he had probably followed one somewhere.

Willow Woman placed the little black one up on one of the poles extending beyond the edge of the wigwom roof.

"Talk Talk," she said, "we will return. Here is food for you to eat while we are gone." She threw a handful of scraps up onto the roof of the lodge next to the crow.

"What are you waiting for?" she said to Young Hunter as he reached the wigwom, breathing hard. "We have been called."

She and Sparrow began to run back in the very direction from which Young Hunter had just come. Shaking his head, Young Hunter pressed his hand against his side where a pain had formed, sharp as a spear point. He looked to his two dogs for sympathy. Danowa and Agwedjiman looked back at him. There was no pity in their eyes. Instead, it seemed as if his dogs were telling him more clearly than words could say that they could see what was really inside his heart.

"Uh-hunh," Young Hunter said, inhaling and exhaling slowly to catch his breath, "you know that I am as excited as those two." He gestured with his head toward Sparrow and Willow Woman. Young Hunter smiled. "And you also know that I am not going to follow the trail they are running on to get there. We will go the quick way."

Even as he spoke those words the two dogs wheeled and began to trot in the direction of the quicker trail up the hills. But they stopped long enough for Young Hunter to catch up with them.

As Rabbit Stick walked, he was thinking not only about the source of the Long River. He was also thinking about stones. There were many loose stones on this trail as it wound its way toward the caves, and there were other stones that pushed their heads out of the earth on the uphill side of the trail just at the height where Rabbit Stick could touch them, gently, saying hello, as he passed by.

There was much to be learned from stones. He would sometimes pick up a stone and look at it, wondering at how no stone was like another. There were so many things that stones had taught the people. Whenever you picked up a stone, it seemed to fit itself into your hand in a way that would give you the idea of what could be done.

There were stones that told you they were made to be used for scraping the flesh from a hide. There were other stones that told you they were meant to be used to crack butternuts. Some stones liked to fly and always found the hands of small children, who were especially cooperative in helping such a stone realize its wish.

According to the oldest story, the Owner Creator shaped the first people from stones. Perhaps he meant them to be strong and self-reliant. Stones were always very much that way. Rabbit Stick remembered how, as a child, he had marveled at the way stones, even ones that seemed quite friendly to his touch, would never complain when they were left out in the cold rain or in the snow.

The one lodged now in his mokasin seemed to have a particularly important lesson to teach him. Rabbit Stick sat down. He had been trying to ignore it, but this stone would not be ignored or work its own way out of the mokasin. He adjusted the rabbitskin robe, which was slung over one shoulder and secured at the waist by his belt of woven basswood, and bent to his mokasin. As he unlaced the leather bindings, he smiled at himself. He was acting just as he had when, as a small child, he had thought that just by thinking about them he could make things happen, make clouds move out of the sky, make birds appear when he pointed ... make stones magically disappear when one was in his mokasin and he was in a hurry to get somewhere and didn't want to stop and unlace and take off his mokasin to get rid of it.

Rabbit Stick reached in and felt around. When he held the stone up, he was surprised at how small it was. It should have been at least as big as a spear point, the way it had been making its presence felt. He looked at it closely. *Did it have a face?*

Rabbit Stick always looked for faces on stones. He had started doing so back before he had the name Rabbit Stick, back when he was a little child known as Big Ant. He did so because of the story of the Stone People and how the Owner Creator had discovered that it was not good to have the people made of stone and so had broken them up into pieces again. One of his grandparents, his father's father, Loon, had told him the Owner Creator did that because the Stone People were too hard on the rest of creation, too heavy-footed. But Loon's wife, his grandmother who was named Sweet Voice, had told him it was because the Stone People became too proud of themselves. They even thought they were greater than the Owner Creator. That was a good reason, and for a time Big Ant, who had not yet become Rabbit Stick, decided his grandmother Sweet Voice must be right.

But then he had heard the same story told by his other grandmother, his mother's mother. Her name was Singing Beaver. She explained that the reason the Owner Creator returned the Stone People to their original shapes by breaking them up into stones was that stones never die. Death was a necessary thing. Because the Stone People never died but continued to have children, there would come a dawn when they would have crowded out all other things. The whole earth would be covered with Stone People and nothing but Stone People. That had frightened Big Ant who had not yet become Rabbit Stick, and he had been certain *that* was the right reason. For many moons after that, he woke up certain that the Stone People were going to return one day and that they would destroy all of the Only People.

Finally, because he was sleeping so badly, his mother's father, his grandfather Cedar Tree, told him the same story a fourth time. Big Ant Not Yet Rabbit Stick was lying with his eyes wide open, looking up at the stars, which were especially bright at this time when the leaves were turning colors, when he heard his grandfather's voice grow louder. He was speaking with his wife and with Loon and Sweet Voice. The old man was saying something about telling a story the right way, about how some stories could frighten a little child who might not yet be ready to hear a story told in a certain way.

Big Ant Not Yet Rabbit Stick was wondering who that little child might be when he felt his grandfather pull the big toe on his right foot. It was the way Cedar Tree always checked to see if he was asleep or, by pulling harder, would wake the boy in the morning when he wanted his favorite grandson to walk with him.

"I will tell you a story that you already know," Cedar Tree said, when Big Ant Not Yet Rabbit Stick rolled over.

The firelight flickered on Cedar Tree's face as he told of the Stone People. But he did not end the story where the other three grandparents had ended it. He went on. He explained how happy the Stone People were to be able to return to the earth. It had been lonely for them to be so tall and powerful. Now that they were stones again, they fitted back into all of creation. "And," Cedar Tree said, "those stones have faces on them. Look at every stone you pick up. If you find one with a face on it, it is one of those that was once part of one of the Stone People. Look closely at that stone's face. You may see that it is smiling."

From that day on, Rabbit Stick had always paid very close attention to the stones. And it did seem as if he often could find faces on them, although usually you had to look on the underside of the stone to find the face. Stones liked to keep their faces hidden. And he would always put each stone back where he had found it unless he had some special use for it. He was not like some of the Only People who were always bringing home stones, piling them around their wigwoms. They did that just because they liked the way those stones looked. Sometimes, when Rabbit Stick walked by some of those piles of stones, it seemed to him as if the stones looked resentful.

But stones did like to be placed in piles at the edge of the Long River. When Rabbit Stick had waded into the Long River at dawn, two days ago, he had made such a carefully piled stone cairn and then placed a fallen blue jay feather at the top of it. It was a visible sign of the sincerity of the words he had spoken that morning to the river and the new light.

He stopped walking, bent down, and picked up a stone. Turning it over, he could see a face more clearly than on any other stone he had picked up before. It seemed as if the eyes in that stone's face were looking back the way he had come. As if to tell him to go back that way. Rabbit Stick sat down to think. He could walk farther before he would have to turn back. If he walked just a little farther, past the mouth of the deepest cave there around the bend in the trail, he would be able to see the long glittering body of the river below, winding its way through the land. It was as if there were another wordless voice in his mind, calling him to go just a bit farther. He put the stone down, being careful to place it just as it had been before he picked it up.

"*Wliwini,* Older Brother," he said to the stone. "You are telling me that an old man should not walk too far from his home. I will not go much farther now."

Then Rabbit Stick began to walk again with long strong strides, uphill toward the bend in the trail.

When Young Hunter finally reached the lodge it was almost midday. He could see the door was open, an invitation for anyone to come within. He ducked his head and stepped inside. Bear Talker was sitting with his back against the wall of the lodge to the sunset direction. He was rubbing his knee with his left hand, stroking downward as if to wipe the pain away that he must be feeling from the large red swelling there. The look on Bear Talker's face was a strange blend of confusion and pride. Young Hunter saw Bear Talker first, for the deep-seeing man raised his hand to catch Young Hunter's attention as he entered. *Be quiet,* that gesture said. *Pay attention.*

Young Hunter looked around the circle of the lodge. Against the north side he saw Willow Woman. Despite his shortcut, she had arrived before him. She was sitting, too, and from the look on her face, a look of barely contained excitement, he knew that something important had been said to her and that he, too, would soon hear it. That worried him even more than the look on Bear Talker's face. Sparrow was not in the lodge. Perhaps he had been sent off on another errand. And even as Young Hunter thought that, he knew for certain where Sparrow was. He had been sent to bring Rabbit Stick. Young Hunter could see it in the eyes of his mind. He saw his friend running swiftly up the trail that led to the place of many caves above the Long River.

And in his knowing of Sparrow's mission, another picture came into Young Hunter's mind. He saw his grandfather's face in a way he had never seen it before. His grandfather's eyes were closed and there was blood on his face. When that image came into his mind, he almost cried out, almost turned and ran out of the lodge. Was it only a waking dream or was it a vision of something that had happened or was about to happen? But as he stood there, held in place by that thought like a person suddenly turned into a tree and rooted to the earth, the voice of his grandmother cleared away the confusion.

"Grandson," Sweetgrass Woman said in a very quiet voice, "sit down by your wife."

Young Hunter turned his eyes toward the southern side of the lodge. At this time of the day, with no fire in the center of the lodge, that side was the darkest, and there in the darkness he saw the figures of two women sitting close together, holding a bundle. His eyes opened to the darkness, and he saw them more clearly: Sweetgrass Woman and Medicine Plant. Medicine Plant's hair, unbraided, circled her face and covered her shoulders like a dark cloud flowing down a mountain. Her face, though, without losing any of the strength he had always seen in it, was softer now. It was because of the bundle she held, the bundle that was a sleeping child wrapped in soft, smoke-tanned white skins.

As soon as he sat, Willow Woman grabbed his arm and held onto it as tightly as someone might hold onto a sturdy branch to keep from falling out of a tree. Young Hunter kept looking at the faces of the two older women. They had something to tell him and he was growing even more certain now that it was something he was not ready to hear.

Within the shadowed mouth of the deepest cave, the light of the Day Traveler touched the edge of a deeper shadow, a shadow that loomed over the cave entrance, a shadow that breathed. Its breath was almost as slow as the motion of the Day Traveler across the sky, but that breath was deep and strong and old. And with each slow breath, the Ancient One sent out that wordless call. Softer than the whisper of a spider's step across its web was that call. It called, and it felt the steps of the one who had heard it coming closer, yet not steadily. Pausing now and then, as if stopped by something.

The Ancient One had only to take a few long strides out of that darkness, and the one who had answered its call would be there, within easy reach. The Ancient One remembered the feel of its long arms reaching out, the sound and the feel of bones breaking and the warm smell of blood. It also remembered watching the manylegs walk unharmed across its gray flesh. Its own mind was not clear as to what it would do when the one it was calling came within reach, stepped within the cave. But it knew that it would not be alone then. And if it was not alone it would be stronger. And the one it called was close, so close its breathing could be heard.

But the Ancient One did not move from the cave, did not step out of the shadow. It did not want to be seen by the light in the sky. It sensed that if it stood and was seen by that light, the Day Traveler would tell others where it was. And because it was alone, the Ancient One feared being discovered. So it waited.

Rabbit Stick sat down and held the two stones in his hand. He had never felt the voices of the stones calling him more strongly than they did now. He had intended to walk a bit farther, just to that spot there where the Long River was a look below. But these two stones had almost lifted themselves right up from the earth to place themselves in his hands.

He let his legs dangle over the edge of the cliff. A small pebble fell, bounced, and fell again. It was a long way down, indeed. As the pebble fell, two cliff swallows swooped and dove at it, as if to tell it to continue on its way and not trouble them further. Rabbit Stick watched the pebble as it went, knowing that the fall would not hurt it, that it would surely find friends to stay with down there below. He smiled as he thought this. He was thinking the same way he had thought when he was a very small child. Thinking so much about stones often affected him that way. Perhaps that was why he felt just now as if he were a little one again being called by an elder. But he would not hear that call. He would sit here with his two friends and dangle his feet.

Rabbit Stick's mind was now working at two levels. At one level he was playing and thinking like a child. At another level he was still an old man, an old man aware that his medicine was speaking to him. Stones had always been his medicine friends—stones and the waters of the river. For some reason, the stones were asking him to think like a child, to be in no hurry to go anywhere. And Rabbit Stick listened to his medicine whenever he felt it speaking to him. He was no deep-seer like Bear Talker. He was not able to explain the how and why of things as Bear Talker did. But he knew when he was being helped by power, even if he did not know exactly how it was helping him.

Rabbit Stick sighed. He looked up at the Day Traveler, whose steps across the sky had taken it almost to the highest point in the sky. He would walk no farther today. He would go back down to his lodge where his grandson was surely waiting for him. And perhaps Sweetgrass Woman had returned by now and a good stew was cooking over the fire. He stood up and carefully placed the two stones down where they had been. But as long as he had come this far, why not take a few more strides up the hill to the lookout in front of the cave, just to look down and greet the Long River?

Rabbit Stick took one step and then another. He heard what sounded like a distant wind coming from inside the mouth of the cave, which was no more than the length of two spears away. He did not know it was the long drawn-in breath of the gray giant. He did not see, inside the cave's darkness, the long arm that was raised up and ready to strike. Instead, he turned to look because he heard the sound of running feet. He stepped back down the trail, away from the mouth of darkness. It was Pabesis. Tongue hanging out, the big young dog was running up the trail with long, surprisingly graceful strides, its eyes on Rabbit Stick. It yelped twice, as if to greet him, and then its grace left it suddenly as its big paws slid on the loose stones where Rabbit Stick had been sitting. Rabbit Stick dove onto his belly, grabbing the big young dog by its hind legs, trying to keep it from sliding off the steep trail. Both of them went over the edge of the cliff together.

CHAPTER TWENTY-FIVE
THE SKY LAND

Long ago, two brothers decided to travel to the Sky Land. The old people of the village told them not to try this. Only those who died could go to the Sky Land. It was a long way to travel, past the end of the world. And why would anyone want to see the place now while still alive? After all, everyone was going to go there one day.

But these two brothers were very stubborn. They kept asking the deep-seeing woman of the village how they could travel to the Sky Land without first dying.

At last, the deep-seeing woman told them what to do. "To go anywhere," she said, "you must walk, placing one foot in front of another. Then, step by step, your feet will take you where you are going."

The two brothers were not sure that they understood, but they felt that at the least they had been told how to begin their journey. They gathered together extra pairs of mokasins and began to pack their pouches.

Their two grandfathers took them aside. First their mother's father spoke.

"Your grandmother does not want to see you go. That is why she has not come here to see you as you leave our village. But she has asked me to give you this. This pouch, which is made of a fisher's skin, has special power," he said. "If you are in trouble, untie its mouth and ask for help."

The brothers thanked their mother's father. Then the older brother took the fisherskin pouch, and tied it to his belt, which was made of strips of woven basswood fiber. That belt was very strong and nothing would break it.

Then their father's father spoke. "Your other grandmother also does not wish to watch you leave our village. She is afraid that you will never return. So she has asked me to give you this spear. Whenever you become lost or are not sure which way to go, throw this spear up as high as you can into the air. Think hard about where you want to go while it is still flying. When it falls, it will point the way you need to go."

The younger brother took the spear.

"Travel well," said their two grandfathers.

Now the two young men began to walk, putting one foot in front of the other. When they reached the Long River, near the big whirlpool, they crossed over it on the rocks above the waterfall and continued. But the way they traveled, going one foot in front of the other, led them off the usual paths, and they found themselves forcing their way through the brush and climbing over the hills. After they had traveled most of the day, they realized they had been going in a big circle. They were back near the Long River where they had started. They did not know which way to go to reach the Sky Land.

"Throw the spear," said the older brother.

The older brother threw the spear as hard as he could up into the air. It went very high and very far. But as it flew, the younger brother could not keep his mind on finding the Sky Land. He thought first of how comfortable his own bed would be if he was in it. Then he thought of going to the Sky Land. Then he thought of how good the food always tasted in the evening in the cookpot in their wigwom. Then he thought again of going to the Sky Land. When the spear finally fell, it landed in the Long River and became caught in the whirlpool, where it floated to the surface and spun around and around.

The spear was out of their reach and they could not get it back.

"You have done well," said the older brother. "Thanks to your bad throw, that spear is not telling us where to go. It is saying where we have gone. That is how we have been traveling thus far. Shall we continue to go in circles?"

The younger brother did not answer him. He sat down and began to eat some of the dried meat he had packed in his pouch. His mouth was soon so full that he did not hear the noise of something moving in the bushes near them. And his older brother was so angry that they had lost the spear that he, too, did not hear those sounds.

The sounds in the bushes were made by the Old Toad Woman. She was one of the old ones who was a great danger to the human beings. Although she was a coward, she liked to lure people into the swamps and drown them there. Then, when their flesh had softened on their bones, she would eat them.

Old Toad Woman looked a bit like a hunched-up old, old woman. If anyone got close enough to see her big eyes and her face which had no nose and her wide mouth which had no teeth, they would see that she was not a human being. But she never let anyone see her until it was too late. She could make her voice very sweet, like the voice of a bird. Little children would follow that voice and so would some of the foolish young men. These two young men looked very foolish. And there was a lot of flesh on their bones. Old Toad Woman smiled and called out softly as she slipped back between the cedar trees away from the river. Her voice was sweet and both young men turned to listen.

"What was that sound?" said the older brother. "I think it was a bird."

"*Nda,*" said the younger brother, "I think it was the voice of a woman calling to me."

"Let us follow it," said the older brother.

They turned their back on the river and walked back through the cedar trees. So it was that neither of them saw the spear float free of the whirlpool. It drifted over to the opposite shore and wedged between two stones in the shallows, pointing toward the sunset direction, the opposite of the direction the young men had taken.

Rabbit Stick opened his eyes. He had been hearing the voice of his mother, telling him that long-ago story of the young men and Old Toad Woman. Her voice had been so clear that he was surprised not to see her leaning over him, speaking more and more softly until he fell asleep. But it was hard to see anything. There was dirt in his eyes, and one of his eyes he could not open, no matter how hard he tried. He tried to lift up his right hand to clean the dirt from his eyes. But when his hand did not touch his face, he realized that he only thought he was moving his hand. He tried to lift his left hand. It, too, would not move. He tried to stand, pushing hard with both hands against the stones. It was hard to do, for the stones seemed softer than moss and kept slipping away beneath his hands. He gathered himself with a deep breath and suddenly found himself standing, his vision cleared. Everything was also much brighter around him—as if he were carrying a torch in each hand. He turned to look down at where he had been. An old man was there on the slope, his face half-covered with dirt and small stones and much of his body buried in the sliding earth which made a long scar up the side of the steep hill. What showed of the old man's clothing—deerskin leggings embroidered with moose hair, part of a belt made of basswood strips woven together, a robe of rabbit fur which appeared to be draped over one shoulder—looked familiar to Rabbit Stick. Pabesis was there, too. The young dog sitting at the feet of that old man turned, looked up at him, and whined.

Rabbit Stick tried to speak; no words came from his mouth. But though he could not seem to speak, everything else felt as it should. *Nda, better.* There was no stiffness or pain anywhere in his body, and it had been a long time since he had chewed any of the leaves he always carried with him in his pouch to make the pain fade when it came. He reached down to the pouch, but it was not there at his side. In fact, he had none of his clothes on. Even though this day had begun warm, Rabbit Stick knew that it was still the time of year when the wind that blew through the trees could become very cold. Even as he thought of that wind, it began to blow, shaking the small leaves on the blanket trees that grew on this slope. But the wind did not feel cold to him. He saw the leaves move, but he did not feel the wind at all. He motioned to Pabesis to follow him, but the dog only whined again and then began to lick the still face of the old one half-buried there. Rabbit Stick thought of helping the old man. Yet the look on the old one's face was peaceful. He was resting there. He did not wish to be disturbed.

Rabbit Stick turned and took one step. As soon as he did so, he found himself on top of the hill at the very place he had been when he had fallen. He looked into the cave. He knew now what it was that was hiding in there. He felt the spider-web touch of its thinking. He saw the confusion in its thoughts. But he did not stay there. He had to go to someone. Another step and he was back in the village. The person he sought was not there. Another step and he was high on the trail up the far hill. Rabbit Stick laughed. It was a laugh without the breath of sound, but it felt so good that he did not care. He could see all the way up the Long River from this place. He could see farther than a hawk's eyes could see. Something else was coming from that direction, something of great power. If he wanted to, he knew that he could leap and be higher in the sky than a hawk's flight could carry it. Then he could see what was coming. He thought of doing that. It would be good to reach the Sky Land. But he could not do that yet. He had to go somewhere else first. He took another step.

CHAPTER TWENTY-SIX
FAST TRAVEL

Young Hunter saw his grandfather enter the lodge. Willow Woman did not see him. Sweetgrass Woman did not see him. Young Hunter wondered why. The way his grandfather entered was so strange that anyone would have noticed, for he came not through the door, but through the solid bark wall. The bark seemed to melt away like snow as he entered and then it was back as it had been before. And there had been the sound of knocking on the lodge's west wall. Once, twice, three times, four times. As if someone were striking the bark wall with a stick. And then Rabbit Stick had come in to stand there next to Medicine Plant and the tiny baby. He stood there now, not speaking, with a happy look on his face.

Young Hunter looked over at Bear Talker. Bear Talker was looking at Rabbit Stick.

Then I am not waking sleeping, Young Hunter thought. *Bear Talker sees him, too.* Young Hunter looked at Medicine Plant. She looked at Rabbit Stick and nodded her head. Rabbit Stick knelt and placed his hand on the head of the small child. The baby reached up a tiny hand and grasped one of the old man's long fingers.

As soon as the child's strong fingers circled his own finger, Rabbit Stick felt something change. He felt a warmth go through him, and he stood and took a step back and began again to fall. ...

Young Hunter looked down at the others seated in the lodge. He did not remember standing up. Medicine Plant nodded to him.

"Uh-hunhh," she said slowly, "you know where to find him."

Bear Talker motioned with a twist of his head toward the door, pointing with his lips as he did so. "Go now."

Then Young Hunter found himself running high on the winding trail that led up to the crossroads of paths below the mossy ledge where he had left his grandfather. He did not know how he came to be running. The last memory in his mind was of Bear Talker pointing with his lips to the door. Medicine Plant's lodge lay two looks behind him, beyond the range of hills.

Have I been given a pair of magic mokasins? The kind that carry you a whole look with each step? That thought came and went from his mind as quickly as he moved up the slope. Stones rolled down as his feet dislodged them. Perhaps Bear Talker and Medicine Plant had helped him with their power. Or perhaps it was just that his own thinking had stopped as he turned and ran. Or perhaps this was what fast traveling truly was.

His grandfather had told him about fast traveling. That although he, Rabbit Stick, could not do it, it was part of his grandson's heritage. Thrower, Young Hunter's father, had come from a line of men who knew how to go that way, how to fast travel.

Rabbit Stick had been close friends with Thrower's father, Walks Easy. Young Hunter had never met him breath-walking. He and Young Hunter's other grandmother had been drowned one spring when they were crossing the ice of the big lake. Perhaps Walks Easy could have escaped, but when his wife, Swan's Wing, had stepped wrongly and fallen through

153

the ice, he would not leave her. That was how Oldest Talker, the deep-seeing woman of the people in those days, had explained it, explained it as clearly as if she had been there by their sides, watching what happened.

Oldest Talker told of how Swan's Wing had motioned Walks Easy to go back. She was already too cold to speak and there was ice forming on her eyebrows. But she waved her hands at him, telling him to stay away. The ice was too thin. He would fall in too. But he had not paid attention. He pushed the birch bark toboggan which held their small, sleeping son, Thrower, and his little dog toward the shore where the ice was thick and safe. Then he tried to pull her free with a basswood rope that he threw to her. When her hands grew too cold to hold on, he had crawled on his belly over the ice to grasp her robe with his own hands and try to pull her up. That was when the ice had given way under him also, and he had gone beneath it, his arms holding his wife close to him as if to warm her with his own last warmth.

Oldest Talker's words led the people to the place where the birch bark toboggan rested near the shore and where Thrower was asleep, kept warm by the skins piled over him and by the little dog which was nestled close to him.

When the ice had gone out the following spring, the people had gone to the place where Oldest Talker told them to go, and they found the two of them there, floated up at the lake's edge, their arms still around each other. Death was not strong enough to come between Walks Easy and Swan's Wing.

Walks Easy's name and his stories were so familiar to Young Hunter that there was a picture of the short, muscular man, vigorous in his middle years—for he had not lived long enough to grow old—in Young Hunter's mind. A picture that came to life sometimes in his dreams. Rabbit Stick told Young Hunter the story of how he and two other friends had gone trapping along with Walks Easy far to the east.

People liked to go on journeys with Walks Easy. No one ever saw him running, yet he was almost always the first one to get there. And when you traveled with him, it seemed as if the distances were much shorter.

One morning, when they were four days' travel from their village, Rabbit Stick had broken his knife. The flint had splintered right down the middle of the blade. It would be easy enough to make a new one, but there were no flint stones in this area that would be right for such a knife.

"If only I had brought my new knife," Rabbit Stick said that night as they sat around the fire. "I had just finished making it and I left it in my lodge."

"Where did you leave it?" Walks Easy said.

Rabbit Stick looked hard at his friend and let a long time pass. The sticks in the fire made popping noises. The other two men with them also said nothing. Finally Rabbit Stick spoke.

"I left it up in the rafters on the sunset side of my lodge."

Walks Easy stood up and stretched. "I am going to walk into the forest," he said. "I will be back soon." He took two slow, unhurried steps and then was gone in the darkness. He was gone only as long as it took for a handful of sticks to be placed into the fire and burn down to embers. When he appeared back in the light cast by the fire, there was a smile on his face.

Again, Rabbit Stick said nothing. He only held out his hand. Walks Easy took another step forward, leaned over, then placed Rabbit Stick's new knife on his friend's palm.

"I am sorry," Rabbit Stick had said to Young Hunter, "that there was no chance for you to know your other grandfather. He made our lives interesting."

Young Hunter had never known his father, either. Thrower had been killed along with Young Hunter's mother when the tree fell on their little trapping lodge far from the village, leaving only the tiny boy as a survivor. If Bear Talker had not been able to see far that day and know of the tragedy, then the little baby would also not have survived. But Bear Talker had come to the lodge of Sweetgrass Woman and Rabbit Stick.

"I've dreamt. I have seen something," the deep-seeing man told them. "Go and follow the northern trapline trail."

And now I have seen something, Young Hunter thought.

As he thought this he felt his legs growing weak. He grasped at the small trees that grew by the side of the trail, trying to pull himself along, but he could run no farther. He went down on one knee, placed his hands against a large stone that had been warmed by the afternoon sun, and breathed in and out deeply four times. He saw the patterns on the stone as he breathed. Great circles of red and blue and gray. He had not seen those patterns on the stone as he ran. The green and yellow of the lichen made pictures on the face of the stone within each of those great circles. He began to read something in those pictures. In the gray circle was the tall shape of a being like a man rearing up over another person who seemed smaller than a small child. In the blue circle there was another shape bent beside what looked like a river. The shape of a woman, perhaps. In the red circle a four-legged being was crushing what seemed to be a wigwom beneath its feet. As he looked at those pictures, pictures no human being had made, Young Hunter began almost to understand them.

Something made a small noise upslope from him. He turned his head away from the stone to look. A jay flew out, calling indignantly. Then, from below the thick branches of a hemlock an arm's length away from him, an animal's head was thrust out and then another next to it.

Young Hunter held his hands out to his two dogs. They came and pressed their heads against either side of his face. They did not try to kiss him. They did not whine or roll at his feet. It was as if they understood that there was no time for such things now. The look in the eyes of both was deep and serious.

"My friends," Young Hunter said, "Agwedjiman, Danowa! Thank you for coming to give me strength. We must hurry now. Our grandfather needs us to come to him."

Then, his two dogs beside him, he began to run up the trail even faster than before.

Rabbit Stick coughed. It hurt to cough, but he could not stop himself from coughing again. He breathed in. It was difficult and he did not like the feeling of it. He had forgotten, it seemed, how hard it was to breathe. It was much easier to move without breathing, to travel as he had just been traveling, travel without taking this heavy body with him.

He opened his eyes. They would not focus at first. Then he realized that his vision was filled by the head of a dog. Pabesis. A growling dog. A growling dog looking at something. Rabbit Stick tried to move his head. He could barely do so. It was as if his head were tied to the ground. But he thought he saw something out of the corner of his eye, there in the direction the dog was looking. Something that moved away as the dog growled. Was it the hunched-over shape of a being like an old woman?

Rabbit Stick coughed again. It was not easy to cough. There was much weight on his chest, dirt and stones and what seemed to be a pine log pressing down on him. He could not move his arms or his legs at all. Only his face was free of the slide of rocks and earth, and even that small part of himself would be covered over if the big young dog moved from its place. But Pabesis did not move. He growled, a deep growl that Rabbit Stick felt as it vibrated the air near his face.

"Old Toad Woman," Rabbit Stick said, his voice weak but clear, "I am not dead. Go back to your swamps to look for easier food there."

He thought of animal people who were able to get out of tight places. *Skoks*, the snake. He tried to wiggle his body like a snake, but all that would move was one arm. Yet that was a start. He thought of his arm as a snake, moving it slowly in a snake's motion. Not too hard; the stones that were held from sliding by Pabesis might come down if he jerked free. Sweat covered his forehead and began to walk down across his cheeks and into his eyes. He did not mind the sweat. It was forcing the little biting ones, who had discovered him now, to move aside or be drowned. He wriggled one more time and felt the pressure lessen on his arm. Carefully, a finger's width at a time, he drew his arm out and held it up.

Small stones rattled free and bounced down the slope below him. He reached down and wiped the sweat from his eyes and waved away the remaining little biting ones. His hand swam into focus and he counted. Ah! All there. None of his fingers were missing. He wiggled his fingers in a rude gesture in the direction of the hunched-over figure, which was fading away now like mist at the edge of a swamp.

"My grandson chased you away once, Old Woman," Rabbit Stick said. "You cannot come back here again." He chuckled at the memory of a six-winters-old Young Hunter chasing what he thought was the Woman Who Lives in the Swamp with his small, sharp spear.

The shape was gone now, but the light of the Day Traveler was bright, blindingly bright in his eyes. Rabbit Stick squinted and held his hand before his eyes to shade them. He let his hand fall down onto his face and felt with his fingers. Again, there was nothing missing. Two eyes, one nose, two ears. Yet that feeling that some part of himself had been ... Rabbit Stick swallowed hard and tried to reach his hand farther down along his body, down there between his legs. But the earth and stones and the buried log held him as tightly as a child in a cradle board, preventing him from feeling anything. He tried to shift his hips under the earth and stone. He did not move, but he could feel the muscles of his hips and thighs strain.

That was good. It meant that his back was not broken. He would not like to be like the old man he remembered from his childhood, the one the people called Crawler, the one whose back had been hurt by a falling branch so that his legs no longer worked. Most thought the man would die, but Crawler was stubborn. After his wounds had healed, he tied his legs together with rawhide so they would not get caught as he moved about. Then he fashioned mokasins for his hands so that he could use them as feet to pull himself along. Crawler had lived on for many more winters before he died, an old man with gray hair. He had seemed happy enough, and he was able to go almost anywhere he wanted, but it was not a way that Rabbit Stick wished to be. And Crawler's wife had not been happy with her man.

"Sweetgrass Woman," Rabbit Stick said, seeing the unhappy face of his wife in his mind, "I hope that I am not going to have to explain something painful to you."

CHAPTER TWENTY-SEVEN
THE DEER JUMP

Sparrow tried to keep himself as small as the bird whose name he shared. He tried to keep his mind empty of thinking. Young Hunter had told the story of how the Ancient Ones seemed to know a person's thoughts. Even as he had thought that, the Ancient One had begun to turn its head slowly in his direction. So Sparrow turned his thoughts to small wings fluttering, to the feel of feathers embracing the wind, to the ways certain berries shine in the sun and taste sweet to a small tongue. He made his thoughts and all that he saw in his thoughts the same as those of the sparrow, and the great, gray head stopped turning his way. Slowly, almost as slowly as a drop of pine pitch moving down the rough bark of a tree, the Ancient One turned its head again to look back down the slope, down the slope where Rabbit Stick had fallen.

Sparrow did not think of that. He thought only the sparrow's thoughts. But when he had come over the top of the hill—approaching the caves from above, a path he had taken to bring him ahead of Rabbit Stick to give the old man the message that he must come to Medicine Plant's lodge—his thoughts had been very human, indeed. He had been thinking of his own ways, thinking as he often thought of how his heart never was able to rest in the lodge of one woman. Wondering why he was not able, like Young Hunter, to let his spirit heal itself in the love of a person such as Willow Woman. Wondering about the long winters of affection shared by Rabbit Stick and Sweetgrass Woman. Wondering that even the deep-seeing people, who often could not find anyone to share their love because the fear of their powers prevented it, even Bear Talker and Medicine Plant had found each other. And in that very human wondering, Sparrow had been feeling more and more sorry for himself. Until he had heard the sound below him.

He had looked down. There, far below, so small that he looked no larger than an ant, was one of Young Hunter's dogs. Sparrow crouched down next to a very large boulder that was balanced right on the lip of the cliff. He liked that boulder for it always made him think of the story of Azeban the raccoon, and the big rock that did not really want to travel, even though Azeban helped it on its way by pushing it over the edge. Sparrow shaded his eyes with one hand and held his other hand up beneath it as if holding a tube of birch bark. He looked through that tube made by his hand, narrowing his focus. A fire had passed along this part of the hill only two winters before, and so there was a clear line of vision down the trail where fire had eaten brush and trees, leaving only leaning stubs. The dog appeared and then disappeared and then appeared again among the sumac saplings and the stones. It was Pabesis. The big young dog was coming up the trail below faster than Sparrow had ever seen him run. There was grim determination in the dog's running and it shocked Sparrow. Where was the dog going and why was it running that way?

Sparrow did not move from his crouching position. He was on the roof of the largest of the caves, on the place that was sometimes called the Deer Jump. Just behind him there were many trees that had acorns and beechnuts. Herds of deer liked to feed there in the time of leaves changing. Hunters could make a drive and bring the deer out of the nut tree woods to this place. A dozen or so people with their arms linked could cut off all escape from this place of the Deer Jump. Then the hunters would speak to them, tell the deer that they had chosen to hunt them but did not wish to kill them all. Only one or two to feed the Only People. Sometimes one of the deer would then choose to be the one to feed the Only People. It would leap over the edge to fall on the flat ledge that was the height of a tall tree below this spot. Then the hunters would unlink their arms and step aside. The surviving deer would walk past them and no one would dream of striking at them with a spear. That was how this place worked.

Although he could not see it, the mouth of the big cave was just below Sparrow. He would have been able to see better down the trail from the cave mouth, but he did not move. The small voice which had no words but came to him from within the little bag he carried tied to his belt was talking to him. Sparrow listened and he did not move from the Deer Jump. Soon he began to hear the sounds of someone coming, soft sounds made by a man accustomed to walking the trails quietly. Though he could not see him, Sparrow knew it would be Rabbit Stick. He would wait where he crouched and then call down. Perhaps it would make Rabbit Stick jump. Sparrow smiled at that thought.

But when Rabbit Stick did appear and came to stand in front of the cave mouth, Sparrow did not speak. What happened made it impossible for him to speak. First, there was a sound that came from below. It came from within the cave and made Sparrow think of a cold wind blowing over bones. Pabesis came up over the edge of the trail onto the ledge, still running fast, straight for Rabbit Stick. And as the old man's eyes turned to the dog, something huge and gray came from the mouth of the cave. Sparrow had never seen it before, but he knew what it was. He tried to shout, but his mouth felt as if it were filled with dry acorn mush. The gray one raised a long arm, reaching for the old man. But just as that long arm swung down, Pabesis slipped on the loose stones of the ledge. Rabbit Stick grabbed the dog's legs, and in a rattle of falling stones, the old man and the dog slid suddenly out of sight over the edge.

Sparrow had closed his eyes then. He heard in his mind one of the few things his father told him before that man he hardly knew went away from him and his mother and did not return. But because his father had told him so little, he had held strongly to those small gifts from that wandering, restless man.

"If you wish to see and not be seen," his father had told him, "you must know when to close your eyes. Your eyes carry your voice. Only look at someone from behind and even if they cannot see you, they will feel your gaze upon them and turn to look. And even if you are concealed, their eyes will find your eyes if your eyes remain open."

So Sparrow closed his eyes. And with his eyes closed he felt the gaze of the great one on the ledge below him. But his eyes remained closed and because of that, those few words from his father saved his life.

The Ancient One looked up and around and then back down the slope. But it did not follow where the human and the four-legged one had fallen. Instead it sat at the edge of the cliff, hunched over, and seemed to become a stone itself.

Sparrow leaned hard against the big balanced rock. He could feel that it would move. But even as he did so, even as his thoughts toward the Ancient One below him were that it should go back into the cave, his power spoke to him and told him to still his own human thoughts. For that Ancient One would hear him. And Sparrow became a bird.

The trail leading up to the caves wound back and forth up the side of the mountain like a snake crawling among rocks. As he struggled up the slope, one of the dogs was always close to him, and Young Hunter often placed his hand on the back of Agwedjiman or Danowa, feeling the way they gave him the strength to continue. It was as if he and his dogs were doing the long dance winding among the wigwoms, the dance where

163

each person held the hand of the one in front and behind as the leader shook his rattle and the song gave their feet strength and pulled them faster and faster about the village. The sun had not moved more than a hand's width across the sky, but he had traveled as far as another man might go in a whole long day's afternoon.

He knew where he was going. He had seen in his mind the place where Rabbit Stick had been. It was the ledge in front of the deepest of the high caves. That was where he had to go. And now they were not far below that place. Just up around that twisted cedar, over those rocks, and around that big standing stone there at the top of the ridge above him. But suddenly he could go no farther. Agwedjiman stood across the trail, blocking his way. Young Hunter pushed him.

"My friend," he said, "move. We must go farther."

But the big dog did not move. It looked straight into Young Hunter's eyes and Young Hunter remembered that look. He had seen it first in another dog's eyes, in the eyes of the dog his grandfather had named Bear Chaser. Bear Chaser had been very old when Young Hunter came to live with his grandparents. One day, when the old people were out of the lodge, Young Hunter had tried to play with the fire. Bear Chaser had placed his heavy old body between the little boy and the flames, and no matter what he did, Young Hunter could not move the dog out of its place, guarding him from the danger of those flames.

Young Hunter went down on one knee.

"My friend," he said, "what is the danger? We are in a hurry. My grandfather has called us to him."

As he spoke, Young Hunter realized that something cleared away from his mind. It was not only concern for his grandfather that had been hurrying his steps. Another voice, a voice without human words, had been calling to him. And in the eye of his memory, he saw that there was something different about the trail. He looked up again. It was far away, at the very top of the ridge, and he would need the eyes of a hawk to see it with absolute clarity, yet something was different. The standing stone there now had not been there before when he had come up this trail.

Young Hunter felt a coldness begin at the nape of his neck and then walk down the center of his back. Agwedjiman looked up the slope and a soft growl came from deep within his throat.

"I see you," Young Hunter said. He said it first with words and then within his mind, without using words. He formed pictures in his mind. Pictures of himself standing with the Long Thrower in his hand, pictures of himself taking one of the small spears and fitting it to the string. He pictured himself bending that terrible weapon which no one else living among the Only People had ever seen, except for Bear Talker and Medicine Plant. Then, as he let the string go, the small spear flew through the air and pierced the throat of the great black animal that hunted human beings. He made another picture in his mind and this time the small spear flew into the eye of a gray giant, a being like a human, but the color of stone, the same color as that strange standing stone which Young Hunter had never seen before. He pictured himself doing this again and again, and he closed his eyes with the intensity of his thoughts. And as he did so, he felt the spider-web touch, the coldness along his spine, disappear. And though it was as hard to grasp as a leaf swirled in a whirlwind, he felt something else. He felt fear, but it was not his own fear. His thoughts had made something powerful become afraid.

He opened his eyes. Agwedjiman no longer blocked the trail. Instead, the big dog sat on its haunches, looking up at him, no longer tense. Young Hunter turned his gaze back up the trail, back to the highest point on the ridge. The gray standing stone was gone.

Young Hunter reached out with his mind. The Ancient One, for that was what he now knew he had seen, was gone. It would not wait for him there at the top of the trail. Yet he did not intend to go that way, even if the way was clear. He scanned the steep hillside. Perhaps he could cut across the slope and make his way by another path. And as he looked, he saw Danowa appear from among the rocks, making his way back toward Young Hunter. The dog bounded across the slope in three great leaps to reach him. As soon as Danowa's feet touched the trail in front of Young Hunter, he turned and whined, looking back the way he came. The message was clear.

Young Hunter motioned with his hand. "Lead us," he said. "We will follow you."

They moved slowly as they cut across the slope. The stones were loose here and the rains of the early spring had loosed the roots of trees. Above and below them were the remains of small landslides, some topped with bare-rooted trees that had walked down the slope from the places where they had stood high above before the earth gave way. Young Hunter looked at one of those trees, remembering how his grandmother had pointed out such a tree to him once when he was only a small child.

"You see, Grandson," Sweetgrass Woman said, casting her eyes for a moment toward Rabbit Stick as she spoke, "there is a tree that thought it wanted to travel. Even though it was no longer young, even though its roots were holding it upright quite happily in the place where it had grown for many years, it thought that it would be more interesting to stand in another place. You see how it ended up—with its roots sticking up into the air wishing it had never decided to leave its home."

Rabbit Stick had said nothing, but later that night Young Hunter had seen his grandfather unpacking a basswood bag he had concealed beneath their bed.

Suddenly, Agwedjiman yelped and turned up the slope. Young Hunter looked. There, a spear's throw away at the end of a recent slide, was a pile of stones, and half-buried in the earth and rocks was a dead pine log twice the length of a man.

The pale branch of another smaller tree stuck up just behind it. Then that branch moved up and down. And a dog lifted up its head just above the branch, which Young Hunter knew now was no branch at all. It was an arm. Rabbit Stick's arm. Both Danowa and Agwedjiman were there now, on either side of the dog, which Young Hunter recognized as Pabesis. But the young dog did not move, and Young Hunter saw that its body was holding back a small wall of earth and stone from falling onto his grandfather's face.

"Grandson," Rabbit Stick called up to him in a weak voice, "I am glad to see you. As the Wind Eagle said to the One Who Shaped Himself, I am not comfortable here."

Young Hunter made his way carefully across the loose stones. One wrong step and they would begin to slide.

"It is all right, Grandson," Rabbit Stick said. "These stones are my friends. They didn't want to hurt me. See how they have gathered all around me. Look how they are embracing me."

Rabbit Stick began to cough and blood flecked his lips.

"Grandfather," Young Hunter said, struggling to keep his voice calmer than the thoughts that flew through his head like a startled grouse, "do not talk yet."

He reached over and stroked the side of Pabesis, who whined and licked Young Hunter's fingers but did not move.

"You have done well, my friend," Young Hunter said. "You have saved our grandfather."

Rabbit Stick laughed. It was not his usual laugh, for it was much smaller and weaker since he could not draw much breath. But it was still a laugh. "It is only right that our young friend should have saved me," he said. "He is the one who brought me down here."

"Grandfather," Young Hunter said again, "do not talk yet." He gently wiped the blood from Rabbit Stick's lips. The blood was not foamy. Perhaps it was not from within the old man's chest.

"Grandson," Rabbit Stick said, "do not worry; I have only

bitten my tongue. But I would be very happy if you would take these friendly stones off the rest of me."

Young Hunter began to remove the stones, placing them aside with care so that the stones would know his respect for them.

Suddenly a loud rumble, almost like thunder, came from the slopes above. Young Hunter looked up, fearing that another landslide had started. He saw dust rise from the ledge in front of the big cave, which was not directly above them, for Rabbit Stick's slide down the slope had taken him far off to one side. Only a few small stones came bouncing down past them.

Young Hunter turned back to his task. He pulled free another stone and then another, stacking them gently to the side. The way they had fallen, it was not that hard. The pine log that had rolled down with his grandfather had acted almost like a lodge pole, spreading the weight of the stones across his grandfather's body, keeping him from being crushed. Now Rabbit Stick's chest was free, and his other arm. But he could not sit up. His long gray hair was buried in the stones and earth that walled up around his head, still held back by the patient body of the big young dog.

Agwedjiman and Danowa sat quietly on either side of Pabesis, licking the places where rocks and sticks had cut him. They did not try to help dig Rabbit Stick free. It was as if they knew that their efforts in this dangerous place would only make things worse. What was needed now was human hands to remove the stones one by one.

All three of the dogs lifted their heads to look behind Young Hunter. He turned and saw someone coming toward him on all fours across the rock slide. It was Sparrow.

"I was up there," Sparrow was shouting. "Up there. Up there."

Young Hunter held up his hand, fingers spread wide and palm out, and moved it across his body. Sparrow stopped talking. His hands were trembling and he breathed hard, but he understood. It was not the time for words. He leaned over, shoulder to shoulder with his friend, to help lift the pine log from across the old man's lower belly. It moved a hand's width, then another hand's width. Young Hunter put his shoulder beneath it and with one great heave lifted it as if it were a man he was wrestling. The log thudded down and then began to roll down the slope, disappearing over the edge of the next ledge a spear's throw below them.

"Grandsons," Rabbit Stick said, "I cannot lift my head to look down there. I am not entirely sure that I want to look down there. Only tell me one thing. Is anything missing?"

Young Hunter brushed his hands along the lower part of his grandfather's body. The deerskin leggings were torn from the jagged edges of stones and there were some small cuts. There would be many bruises, but nothing seemed broken. Then he noticed.

"Grandfather," he said, "can you not feel it? There is one part of yourself gone."

"Ahhhhahhhhh," Rabbit Stick said. "Do not tell me that my ... "

"It is so, Grandfather." Young Hunter put his hand on Rabbit Stick's foot where the mokasin must have been lost in the long slide down the slope. "The small toe on your heartside foot is gone. Perhaps it does not hurt now. The cut is clean, as if taken off by a knife. It is hardly bleeding and ... " Young Hunter paused and looked down at Rabbit Stick with curiosity. "Grandfather, why are you laughing?"

"Nothing, Grandson. I am only an old man feeling foolish. But I am still not comfortable. Is there no way you can pull my hair free? I feel like the young man who tied his hair to the log so that he could not be carried off in his sleep by the young woman who said she wanted to marry him but was really an owl."

"I remember the story, Grandfather. He was one of the Mouse People."

As he talked, Young Hunter tried to move more of the stones and earth piled on top of his grandfather's long hair, which must have fanned out behind him as he fell. He tried to reach his hand around the body of Pabesis. But the big young dog kept its body pressed back against the slide and looked up at him in a way that spoke as clearly as words. As soon as Pabesis moved, the slide would come down onto them.

Sparrow tapped Young Hunter on the arm.

"This," Sparrow said, holding out the small flint knife he had taken from the leather sheath near the pouch on his belt.

"He is right, Grandson," Rabbit Stick said, reaching up a hand. "This hillside wants another part of me. It is better that it should be my hair than my head! Hurry now! If Pabesis is not getting tired, then surely he will soon have to empty his bladder, and I do not wish to still be in this position when that happens."

Young Hunter began to saw at his grandfather's thick gray hair. It was not easy to cut it, but the flint blade was sharp and the hair gave way strand by strand. As he cut, he saw that Pabesis' legs were shuddering. They were braced firmly against the earth, the strong muscles tensed, but his claws were beginning to slip on the stones, and it was clear that the dog could not hold much longer. Sparrow saw it too. He braced himself and put one arm around the dog, the other on the largest of the stones just above them, a stone that would surely give way.

"Up there," Sparrow said, pointing with his chin, "I was just breaking my back to make a big stone move. Now I am trying to stop one from moving."

Young Hunter was on the last strands of hair. He pointed with his lips, casting his gaze around as he spoke, making certain that his grandfather and Sparrow and the three dogs all heard and understood. "We must all go that way," he said. He dropped the knife. There was no way to hold it, no time to put it back into its case. He grasped Rabbit Stick's arm and shoulder.

"Now!" he shouted, pulling his grandfather up and over his own shoulder.

From the corner of his eye, as he rose with his grandfather's weight, he saw Sparrow dig a hand into the loose skin on Pabesis' neck. The big young dog was being pushed down by the earth. It could not pull itself free. Then Sparrow yanked hard and the two of them, young man and dog, came stumbling and running behind Young Hunter as he carried his grandfather. Something struck against Young Hunter's leg and a pain as sharp as the stab of a spear point shot through him, though he managed to still stay erect and keep moving. The earth was shaking. Even the dogs, on four legs, were having a hard time keeping on their feet, barely dodging the stones that were now coming down all around.

Young Hunter continued to run and stumble himself, not quite falling, one hand held up to catch himself, the other holding his grandfather firmly over his shoulder. In the midst of it all, Young Hunter heard a sound that was strangely soothing and made him forget the pain in his leg. It took him a few breaths to realize that he was carrying that sound. Amidst the roaring of the rock slide and the cracking of the limbs and trunks of trees as they fell, he was feeling that song more than hearing it, feeling it vibrate through his body. His grandfather was singing.

Kuai hai yo wey
hai yo wey hi
kuai hai yo wey
ho yo wey

Although Rabbit Stick's voice shook from the shaking of the earth beneath them, it was a powerful song that Rabbit Stick sang, a song for good traveling.

But as Young Hunter and Sparrow and the three dogs ran and stumbled, it seemed as if the whole mountain were shifting beneath their feet and they would surely be carried to their deaths in the great slide of earth and trees and stones.

CHAPTER TWENTY-EIGHT
DOWN THE RIVER

Angry Face had come a long way down the Long River. Her little dugout was one that she had made by herself many seasons ago from the trunk of a basswood tree. It had been long work, placing the burning coals on top of it and then chipping away the charred wood. Few people made a dugout all by themselves, but she had felt that no one would care either to come close to her or help her when she worked. So she had made it half a day's walk down the river from the village of the Below the Cliffs People, then hidden it well.

Why had she made it? Perhaps because it was still in her mind somewhere that the curing woman down the river, the one called Medicine Plant, might help to make her face less ugly. This boat could carry her down to the river village of those who called themselves the Only People.

It had been easy to gather the basswood inner bark, for it was the time of year when the flow of sap made the trees loosen their blankets. With her sharp stone knife she had peeled enough to make a long, long coil of braided bark rope that she kept with her, one end of it tied firmly to the boat so that she could keep it from drifting away whenever she ventured out of the river.

Since her childhood she had heard of places in the river where there were dangerous waterfalls. It was one of the stories the parents in her village told the little ones to keep them from venturing too far down the river on a floating log or a raft. She smiled at the thought of the children playing in their river. The thought of children playing had always put the sun into her heart, even though the children of her own village had stopped playing with her after her accident, even though she knew that one with a face as ugly as hers would not find a husband and have children of her own. But her smile at the thought of the children of her village, a smile that softened her angry face and made her scar less prominent, vanished as she remembered. Only a few of the children in her village had survived. And that village, the village of the People of the Bear, was no more.

She thought again of the waterfalls. She had come to only one small waterfall before this one and she had been floating for two full suns. This one that she had been hearing for a long time, whispering, growing louder, and now growling around the next bend, was the first big one. She knew that she was now ahead of the great beast. At least a day's travel. Three days before she had come to the place where its fresh tracks had led off to the east from the river, up an old trail along a stream that led into the wider flow. She had followed it long enough to know what it would do whenever it came to such a stream. It knew enough of the humans it hunted to know that people would have their little villages along such streams. So it would range up the small valley on the trails the people had made, seeking any humans who lived there. Three times now she had followed it as it did this, and she had come upon the remains of the people and their smashed little clusters of wigwoms.

She knew that she could not follow the Walking Hill too closely. Twice now, the great beast had smelled her or heard her and come back, looking for her. But she had learned how to escape it. She must find a place where she could not be reached or seen; she must sit there without moving, not just for a few breaths, nor even for as long as it takes the Day Traveler to move an arm's length across the sky, but until the day was ended and the night fully come. And perhaps even longer. She had sat that way once for a full day and night, within the high crotch of a pine tree so large that next to it the great beast looked no larger than a horned beetle at the base of a reed. She did not look out to see if it was there, but she sensed it, felt it below her. Angry Face was not one able to touch the thoughts of others, yet she felt the presence of the great beast, the Walking Hill, as if it were the spark from a fire that had sputtered onto her skin. She could feel the heat of its anger. Even when her hearing, keener than that of any other person she had ever met, did not warn her of it, she sensed the Walking Hill. She felt a tightness at the base of her neck and knew that it was close.

She carried with her now in her fisherskin pouch the strong-smelling plants that she had gathered to cover her human scent, the same plants the hunters in her village had always used after coming out of the sweat lodge before going to hunt their brother, the bear. Each morning she bathed away her sweat and wiped her arms and legs, her face, and her chest with the plants. Then she followed its trail, trying each time to reach the people before it reached them. And each time, failing. But this last small stream that the great beast had decided to follow was different. She knew that the small circle of a dozen wigwoms once located on it was now empty. The Little People, the ones who do not show themselves, but are always watching, had grown angry with the ones who lived up that little valley. The people of that valley had grown careless in the way they hunted. They had not shown the proper respect for the bear, in particular, and the forest spirits are the special friends of the bear. So the forest spirits had made it impossible for the people to stay. They had spoiled each hunt the people tried, leading the animals away so that there was no game for the villagers.

Finally, two winters before, the people of that valley had given up. They knew they had to move. Because the people of that little valley also called themselves People of the Bear, they had come back upriver and joined with her village. Only ghosts would be at the campground where their lodges had been left behind. Now, at last, she could get ahead of the Walking Hill and reach whatever people lived downstream first. But its legs were long and she would have to travel fast. *As fast,* she thought, *as the flow of the Long River.*

Angry Face squinted her eyes against the sun as she looked down the river, pushing her boat closer to the near bank as she did so. Perhaps, below these falls, she would come to the place where that deep-seeing woman lived, the one called Medicine Plant, the one who could heal scars. She turned aside that thought and the hope that it stirred in her. She had no room for hope. It made her mind less clear. She could think of only one thing at a time now.

She put her cedar paddle in the bottom of the boat next to the spare paddle that already lay there. Then she used her long pole, a peeled ash sapling, to push her boat close to the bank. As soon as it touched, she jumped lightly out and climbed up the rocky bank, uncoiling the basswood rope tied to the dugout that drifted back toward the current without her. She found a hemlock tree, looped the rope around it several times, and then walked ahead to look at the falls. The water was still high from the melting of the snows, but the falls here next to this bank were a long series of gradual steps. The dugout should be able to ride over the rocks here without breaking. She could loop the rope around a tree by the edge of the falls and let the dugout down gradually. This would be the best place. She was glad she had not tried the other side of the river where the water foamed and leaped at the base of the falls.

Angry Face looked carefully at the water flowing toward and then sweeping over the falls, and as she watched, something came down the river along the other bank where the falls were highest. It moved faster than any raft or dugout that she had ever seen. It was like a large leaf, as pale as a seagull, and it seemed to have something riding on top of it or within it. Was it a very small person? It was hard to tell from this side of the river. But as it reached the falls, the little figure within that strange boat raised up both hands—as if in exultation. A high, echoing cry came drifting across the water to her as the white boat leaped over the edge of the falls and disappeared into the foam below.

CHAPTER TWENTY-NINE
PEOPLE OF THE BEAR

It happened within the days of the grandparents of those who now lived and were grandparents themselves. A man and a woman from the northern village that became known as the village of the Bear People walked far into their hunting territory. It was just at the time when the leaves begin to change color. They took with them their son who was only seven winters old. As they walked along the river, the woman remembered something that she had left behind.

"I will go back and get it," said her husband. The woman sat down to wait with her son, but after a while she began to wonder what had taken her husband so long.

"Go and see what your father is doing," she told her son. Although he was only seven, he already knew a great deal about hunting and fishing and often went into the woods by himself. One of his favorite pastimes was to make little spears and then stand by the river and catch fish. So his mother was not worried that he would get lost on the trail.

The boy ran back along the trail. The woman waited and waited, and at last her husband came back up the trail.

"I see our son found you," said the woman.

"I have not seen him," said the man.

Then the two became worried. They both went back along the trail. At first they found some of his tracks, leading down to the river. They could see where he had picked up stones to throw into the river. Then his tracks led up onto the rocks and his trail ended. They searched and searched, but they found no further sign of their son. All that they could find were many bear tracks.

So they went back to the village. Many people joined them in the search. The search went on all through the night, as men and women walked the trails, carrying torches of birch bark and calling the boy's name. They searched all the next day and night. Perhaps the boy had fallen into the river and been swept away by the current and drowned. Still, the people from both sides of the village continued to search. They searched all through the winter.

When the spring came again and the ice went out and it was the time when the bears leave their winter sleeping places, an old woman was walking along the river and found something in the sand. There, among the tracks of the bears who often came down to the water in that place, she found some small sharpened sticks that had been used as fish spears. So she knew that the boy who had been missing for so long was living with the bears and had come down to the river to fish for salmon with them. She went back to the village as quickly as she could and called the people together.

"Our boy who is missing," she said, "our little nephew, I know where he is. He is living with the bears."

Then the people understood. This kind of thing had happened before. Sometimes the bears would see a young boy or girl out alone in the woods and take a liking to them. The bears would sing sweet songs to attract that young person, and then they would take the child away to live the life of a bear. The boy's mother and father and the other people of the village began to search. But although they searched long and hard, they found no other trace of the boy.

Like most of the villages of the Dawn Land People, that little village had two sides that were always in friendly opposition to each other. It made certain that even in the smallest of villages, life would always be interesting. When there were races or games of any kind, the north side always went against the south. On the north side of the village, the people were said to be friendly to strangers, and so the people on the south side always made certain to be suspicious whenever new people visited. The north people always tried to be very honest when they played games, and the south people always tried to cheat in any way they could. The people on the north side of the village were said to be hardworking, and so the people on the south side tried hard to be lazy. And, of course, the two sides always gossiped about each other.

The missing boy was from the north side, but, of course, both sides of the village tried their best to find the missing boy—except for one man from the south side. He was said to be the laziest man in the village and he prided himself on that distinction. He was so lazy that he would not even bother to crawl into his own lodge when he was tired. He would just lie down and sleep right in the middle of the village. Because of that everyone called him Malkoke, Lazy One.

One day, after everyone had been searching for the lost boy who had been taken by the bears, a group of four searchers returned to find Malkoke sleeping in front of someone else's lodge. One of the four men kicked him in the leg to wake him, and the others began to insult him.

"You are the only one not helping," said the first man.

"You are the laziest of all human beings," said the second.

"You are so lazy that you would not even get up if your mokasins were burning," said the third.

Malkoke opened one eye and looked up at them with a smile. Their insults did not bother him at all. In fact, he took them as compliments. And, after all, none of them had said anything that was not true. Only two moons ago he had been found sleeping with his feet in the fire and smoke rising from his soles. When someone had told him that his mokasins were about to catch fire, he had only lifted his head to look down and then said, "That is true, indeed. Someone should move that log back away from my feet."

The fourth man looked at him. He knew how much this man prided himself on being lazy, but he also knew that Malkoke was the best hunter.

"Brothers," the fourth man said, turning to the other three, "we should leave Malkoke alone. He does not want anyone to know that he no longer knows how to hunt."

Malkoke sat up. "That is not so. No one has asked me to help yet."

"Help us find the lost one," the fourth man said.

"Since you have asked me, then I will do it," said the lazy man. He stood up and went to his wigwom to get his bow and four arrows. Then he went into the woods and went straight to the cave of the bears, where he knocked on the stones at the cave's mouth with his bow.

"Come out," he shouted.

Within the cave, the bears who had taken the boy heard the knocking on the stones and the sounds of the hunter's voice.

"You must stay here," said the old man bear to the boy. Then he ran out of the cave, holding a birch bark basket full of meat in his paws.

The hunter fired the first of his arrows, which struck the birch bark basket. As soon as the arrow hit, the old man bear dropped the basket of meat and ran on, unseen, back into the forest.

"Do not leave this cave," said the old woman bear to the boy. Then she ran out of the cave, holding a smaller birch bark basket filled with meat.

The hunter shot the second of his arrows and it struck the basket. The old woman bear dropped the basket and ran on, unseen, back into the woods.

Now only the boy and the young bear cub were left in the cave.

"Remember what my parents told you and you will not be harmed," said the young bear. Then it, too, ran from the cave carrying a birch bark basket filled with meat.

The hunter shot the third arrow and it pierced the birch bark basket. Just as his parents had done, the bear cub dropped the basket and vanished into the forest.

The hunter walked over and looked at the three bears that lay dead in front of the cave. His arrows had struck each of them in the heart.

"Thank you for giving your meat to my people," the hunter said. Then he went inside the cave and found the boy crouched in a corner. He was dirty and crying because his relatives had been killed.

When Malkoke took the lost boy back to the village, everyone praised the lazy man. Everyone gave him presents and food, and he was happy.

But the boy who had been taken by the bears was not happy. It took a long time for him to grow accustomed to human beings again. He ate and acted like a bear. His hair was very black and thick, and there were bristles growing on his back and shoulders. However, he finally grew used to people, and when he grew up became a very important person in the village. He married, and his children called themselves Bear People. They moved far to the north of the Thirteen Villages and marked their hunting grounds with the sign of the bear paw or with pieces of birch bark cut into the outline of a bear. After a few generations, it became known as the Bear People village. And as long as they treated the bears with respect and thanked them for giving their flesh to the people when they were hunted, things went well in that village. Bad luck only came when the people stopped treating the bears with the proper respect.

That was the story which told itself in the walking thoughts of Angry Face as she coiled up the basswood rope at the base of the falls. She had found herself thinking of that story because of the bad luck that had come to her village. How the last bit of bad luck had been the coming of the Walking Hill, itself like a great stiff-legged bear. The eyes of her mind blurred with the anger and pain of that coming, and she could not see the lessons within the story that told itself to her.

The story had come to her after she saw the strange boat go over the falls, after the one in that boat waved to her and then disappeared into the foam. Although she had looked hard, she had seen no further sign of that little boat or its small passenger below the falls. Perhaps it was one of the Little People. They were, like the forest spirits, friends of the bears. That was why that story came to her, she decided. Seeing the Mikumwesu was meant as a message for her. Perhaps it meant that she would succeed in the two things that she now lived to accomplish.

Those things were as clear in her mind as was the scar on her face in her reflection in the clear pool below the falls. First she must warn any human beings she could find before the Walking Hill reached their villages. The first village, another village of the Bear People, was just over the next range of hills, only a look away. She knew she would reach it before the Walking Hill and that she would be able to convince the people to flee downriver.

The thought of reaching that village before the great beast made a grim smile come to her twisted face, for she knew how angry it would be when it did not find any human lives to crush beneath its feet. But there was no happiness in her smile. The spirit within her had spoken to her clearly and told her that she would find happiness in only one way, a way she had not yet discovered. That way was the second thing she must do—find some method to destroy the monster that had killed her own village.

But first she had to warn the people in the village downriver, warn them in a way that would make them act and not question her warning. How could she do this?

As Angry Face thought, she finished putting the long coils of rope into her boat. She knelt by the river to wash her hands, and as she did so she felt the slipperiness of the bank. Digging her fingers in, she lifted up the pale clay and held it in the palm of her hand. With three fingers, she scooped some of it up and wiped it across her thigh, seeing how it clung, drying onto her skin and growing even paler as it dried.

Sweetgrass Woman handed the cup to Medicine Plant. The deep-seeing woman looked at her with a stare that seemed hard enough to break stone, but Sweetgrass Woman simply smiled and continued to hold out the cup.

"If you were any other woman who had just borne her first child," she said, "you would not hesitate to drink this."

"This may be so," Medicine Plant said, "but few other women know as well as I know just how bitter this drink tastes."

She took the cup and moved it back and forth between her hands so that the well-boiled yellow ash leaves swam back and forth in the warm liquid like boneless fish. But as Sweetgrass Woman knew, it was the right thing to drink to cleanse herself now that the child had been born. Shaking her head once, she lifted up the cup and drank.

Willow Woman watched as she sat holding the new child. The baby was sleeping now, but even asleep it seemed to her as if it were more aware than any newborn baby she had ever seen. Perhaps it was only because she expected the baby to be powerful—as the child of two deep-seeing people. She and Young Hunter had talked often of such things, of the way deep-seeing people such as Medicine Plant and Bear Talker made themselves more impressive in the eyes of other people. Not just to fool them, but to give people more trust in their powers to heal and help.

She remembered well the first time Young Hunter had come into their lodge eager to show her a new trick that Bear Talker had given him.

"Watch," he said, "I now know how to turn into a monster bear. But it is dangerous," he added, "for as a bear I may forget that I was once a human and I may eat you alive."

He had his back to her as he spoke those words. Then he spun around, his arms wide, his mouth open, and two huge fangs protruding from his jaw. Willow Woman had screamed and then hit him hard with one of her digging sticks—so hard that it knocked the two bear teeth fastened together with a piece of rawhide right out of his mouth.

"Ah," Young Hunter said in a rueful voice as he picked himself up from the ground, "did I not warn you that this was dangerous? Still, though I have lost my terrible teeth, I still have the power to catch any unsuspecting victim and tickle them." He grabbed at Willow Woman who stepped aside and tripped him, a wrestling move that Young Hunter had taught her only a few days before.

He stood up again. "I can see," he said, "why it is not a good idea for a man to share everything he knows with his … "

But Young Hunter did not finish his words, for Willow Woman threw him to the ground a second time. This time, though, she did not let go of him when he fell, and the laughter they shared required only a few heartbeats to soften into whispering.

Willow Woman looked down at the baby's sweet face and smiled. Then she watched as Sweetgrass Woman lifted the bundle of dry grasses that held the umbilical cord wrapped in bark and carried it outside. There she would burn it. Sweetgrass Woman had explained that doing this would make certain that the child would not be one always snooping around and prying into other people's lives. Willow Woman had bitten her tongue then to avoid wondering out loud if the midwife had failed to do that chore on the day Sweetgrass Woman was born.

Willow Woman looked back at Medicine Plant. Lying there on her bed, the deep-seeing woman looked tired, but satisfied. The two of them were alone now in the lodge. Bear Talker had left long ago to go and follow the trail of Young Hunter, to see what had happened to Rabbit Stick. There was a small feeling of worry somewhere inside Willow Woman, like a very small fist beginning to close tighter and tighter.

"Daughter," Medicine Plant said, "I am feeling weak, but I can see something now. I see that your husband and your grandfather are well. Let go of your fear, Daughter."

Willow Woman let out the breath she did not know she had been holding.

"*Wliwini,*" she said. "Thank you, Mother. Can we talk now of what we will do with our little one in the days to come?"

"Uh-hunh, Daughter, we can talk a little. Then I will sleep. But come to this side of the fire. I want to talk softly so that only our ears will share the words."

Medicine Plant lifted herself up on her elbow and began to reach into the small basket behind her. She stopped, looking up to be certain that Sweetgrass Woman was well outside, and then pulled out two birch bark cones.

"We can also share this maple sugar that you brought to me, Daughter. It will take the taste of that awful drink from my mouth and sweeten these words that I have for you."

Mikumwesu's heart beat very fast as he sat in his birch bark boat, holding fast with his hands to the overhanging alder branches by the edge of the Long River. He was certain that he could not be found in this place of concealment. The swirl of the river had cut into the bank here, where clay glistened on the river's bed and in the earth just above the surface. In all of the many winters he and his parents had lived close to the human beings, he had never allowed himself to be seen by one of the big people before. Even before he had come to the falls he had sensed that woman there. He could have stopped before the falls, but a recklessness came over him as he realized that he wanted to be seen.

185

So he had raised his arms to wave and had shouted as his boat crested the edge and flew over. He had no worry about tipping over or being caught in the turbulence below. His little boat was light and strong, and his own weight was no more than that of a small human child of a few winters. The waters of the river and the falls along it held little danger for a little one. And even if he had somehow fallen from his boat, he could swim almost as well as an otter. In fact, the otter and the beaver peoples had been among his best friends when he was very young. Sometimes, even though they were old and their limbs so stiff that they could no longer spend a whole day within the embrace of the river like their son, his parents had come and played with them.

He smiled within himself thinking of otter games. Mikumwesu thought of how the otters would play the stone game—dropping a flat rock to the bottom, then diving down to bring it up balanced on their heads. He was almost as good as an otter at diving deep, and he loved few things as much as using their slides with them—flopping onto his belly, headfirst, and shooting down the slick mud and grass into the water.

Beavers were quieter than otters, yet he loved them almost as well. Their games were slower ones, but they would sit next to him and comb his long hair with their gentle paws. He was always a welcome guest in their lodges, curling up in the comforting dark while their little ones would snuggle against him or wrestle with each other on the lodge floor. To let them know how much he appreciated being their guest, he would be sure to chew at least some of the tender bark off the sticks they offered him.

With such good friends among the animals, it was interesting, Mikumwesu thought, how he always found himself watching those big ones, those tall people, yet he never tried to speak with them or play with them. He and his parents used to leave little presents for them, though, by the edge of the river where there was clay. They would make little shapes in the clay and place them where they would be found. When the tall people took those gifts, they would always leave something in return—some of the smoking herb, a little food, something made from stone or a small bark basket. All of those were things that Mikumwesu and his parents could as easily have gathered or made—and made better, yet there was something endearing about the clumsiness of the tall people. They were so much like children who somehow grew unfortunately large and thought they were adults but were really just small ones in the disguise of a big body. And though Mikumwesu and his parents never showed themselves, the tall people always knew they were there. That was why they left little bark plates of food on the trail. At this time of the year, when the sweet smell of cooking maple sap filled the forest, they had also left little cones of bark wrapped around offerings of maple sugar. Those had been Mikumwesu's favorite gifts, and he had taken special delight in picking those up and bringing them back to his parents, knowing how they loved that special taste. The tall people even spoke aloud to the forest at times, as if they sensed Mikumwesu and his parents listening. But more often than not, they would look in the wrong direction or would speak to a passing fox, thinking it was one of the Mikumwesu in the shape of an animal. Mikumwesu smiled. It had always been amusing to watch those clumsy tall people. It was enjoyable to think about them.

So on a special ledge in their cave, Mikumwesu's parents kept the baskets and arrowheads and pipes made of clay that the tall people left them as gifts. Mikumwesu had left all of those things there. They would stay there forever, keeping the spirits of his parents company.

From his hiding place under the overhanging branches, Mikumwesu's keen eyes watched as the big woman with the angry face continued down the bank on the other side. She was no longer looking, with either her eyes or her heart. Mikumwesu felt all of the sadness inside her. It was like the feeling he sensed one morning after a heavy rain, when he had gone out and found that the hollow tree where a family of raccoons lived had been split by lightning, killing all but one small cub. That sadness felt by the cub whose family had died was much like the sadness he felt coming to him like waves of cool rain across the Long River. It made him want to come out from under the alders and call to her, do something to delight her or make her laugh. Yet he did not move. He knew he could not adopt her and care for her as he had that raccoon cub. Within her sadness there was also an anger-pain, and that anger-pain he recognized too. It was like the anger-pain he sensed from the great beast, the Walking Hill, which was at war with all living things now. And, once again, Mikumwesu wondered why he had decided to make this journey down the river and what it was that he intended to do.

CHAPTER THIRTY
THE CLOSED CAVE

"Old bodies do not have as much blood as young ones," Rabbit Stick said as he tapped his foot with a finger. "You see, I have given all that I am going to give for the earth of this hillside to drink."

He lifted up his foot and shook it to make sure that the bandage that Young Hunter had bound on it would hold firm.

Young Hunter held out his hand and Rabbit Stick grasped it, even though he did not really need his grandson's support to stand. Sparrow handed the old man a walking stick he had shaped from one of the young trees dislodged and broken in the rock slide. Rabbit Stick took the cane. He did not really need it, but it would make the young man feel useful if he accepted it. Then he sighed, feeling a deeper weakness than he had been willing to admit. He sat down on the slope, shaking his head. It had been close, but they had managed to escape without further injury—all six of them, men and dogs alike.

Pabesis, freed of the responsibility of acting like a grown-up, was now frolicking around and making a general nuisance of himself. He had picked up the arm-long, broken-off end of the stick that Sparrow had shaped and was running wildly with it, trying to get the others to chase him.

Danowa had already knocked the young dog down once and stood over him growling until Pabesis had bared his throat in acknowledgment of the older dog's superior place in their family. But as soon as Danowa had stepped away from him, he had crawled back on his belly, grabbed the stick, and begun to tear back and forth again.

Young Hunter held his chin with his right hand and watched. Ktsi Nwaskw truly must have loved the dog people. Few humans were able to clear their thoughts so quickly or completely of danger or difficulty overcome. Only a few heartbeats ago Pabesis had been holding back a deadly rock slide, and now he was acting like a small avalanche himself. It was a good gift that the dog people had been given. Then again, the dog people were a gift in themselves to the humans. A dog like Pabesis, with his crazy antics, could help humans forget their troubles. Even as Young Hunter thought that, Pabesis decided to run in between two young trees. But the stick that he carried in his mouth was wider than the distance between them. With a resounding *thwack*, the stick struck the trunks of both trees and Pabesis went rolling head over tail.

Rabbit Stick leaned his head back and laughed, and the two young men joined in his laughter. Even Agwedjiman and Danowa, sitting smugly and sedately on their heels, opened their mouths wider and seemed to smile.

"My friend," Sparrow said, drawing Young Hunter off to the side, "will our grandfather be all right if we leave him here for a bit?"

Rabbit Stick answered the question before Young Hunter could speak.

"Sparrow," he said, "I have lost a toe, but not my ears. Go ahead and fly wherever you want. I have seen your eyes looking back up to the top there. See whatever you have to see up there. I will wait here with my three four-legged friends."

Rabbit Stick lifted up a hand to pet Pabesis and then pushed the young dog back as it tried to climb into his lap in its eagerness to be petted.

"Hmm. Perhaps I will not be safe," Rabbit Stick said.

"After all, this young dog here has almost killed me more than once. But he has also saved my life one time today. So I think I will trust him. Go."

Sparrow led the way and Young Hunter followed. Now that he was no longer walking in a dream, as he had been to reach this place, he was slower than Sparrow again. Fast traveling was no longer with him. Sparrow, though, leaped from one rock up to the next almost as if he had invisible wings, and it was all Young Hunter could do to keep up. It was not easy going. Another rock slide, the one Young Hunter had heard before Sparrow appeared, had slanted across the trail higher up, and the trail had been wiped away as cleanly as if a giant hand had swept across the mountain.

When Young Hunter reached the ledge—or what was left of the ledge, for half of it had been broken away and gone down the steep slope—Sparrow was waiting for him. His eyes were focused on the place in the hillside where there had once been the mouth of a cave. The great stone that had fallen from above was now wedged into that mouth and many other stones had piled up around it.

Both young men stood for a long time, looking without speaking.

"I made it fall," Sparrow said at last. "I saw, there in front of the cave, one of the gray giants that you told me about. It was as still as a stone, but it was an Ancient One."

"I believe you," Young Hunter said. "It seemed that I saw it looking down on me before the rock fell."

Young Hunter walked over to the great rock which was at the heart of the boulder slide that had obliterated all sign of the cave. He placed the palms of both hands against the face of the stone and leaned his cheek against it. He closed his eyes, trying to listen not just with his ears, but with the inner hearing of his heart. He heard nothing. Yet somehow, he knew that it was not yet ended.

"It grabbed at your grandfather just as he fell," Sparrow said.

He was standing close to the edge now, looking down at the long scar stretching all the way into the valley below them. The Long River was clearly visible now that the trees had been cleared away by the river of earth and stone that had flowed down with such power.

"But it missed him," Sparrow continued. "Pabesis knocked him aside first and they went over the edge. Then I started the rock rolling. It leaped back into the cave before the rock hit. It must be buried in there." Sparrow jerked his chin back to point at the pile of stones.

Young Hunter removed his hands from the great stone and walked over to stand beside Sparrow. He looked out, looking up the Long River to the north. For a moment, it seemed as if he saw something there, just at the point where the line of the river disappeared. It was a giant shape like that huge, angry being he had seen in his dreams, in his vision of Big Raccoon's death. The shape hovered over the river and seemed to be moving in their direction. Then, like morning mist vanishing in the heat of the sun, it was gone. Young Hunter looked down and his eyes were caught.

"Perhaps," Young Hunter said, "it did not completely miss him."

He stepped closer to the crumbling edge of the cliff and carefully bent over to reach down and pick up the thing that had caught his gaze: his grandfather's mokasin. It was torn almost in half from the swift blow of the long, sharp fingernail of the Ancient One. Within the torn mooseskin mokasin, curled in the tip like a brown stubby root, was Rabbit Stick's missing toe.

CHAPTER THIRTY-ONE
BY THE RIVER

Sunrise had come and gone more than once. But within the cave there was no sunrise and no sunset. The Ancient One still sat in that darkness, its left hand holding his right arm tight across its body. The huge stone that closed the cave mouth had struck that right arm as the gray giant leaped back into the cave to avoid being crushed. It knew that the arm was hurt badly, but knew also that by holding it in place this way, it would heal.

The Ancient One did not worry about food. Hung back within the cave were what remained of the bodies of a deer and a young caribou. And there was water seeping down the cave walls. It did not have to see to find that water. It was used to the darkness and where it sat, the Ancient One had only to lean over against the cold, moist wall to drink from that slow trickle of water, bitter as the roots of the spruce trees that laced the mountainside.

Sweetgrass Woman did not look up toward the smoke hole in their wigwom. As she busied herself in the lodge, she did not look up. She moved things around, stirred the food in the pot, picked up the basket she had been weaving, and then put it down again. She leaned over and began to work on the floor, a thick, sweet-smelling covering of hemlock boughs laid down and woven together to make a comfortable, springy surface under their feet. She pulled a bough free, looked at it, then wove it back in. But she did not look up.

"Old Woman," Rabbit Stick said, limping over to squat beside her, "are you going to do this all day?"

She did not answer. Instead, she stood and ducked out through the door of the wigwom.

Rabbit Stick sighed. He reached up high and unwrapped the sinew string from around the stick laid across the smoke hole above the fire. As he stepped outside, Sweetgrass Woman went back into the lodge. It was clear that she was serious. To have gone this long without talking was not easy for her.

Rabbit Stick sighed again. Young Hunter, who had been sitting with his back against the cedar tree closest to their lodge, stood up and came over.

Rabbit Stick held up the sinew string.

"Your grandmother will not say anything," he said, "but I know what she wants. She wants me to remove this from our lodge."

Rabbit Stick reached out one finger and very gently set swinging the brown stubby object tied to the end of the string.

"You see," he said, "it is already curing. It will tan in the smoke like good buckskin."

He held it to his nose.

"It does not smell bad at all."

Rabbit Stick held out his severed toe to Young Hunter, who looked at it with uncertainty.

"What do you want me to do with this, Grandfather?"

"The fish racks," Rabbit Stick said. "Take it down by the river and finish the smoking of it there."

Rabbit Stick looked around to be sure Young Hunter's grandmother could not hear him. As he did so, Sweetgrass Woman came out of the lodge door and walked past the two of them, still without saying a word. She walked straight ahead, not looking back, her feet on the path that led out of the village. It was clear that she was either going to visit Medicine Plant and her new baby or heading in the direction of the maple trees where Willow Woman was making maple syrup. Rabbit Stick watched until she disappeared from sight. Then he turned again to his grandson.

"My dreams have told me that I must do this," he said. "This limp will not disappear until I again have all of my ten toes with me. Once it is completely smoke-tanned, then my toe can go into my pouch here, or maybe I can wear it around my neck on a thong—a long thong so it will hang under my shirt where your grandmother cannot see it. But do not dangle it from your hand as you walk. Pabesis may be around and grab it. Since your grandmother tried to give it to him four days ago he has been looking at it as if he knows he is supposed to have it!"

Young Hunter fought to keep the smile from coming to his face. His grandfather was serious about this and he must be serious also. He reached out and took the string from his grandfather's hand, wrapped it around the toe, which felt surprisingly dry and cool to the touch, and turned toward the path down to the Long River.

It was the time of first light when the people had heard the cry from the center of their village. It was a high, piercing scream, the ululating voice of a woman, and it had woken everyone in the village in a way that made them all wonder if they were not waking into the middle of a frightening dream. As people listened from their beds or stumbled from their wigwoms, they realized that the scream was also a song, a medicine song they had not heard before. It was filled with the kind of power that could only come from pain and vision.

The sight that had greeted them as they all drew close to the central fire of the small village circle had been even more disturbing. A tall, strong woman stood there, her body and her

195

face lit by the light of a fire that had been built up to burn hot and high. She had painted herself with clay and charcoal so that half of her face and body was white and the other half was black, and that painting of herself was a warning of great danger. Her face was terrible to see, distorted beneath the paint in a way it seemed no human face could be. And her song, a lamentation for the death of all the humans up the river to the north of them, was as cold as a wind in the time of long nights.

As she sang and moved back and forth in front of the fire, she kept throwing into it pieces of birch bark cut into the shape of a bear. The people recognized those pieces of birch bark. They were the markers made to show other humans that they had reached the edges of their hunting grounds. Somehow, this frightening woman had gathered all of them and was burning them now in front of the village.

The wisest woman in the village, a white-haired grand-mother known as White Goose, who knew something of medicine and healing, stepped close to the frightening woman, holding up a hand. White Goose was the sagamon for this small village of a few families, which had split away from the bigger Bear People village to the north less than a generation ago, trying to get away from the bad luck that always seemed to haunt them.

The frightening woman stopped singing that terrible song and looked at the older woman. She did so with her eyes wide and unblinking, and it was unnerving to see. Most of the people close behind White Goose turned their eyes away. But White Goose leaned closer. She thought she recognized this person as a member of the farthest north of their villages, a young girl White Goose had seen ten winters before when she traveled to visit relatives there. Surely there could not be another with a face scarred that way.

The sound of the wood cracking in the fire and the *whisss* of sparks rising up was all that could be heard as the two women stood there while the other people of the small village held their breaths to listen.

"Granddaughter," White Goose said, "why are you frightening us this way?"

Angry Face glared at her without blinking and then lifted her head and screamed again, a scream that was louder than that of the long-tailed cat and more terrible because it came from a human throat.

White Goose felt her own knees grow weak, but she forced herself to continue to stand straight.

"Listen," Angry Face growled, "listen to me now, foolish ones. One of the old monsters is coming to kill you all. It is a hill that walks, it has death in every footstep, it will tear the trees from their roots with more force than the whirlwind. It has destroyed my village and all the other villages to the north. Most of the people I knew are dead. Look into my eyes. You will see their deaths remembered there. By this time tomorrow, only ashes will remain of this village. If you do not wish to have your bones mixed with those ashes, you will flee. Flee down the Long River now!"

As Young Hunter carried his grandfather's toe toward the Long River, he thought of all that he had to be thankful for. His grandfather was alive, having escaped great danger, and Medicine Plant's child had come into the world healthy and strong. Perhaps the threat of that one last Ancient One was gone from the land, and perhaps his vision of something terrible coming toward the people had only been his imagination. It was hard to believe that anything bad could happen on a day like this. Even the small biting ones, the *peguesak*, had lessened, and he no longer had to wave his hands in front of his face to keep from breathing them in.

So as Young Hunter walked toward the river, he spoke first in his mind and then aloud the words of thanks for the gifts given this season by the flowing waters. It was commonly done this way when one went down to the river in the time of fish spearing, to give thanks as you approached the river, letting the river know that you were coming and that you appreciated what it was about to give to you.

Old one, long one
wliwini
Kwanitewk,
wliwini
for the fish
wliwini
for the small and big fish
wliwini
for feeding the birds and animals
wliwini
for feeding the Only People
wliwini

As Young Hunter neared the river he heard the sounds common to this season, this Moon of the Fish Running. He heard not only the loud whispering roar of the river over the stones and the high, piercing calls of the many fishing birds above the river—the ospreys and the eagles—but also the voices of the dogs and the people. The dogs always came to the river at this season, and it was hard to find even a single dog that would remain in the village when the people were spearing fish. The dogs were whining and yelping at each other and sometimes growling as they fought over the scraps thrown to them by the people as they fished and then cleaned their catches for the smoking racks.

Although not as raucous as their dogs, the people were far from silent. Young Hunter could hear them chanting their fishing songs and calling and joking to each other from the places where they stood on the banks with their long fishing spears, from one end of the rapids to the next. Both men and women were spearing fish, for the run was a bigger one than had been seen in many years; everyone was eager to get enough to have plenty for their own families and to get even more to give away or trade with people from villages that did not come to the river.

The fish that were running up the river now were the smaller ones. Not the big salmon, some of which were as big as a small child. They were the shad, the fish with the shining bodies, that came now in waves, pushing upstream, whipping through the currents. Some of the children, playing near the river or trying to catch fish themselves with spears smaller than those of their elders, waved to Young Hunter and he waved back.

If it were still the time between frosts, the time when the nights were long, those children would have come to him and asked him for a story. Even though he was a young man, Young Hunter was well known as one of the better storytellers among the people, and when the fires burned and the snow was deep, there were always at least a few children sitting in the bigger lodge with Young Hunter and Willow Woman and his grandparents. Young Hunter usually tried to get Rabbit Stick or Sweetgrass Woman to tell the stories, for he still loved to hear them told by the grandparents who first gave the stories to him. Though his grandparents might tell one or two tales, Young Hunter himself always seemed to end up being the one who sighed, leaned forward, and spread his hands wide to begin to weave a long series of stories from the old times or—and the children especially loved this—to tell of his own travels, how he walked into a story himself.

The children knew well, of course, that this was not the season for stories. It was said that telling the old stories after the leaves had broken out of their buds would bring bad luck. Those leaves themselves might listen and forget to grow properly. The snow might hear the stories being told and return, thinking that it was not yet spring. And even if that did not happen, because stories were so powerful, certain other living beings around them would want to hear the tales. So wasps and hornets would come into the lodge and, wanting to get as close as possible, land on the lips of the storyteller. Snakes, too, liked to hear stories and they would crawl into the lodge to listen. It was not that the stories went away. They remained there in the thoughts of the people, and Young Hunter still followed the paths of those stories in his mind whenever he came to a problem and did not know which way to turn. It was only the speaking of the stories that was unwise now that the land had again turned green and the young man, Spring, had driven away Old Winter once more.

Young Hunter stood on the hill above the river and looked down along the rapids. There, at the fishing spot they shared between them, were his brother-cousins. Red Hawk and Blue Hawk were both spearing fish from two elbows of stone that reached out into the rapids. Their drying racks were set up on the bank not far from the stream and smoke rose from the fires that Sparrow was feeding. That smoke bathed the many split-open bodies of fish spread on top of the racks. As soon as the fish were darkened and so dry that moisture no longer dripped from them, they would be ready and would keep for several seasons without spoiling.

Young Hunter folded his arms and watched. He loved the rhythm of people's movements as they worked at this work that was also play. Red Hawk and Blue Hawk each held a long spear, a straight, peeled, spruce pole twice as long as they were tall. At the end of the pole, a fire-hardened spike of wood was seated firmly into the split end of the spruce pole and bound in place with sinew. To either side of that spike were the grippers, two pieces of wood rounded on the inside and tied on so that, like a thumb and finger, they would slip around the body of any fish the spear struck and hold it firmly after it was pierced.

Both the young men were singing a fishing song, and first Red Hawk would throw and then Blue Hawk would throw, as the fish, liking the sound of their singing, swam beneath them. They threw their spears down in such a way that, if they missed, the spear would go deep and then come straight back up out of the water, leaping back into their hands for another cast. This was why their spears were given names. Anything given a name would recognize that name when it was spoken and—if it had been treated well by the one who named it—come when it was called. It was clear that Red Hawk and Blue Hawk treated their spears with love and respect.

Young Hunter looked over at the drying racks. Sparrow was arranging some of the fish that had just been thrown over to him by Red Hawk and Blue Hawk, and which he had gutted and spread wide with a few quick strokes of his sharp knife. The intestines of the fish were grilling on the coals at the edge of the smoking fires. Young Hunter could smell them cooking, and he remembered that, even though the Day Traveler was in the middle of the sky, he had not yet eaten. Unlike wintertime, when people seemed always to be thinking of food, these long days kept one so busy that eating was often the last thing one remembered—until a good smell like this touched one's nose.

Young Hunter looked down the slope between him and the fire. The angle was about right and he decided it might be a suitable time for him to try his trick. He had begun trying to learn it after he had seen something the previous winter. He had been hidden in the thick boughs of a cedar tree at the end of a small hill, watching two game trails that came together below him. He was not hunting, but just watching to see what he could see. His uncle, Fire Keeper, had taught him long ago to do this.

"A good hunter," Fire Keeper always said, "watches before he hunts. One can never spend enough time in the forest simply watching."

That day, as Young Hunter watched, a lynx had come down one trail, not knowing a wolverine was coming in the same direction on the other trail. Suddenly coming upon the wolverine, the lynx had leaped so high and so far backward that it flipped in midair, landing on its feet.

Young Hunter stood, turned his back, and held his hands in front of him. If he jumped and threw his arms back hard, the way the lynx had done, then he would surely land on his feet. He held his hands out, thinking of how he would arch his back as he jumped. But he did not jump.

Instead, the story came into his mind of Rabbit. Rabbit had been invited to dinner by Otter. When Rabbit arrived at Otter's house at the edge of the Long River, Otter had not yet made dinner.

"My friend," Otter said, "I will go get our dinner now." Then Otter threw himself down on his belly, slid into the water, and disappeared beneath the surface. When he came up, he had two big fish in his mouth.

After they ate, Rabbit thanked Otter.

"My friend," Rabbit said, "come to eat at my house tomorrow."

When Otter arrived, Rabbit had not yet begun to make dinner. But he had made a sort of a mud slide leading down into the water of the pond near his home.

"Wait here," Rabbit said, "I will go and get our dinner now." Then Rabbit threw himself down on his belly. But his long legs and his fur caught in the mud and leaves, and he was not able to slide. He pushed and pushed, but all he was able to do was roll down to the water. In he went with a splash and sank beneath the surface. When he came up, his mouth was full of water and he was coughing.

"Help me," Rabbit gasped before he sank again.

Otter dove in and pulled Rabbit out. He jumped up and down on Rabbit's belly to push the water out of him. Then Otter dove into the pond and came out with two big fish.

"You can eat these," Otter said. "I am going home. I am tired of your foolishness."

Young Hunter turned around and lowered his hands. *I am not Lynx*, he thought and, tapping his nose and upper lip with one finger, *I am also not Rabbit*. He walked down the steep path to the fish-smoking racks.

Sparrow looked up at him as he approached. "The fishing is good," Sparrow said. "We've had to make even more racks."

The smells of the wood smoke and the fish blended together in a wonderful way that made Young Hunter appreciate the hopeful look on the face of a dog that lay waiting a few paces away from the racks. A sleek brown female called Squirrel, she lifted her head as Young Hunter passed, and he ran his hand along her neck. Squirrel was only slightly older than Pabesis and she belonged to Red Hawk and Blue Hawk, but she was also very interested in Agwedjiman. Thus far, the leader of the dogs had ignored her whenever she came his way, curling his lip slightly when she became too familiar. But Squirrel was persistent. Young Hunter wondered if Agwedjiman, who had not chosen any of the other female dogs in the villages as his mate, had not finally met his match.

Young Hunter looked over the racks. The middle one there would be good. He unwound the rawhide string and leaned over to tie it firmly in the very center of the rack. Then he stepped back to look. It was good. Rabbit Stick's small toe hung right under the middle pole of the rack where the smoke was thickest. Now he would just have to be sure to be here when the racks were unloaded. He stepped back and looked over at Sparrow. Sparrow seemed not to have noticed what he was doing. Good.

"Shall we take a turn with our spears now?" Young Hunter asked.

Sparrow motioned with his chin toward the two fish spears which had been leaned carefully against the cliff that came down close to the water, above the rapids where the fish ran the thickest.

"Our spears are there, but … "

The wind changed and thick smoke from the fire swirled up into his face. Sparrow closed his eyes and turned quickly away from the fire, coughing.

"Red Hawk and Blue Hawk have been out there," he continued when his throat had cleared, "since the Day Traveler was only two hands high and now it is almost midday. I have motioned to them to come in, but they have been too busy to look my way except when I am not looking at them! I would have to leave the smoking racks, and I am not sure that Squirrel here will be as well mannered as Agwedjiman when I leave her alone for a while."

Young Hunter nodded. Few dogs were able to resist the temptation to steal from the smoking racks when no human was around to prevent them from doing so. Agwedjiman and Danowa could be trusted to guard the racks from an animal, including other dogs, that might be attracted by the good smell of smoked fish. Young Hunter had not brought them with him. Their place was to stay close to his grandparents and to Willow Woman. The Ancient One may have been buried in the cave, yet Young Hunter's inner voice had continued to speak to him, warning him of dangerous things coming for them all.

Squirrel, who had been given her name for her ability to reach high places when something good to eat was hung there—such as the top of a smoking rack or the very peak of a wigwom—was not to be trusted alone with these fish.

"I will walk out and tell them it is their turn to eat smoke," Young Hunter said.

The way out to the fishing spot on the two elbows of rock that thrust into the Long River was over stepping-stones, and the water flowing around them sparkled with light and sang a long flowing melody that seemed to match the fishing song

Red Hawk and Blue Hawk were singing together as they thrust, bent, lifted, and then thrust again with their spears, catching fish after fish that they tossed into the woven baskets on their backs.

Young Hunter jumped lightly from one stone to the next. Soon he was close to the first of the brothers. Red Hawk was just lifting his spear to thrust again at a shad coming up the ripple toward him when he stopped and looked, not downstream, but upstream. Young Hunter followed his gaze and saw what his friend's stunned eyes saw. He saw it as it came floating down on the swift current, half submerged. He saw it as it caught on the rocks of the shallow bottom and then rolled, turning a face as pale as the Night Traveler's up to the sky. The eye sockets in that long-dead human face were empty.

CHAPTER THIRTY-TWO
FLAMES

Walking Hill stood on top of the height of land above the channel of the river. He had followed the long, narrow valley for two days, but he had found none of the hated upright ones. All that he had found had been the empty piles of brush where their scents were stale. He had trampled them, scattering them in pieces through the clearing where sumac trees were already beginning to grow up between the wigwoms. But he had found no fires; he had found nothing to kill. The only flame that remained was in his memory, but it was burning hot. And it deepened his anger.

Now as he stood on the hilltop, he saw the land widening below him. It stretched out a long way before it came to more water, a lake wider than the Long River which he had left behind. He could go down that hill in the direction of the wide water. There would be more of the upright ones here in this new valley. But he did not go down the hill. He remembered that behind him there were some who had escaped. He remembered that his pain had come from behind him, not from the direction in which the sun was setting. He might come back this way again when he had wiped out all of those behind him, but not now. He felt the Long River calling him, and he turned and began to walk again toward the direction of the rising sun.

Red Hawk knelt and snagged the torn sleeve of the dead man's deerskin shirt with a forked pole. The waterlogged leather slipped free. He caught the sleeve once more with the pole and pulled again. Both the sleeve and the right arm of the dead man tore away from the mangled, bloodless body, which rolled and then went farther down with the current. Red Hawk held the stranger's arm for a moment at the end of the pole. As Red Hawk dropped it on the stones by his feet, knelt down, and began to vomit, Young Hunter found himself thinking how glad he was that he had not yet eaten that day.

Blue Hawk was standing at the edge of the rapid looking down at the body, now lodged on the second elbow of rock. He would not touch it with his hands or with his fishing spear. If he touched it with his spear, then that spear would have to be broken and burned, for it would carry in it the touch of the death of a human being.

Young Hunter pulled a long, thick piece of driftwood from the place where it was wedged between two stones. The broken branch on the end of it was like a hook.

"We are sorry to treat you badly," Young Hunter said as he maneuvered the hooked end of the branch so that it caught around the waist of the dead person. Blue Hawk grasped the branch with him, and together they managed to work the body free; then, walking down along the edge of the river, they took it to a sandbar below the rapids. By the time they got there, many people were waiting for them. The fishing and the fish racks had all been forgotten.

Red Hawk pushed through the crowd, holding a second piece of driftwood. He gently placed it under the one intact shoulder of the drowned person, and the three young men pulled the body up the rest of the way onto shore. Then Red Hawk went back and, using two smaller sticks to pick it up, carried down the arm that had loosened from the drowned body and placed it on the sand so that it almost seemed to again be attached.

Flies were already beginning to come around in great numbers. The smell of the dead person was very strong and only the great hole torn in his chest and belly kept the body from bloating. It was said that the breath a person kept within himself when he or she drowned would always seek to rejoin the air and thus carry the dead one up to the surface with it.

Young Hunter covered his nose and mouth with one hand and leaned to look as closely as he could. It was as if a spear twenty times larger than any spear he had ever seen before had pierced the man. Perhaps the body had been thrown against a jagged log at the river's edge. But if that was so, would not the body have stayed stuck to that log? The man wore a leather thong around his neck and on it bear teeth were strung. If this was a man from one of the villages of the Bear People, then he had floated a long time downstream. The villages of the People of the Bear were far upstream, farther than Young Hunter had been. But there was no way now of knowing who this man was or who he had been. Only his deerskin clothes had kept his body together. Surely it would have fallen apart and been eaten by the fishes by now—as his eyes had been eaten away and soft flesh everywhere was peeling from his bones.

Young Hunter held one hand just above the dead one's chest. As he did so, even though his hand was not touching the man's flesh, he felt how cold the bone-spirit had become, how much it needed to be warmed and taken care of for it to rest. He felt also the presence of that same great angry being he had seen waiting below the huge pine tree when he shared the body of Big Raccoon. It was the beast that had caused this man's death; its great tooth had pierced this man's body.

Young Hunter lifted his hand, knowing that the coldness of death had been transferred to his fingers. He pushed his hand down deeply into the moist sand which had been warmed by the light of the Day Traveler, letting the earth drain away that feeling from his fingers.

"What shall we do?"

Young Hunter turned. It was his uncle, Fire Keeper, who spoke. And the words were not spoken idly, Young Hunter suddenly realized. They were directed at him. Despite Fire Keeper's age and his wisdom, despite his position as the sagamon of the Only People, he was asking Young Hunter what to do.

Young Hunter's head spun as he stood up—perhaps it was from the awful smell of the dead person, perhaps from the responsibility such a question placed upon him. But he honored the question by speaking calmly, without uncertainty.

"We cannot carry him far. But his bone-spirit is cold from being so long in the river."

Young Hunter looked toward a little hill a long spear's throw above the sandbar. "We will make a fire for him there. And when the fire is done, we will bury his bones in that spot."

Fire Keeper nodded. His nephew saw things clearly. Without speaking, he went to gather the wood for the fire. Others joined him, and by the time Young Hunter and Red Hawk and Blue Hawk brought what was left of the Bear People village man up to that fire, carrying his body on a wide piece of elm bark, it was ready. A bed of sticks had been prepared, and more wood, piled up to the height of a tall man, lay close to it, to be used to feed the flames. They carefully rested the dead person on top of the bed of piled sticks, which had been raised up on larger pieces of wood to allow the air to feed the flames. The necklace of bear teeth had come loose as they moved the man's body, and Young Hunter hung it on a forked stick well away from the pyre.

Young Hunter and Fire Keeper made a new fire, the two of them working a hand drill. It would not be right to borrow the flame from any of the fish-smoking fires still burning next to the fishing rapids. Fire Keeper placed the glowing coal in the tinder bundle, blew it into life, and then placed it into the little wigwom of very dry sticks at the sunset side of the pyre. Young Hunter carried the flame to the upriver side, the sunrise side, and the downriver side until the circle of the fire was complete. Then, as the flames rose up high, embracing and warming the body of the person who lay there, the other people left the hill. Only Fire Keeper and Young Hunter stayed. They would stay there for the rest of the day, keeping the fire burning until only fragments of bone were left. Then they would wait until the coals had died down to ashes. Then they would make the hole and rake into it all that remained of this person whose name they did not know, but whose body had finally been made dry and warm again, healed into rest by the flames.

Willow Woman poked the end of the sticks into the fire. When they had burned down, she would use the two peeled and forked green poles to lift out the heated stones and drop them into the trough filled with the last of the sap from the maple trees. Agwedjiman, sitting on his haunches beneath a nearby tree, swung his head around at the sound of the sticks scraping the coals, then turned back to gaze toward the north.

Wli, wli, wli. The word was spoken again and again from above Willow Woman's head. *Good, good, good.*

Willow Woman looked up, knowing what she would see. Talk Talk, the young crow, flapped her wings on the branch above. In the days that had passed since Willow Woman had rescued her from the long-tail, she had recovered her ability to fly, but she showed no desire to leave Willow Woman for long.

Willow Woman smiled as she thought of how she had at first assumed Talk Talk to be a male. She should have known better. Few men ever learned to speak meaningful words as quickly as did Talk Talk.

"Your little friend is *not* a boy," Medicine Plant had told her, when Willow Woman brought the young crow to the lodge on the hill. Medicine Plant had looked into the young bird's eyes with that special way a deep-seeing person has. "And she has taken you as a sister."

Wli, mziwi, wli, said Talk Talk.

It was true. All was good. Their lives here were good, indeed. The child of Medicine Plant and Bear Talker was well and strong. Soon he would be old enough for Willow Woman to begin helping even more in caring for him. Rabbit Stick's foot was almost healed, and the danger that had threatened the people in the form of an Ancient One—as Young Hunter had told her—was now gone thanks to Sparrow's quick thinking. And as if to reassure them that their lives would continue to be blessed, the season of maple syruping had been an especially good one, lasting many more days than in any other year anyone could remember. When the flow was as strong as this, it meant that everything would be abundant. The tribes of fish were already coming up the Long River in great numbers. This would be a year in which the food and medicine plants in the woods would grow in profusion. There would be many geese and ducks to hunt, and the deer and the caribou, the elk and the moose would be plentiful. The flow of the maple sap told them this, for it was the first harvest.

"All things are connected, Daughter," was how her mother, Near the Sky, had explained it. She remembered the first time she asked her mother how this could be. It was her first time of her body cleansing itself, and it had come exactly with the fullness of the Night Traveler. So, when she and her mother, whose cleansing time had also come, went to the women's lodge—which no man ever entered—she had found herself in the company of many other women, including nearly all of the girls her age and older and many of their mothers.

"It is because the Moon is our grandmother," Near the Sky had explained. "She tells us when it is time for us to have our special time, our time when we rest and tell stories to each other and play games. A time when no man can bother us to ask us to make food, or tan hides ... or anything else."

Willow Woman used her green pole to push the burning sticks over the tops of the stones, making sure they were well buried in embers.

Everything is connected to everything. The flow of the trees, the flow of a woman's body. *The new life of the plants coming from the brown earth and the leaves coming from the bare branches of the trees were connected to the way a woman's body could bring forth the new life of a child.* Willow Woman felt strong and good as she thought these things. Talk Talk flapped down from the limb above her and landed on her shoulder to peck gently at her ear.

Mziwi, wli? said Talk Talk.

"*Mziwi, wli,*" Willow Girl answered.

CHAPTER THIRTY-THREE
SONGS

"Sing with me, Nephew," Fire Keeper said.

The fire had burned to ashes, and the ashes and bones had been lifted up and placed into a roll of elm bark. They stood next to the mound of earth that had been piled over the remains of the one whose body had come down the river. The bear claw necklace had been buried there, too, placed gently into the roll of elm bark. It was the last of that man's possessions that he had with him, and so it was meant to go with him on his journey to the spirit land. A forked stick had been placed in the center of the newly dug earth.

It was the job of Fire Keeper, as the head of the village, to sing the death song whenever someone was buried. He had never asked anyone to sing that song with him before. But Young Hunter did not refuse. He knew that he could not refuse, nor could he say he did not know the song. It was well known that Young Hunter was one of those who needed to hear a song only once to have it always in his heart.

They stood together and sang the song to each of the directions. It was the greeting song and the farewell song as well.

Ya niga we ya
ni ga we

213

ya ha ah
ni ga we

It was a song to help the spirit of a person who died to travel safely on the long journey. Perhaps it would help that person's spirit find its way back to another life as a real human being. It sang also to the earth: *Nigawes*, Our Mother. Our Mother from whom we came and to whom we will return.

The Day Traveler began to sink beneath the trees as they finished the song. Young Hunter lowered his gaze from the sky to find that several people had returned. Red Hawk and Blue Hawk, still holding their long fish spears, Sparrow, and half a dozen other people were standing in a circle around them. From the look on their faces as the other people gazed at Fire Keeper, Young Hunter knew that they had something to say. He also felt something within him speak. It came from that place within himself which he always felt touched by song. It was that voice without words, and it was saying that something was about to begin. It was as if he had already heard the words that his shaken friends now spoke.

"There are people, many people ... " Blue Hawk began. Young Hunter saw that his friend held his fish spear with both hands and was leaning on it as if to keep from falling.

"Upstream, around the bend by the river ... " Red Hawk said. He, too, held his fish spear tightly and was twisting his hands so hard in opposite directions that small creaking noises came from the wood.

"They built a fire to announce their coming, and so we went to their smoke and they told us they ... " Blue Hawk continued.

"Had come from upriver, from the lower villages of the Bear People; they are seeking refuge with us because ... " Red Hawk said.

"A monster ... " Blue Hawk said, lifting up his spear.

"Has killed all the other Bear People ... " finished Red Hawk.

A long silence fell over them. They could hear the sounds of the Long River, whispering and singing over the stones. The calls of the birds that always came when the darkness grew close seemed louder and clearer than Young Hunter had ever heard them before. He could hear the crackling of the fires still burning down on the shore and the whispering voices of the new people gathered there, the ones who had fled from something terrible to the north.

This has happened before, Young Hunter thought. He felt himself divide, saw himself standing there in the midst of all the people, all those who had been part of his life since his life began and those who were new to him. He looked at the circle of people, himself included, from eyes that seemed to be lifting up above them as a hawk lifts up when the wind rises under its wings; he saw, even farther below him now, his own body collapsing and falling forward into the arms of his uncle. Then all of that was left behind and he was rising swiftly above the Long River, looking north with the last dying light.

The Ancient One had been working at the last stone for a long time. Its hands were almost as hard as the stone and its muscles creaked as it pushed and pried. Both arms were strong again now, but it had eaten the last of the meat it had hung in the cave and it knew that it must leave soon or it would begin to grow weak, perhaps too weak to get out by this one way it had found.

The eyes of the Ancient One were good in the dark, much better than the eyes of the small ones who walked on two legs. So it had not been difficult, even in this darkness, to find the small fingers of light that filtered from far back and up in the great cave. This cave had not been hollowed out by the flow of water, but had been shaped by the motion of the hills and the great boulders, rocks sliding down and piling over other rocks, leaving spaces between them. And if the stones were small enough, they could be made to move again.

215

The Ancient One had found this one place several sleeps ago. But it had waited until now to try to break through, waited until its own strength was greatest. It edged its long fingers in between the earth and stone, and the thin ray of light grew larger so that it could see out, out past the thin root of a tree to the sky. A small bird was singing on that tree. The Ancient One drew its hand back. There was too much light, still. And the songs of the day meant only that there was danger, that it might be observed. Only when the bright eye was gone from the sky would it be safe. It had already made the mistake of showing itself in that light, and so it had been seen by the dangerous one, the small one who carried in his mind the images of the Ancient One's own destruction. Then had come the falling of the stones which almost crushed it. So the Ancient One knew that only the dark time would be safe. Then it would break free.

And then? It did not know what it would do then. It did not try to think beyond that moment of breaking free. When it tried to do so, the fear and the great lonely confusion came back again, and it found itself unable to move, able only to curl its great arms around itself and push itself back into the corner of the cave. So it would not make the mistake of trying to think ahead again. It would think only of the sweet darkness coming and of the feel of the stones moving as it thrust its great shoulders up, up, toward freedom.

Young Hunter felt himself pulled toward the north. There was something to see there. He saw, as if through a mist, a great shape farther to the north near the river. It was four-legged and powerful. It was dangerous and angry, and he knew that it carried death in every step it took. But he would not go farther to see it now, for he saw two other shapes farther down the Long River, two-legged walkers. One of them, the closer one, was very small. The mind of the little one was very good and very clear. It brought a smile to Young Hunter's heart, but as his spirit mind reached toward the little one, he felt the little one's mind draw away and seek to hide. Young Hunter's spirit eyes looked away. It was not right to intrude. He would wait until the little one sought him.

He turned his vision now to the other figure, the one on the opposite bank of the Long River. The other shape was farther away. It had the face of a woman. That woman's face was lovely, but it was twisted with a deeper sorrow than he could ever remember seeing. He felt drawn toward that woman. Perhaps there was something he could say to her that might help. Yet that part of him, that deep-seeing part which had risen free, knew that it was not to the north that his spirit form must now travel. Instead, he found himself turning to the side, back to the village where his grandparents and his wife were waiting.

He could see them below him now, though they could not see him. They sat around the evening fire in front of the two joined-together lodges. Seeing this way, Young Hunter could look into their hearts, and as he looked, he saw nothing there that surprised him. Their hearts were as open to his spirit eyes as they were to his waking, breathwalking vision.

He looked at Rabbit Stick. Rabbit Stick was twisting plant fibers, over, back, twirl, over, back, twirl, into a strong string for a fish line. The knotty strength and the wry humor of his grandfather were written on his heart as clearly as pictures marked onto the side of an old, strong message tree, pictures showing one which way to travel to find those who had gone before. Yet as he looked into Rabbit Stick, the old man looked up from his work, as if seeing him—even though Young Hunter knew from all that Bear Talker and Medicine Plant had taught him that this spirit form could not be seen except by those who have traveled this same way. Rabbit Stick smiled and looked back down at the cordage line which, like his life, grew longer with each turn.

Young Hunter turned his eyes to his grandmother. Sweetgrass Woman was putting aside a special portion of the food, a good stew made from the caribou Young Hunter had brought down with his spear the day before. Young Hunter knew it was being saved for him, but would be hidden so that she could tell him he was so late that they had eaten all the food—before bringing it out and giving it to him. The haunch of that caribou hung behind her near the wall of the wigwom. What was written in her heart was a wonderful blend of caring and curiosity; she was as curious as a raccoon. And there was patience there, too, not so much with herself as with others.

Then Young Hunter looked at his wife. He saw how strong her arms and shoulders were as she worked on a piece of birch bark, folding it so that she could lift it up and bite it, leaving patterns like flowers and circles and snowflakes when the bark was unfolded. It was a game that children played, making patterns in the newly peeled birch bark that way. And Young Hunter knew that she was doing it to delight him when he returned to the lodge; she would hand him the bark and ask him if he remembered the first time she had given him such a folded piece of bark, when she was a small girl shyly holding it out to him from behind a tree and then running home with her face turned away. What he saw in her heart was the purity of a child's heart, yet also the strength and the passion of a woman. He saw her listening wisdom and the laughing spirit that delighted in sharing its joy with everything that lived. Any being that saw and felt that spirit of hers could not help but be moved by it, could not help but feel blessed by it.

But as Young Hunter looked at his family and into their hearts, he also felt, like drops of cold water on the back of his neck, the imminence of something—more than one thing. He felt, from two directions, death hunting his family.

Young Hunter lifted his spirit eyes toward the sunrise direction, and as he did so his vision was grasped by something that drew him to itself so swiftly that the village was left behind. A long gray arm breaking free of the earth like a limbless sapling sprouting with unnatural speed. The hand at the end of that arm opened as he rushed toward it. Then a deep voice spoke.

"Nephew, have you traveled far?"

Young Hunter opened his eyes and looked up. His uncle, Fire Keeper, was holding him by his shoulders. It was no longer the sunset time. The night was divided into four parts. First came the light-going time of evening, then the full-night time of darkness. After that was the going-on-into-darkness time and then the time of middle-night. When the light began to return, the night was ended. That time of the first faint returning of the light was called going-into-the-dawn. It was full-night now. Young Hunter could tell that by the positions of the *awatawesu*, the little far-above beings glittering brightly in the Sky Land over their heads. Like a broad belt slung over the shoulder of the Sky Land, the spirit trail sparkled above them. At the edge of the sky, the Night Traveler was just in *p'keniha'do*, her time of filling up, so her brightness did not lessen the brilliance of the star-belt road through the Sky Land.

Fire Keeper looked up. "Did you travel along the Sky Trail, Nephew? We saw a small star falling toward us just before you opened your eyes again."

"Not that far, Uncle."

Young Hunter stood and stomped his feet. His head was awake, but his legs were still walking in his dream.

"When you were born," Fire Keeper said, "that same star fell down toward your mother's lodge. I saw it and your grandfather saw it. I do not know if you have been told this before. Your grandfather began crying when he saw that star and then heard your voice. He said that he knew your voice because he had heard it when he was a very small boy. It was the voice of his own grandfather, so he knew that the old man's spirit had come back and would guide your body well. He said how happy his heart was, and he kept crying and crying.

"Your father, Thrower, did not know what to say. He had never seen his father act that way before. He was wondering if he should start crying, too, when your grandmother finally came out of the birthing lodge and told Rabbit Stick that if he did not stop crying she would dump a bucket of water over his head. Everyone quietly moved away from your grandfather then." Fire Keeper chuckled at the thought. "They knew your grandmother meant what she said."

Young Hunter smiled and then shook his head. He felt as if cobwebs clung to his face.

"Uncle," he said, "I have seen great danger to our people. I have seen it close at hand and I have seen it coming down the Long River. What can I do?"

"Will the danger come to us tomorrow?"

Nda, a voice said, *it will not come before the Day Traveler has wakened and slept four more times.* Young Hunter shook his head like a dog shaking off water after coming out of the river. It was Young Hunter's own voice, speaking before he knew he was speaking, saying words that Young Hunter knew to be true even though he did not know he had held that knowledge.

Fire Keeper placed a hand on his nephew's broad shoulder. It was good to feel the honest strength there. Young Hunter was truly a young man like the ones in the old stories, a young man chosen by the Great Mystery, to be ready when the people needed help. It made Fire Keeper feel proud to be the uncle of this young man, to have him to lean upon in difficult times. But it would not do to let him know how much his uncle needed to lean upon him, or to let him know that his uncle was even more uncertain than he.

"Nephew," Fire Keeper said, "what you must do now is start walking one step at a time and go home to your wife and your grandparents. Go one step at a time. The dawn will greet us soon enough. I will go back and talk more with White Goose, the old woman who led these people down our river. When the sun is two hands high, we will gather all the people together, and then we will decide what must be done."

CHAPTER THIRTY-FOUR
TRAILS

When Sparrow opened his eyes, it was not yet dawn. He was sleeping close to the fires beneath the fish-drying racks and he was warm, even though the night had grown cool enough for the frost to return and for small crystals of ice to form at the edge of the Long River where its waters eddied into quiet pools.

He raised his head without sitting up. He could see the dugouts of the upriver Bear People. Their dark wood was pale and patterned white where the moisture held by the rough sides had been touched by frost. Mist was rising from the surface of the Long River, making shapes that seemed to be as aware of Sparrow's gaze as he was of their motion. At first they looked like trails, like the trails in the snow that he had looked down upon from a bluff one day in the season of long nights. Trails that were as pale as the land that held them, trails that flowed back into the shape of the hills and became lost as his eyes tried to follow them.

But then the mist danced and seemed to draw itself together. It thickened, and its shape became almost that of a person. Yes, the shape of a person, the shape of a woman. ... Sparrow's heart jumped. It seemed as if the mist had made itself into that very woman Sparrow saw when his mind was held in sleep, but was never able to find when his eyes were open. Tall that woman of mist was, even taller than Sparrow himself, walking straight and gracefully. It seemed as if she were walking across the water to him, and he began to sit up, feeling that if he only knew the right name to speak, the mist would indeed take on human form and come to him, come walking to him from his dreams. But before it reached him, the first small breath of the morning came, a breeze that swirled and scattered the mist. For a moment, Sparrow's lips shaped themselves toward a lonesome song, the song a young man would play on his flute to catch the attention of the young woman he fancied. Then he shook his head. That woman he dreamed of did not exist.

He sat up and looked down along the water's edge. There were new fires there, made by the people from upriver. A whole village of them had arrived and more were coming, from what they said. But what good would their flight do them if the monster that followed was as terrible as they said. A hill that walked, a creature no spear could kill?

Sparrow tried to look into himself, to hear the voice of his own spirit guide, as Young Hunter did so often. It was known that everyone had such guidance. But some people were unable to hear that voice clearly, while others walked with it every day as if it were a close friend. Sparrow was one of those who was deaf to the voice of any guide other than his own quick thoughts.

"You think too fast." That was what Bear Talker said to him. "You must sit alone with yourself and not always be moving. Even when you sleep you do not stay still. You are even running from yourself in your dreams."

Sparrow jumped to his feet. He climbed onto the highest stone at the edge of the river, spread his arms as if he were going to fly, and then he jumped, diving headfirst. But before he hit the stones below, he spun around in the air to land as lightly on his feet as if he had just stepped through the door of a lodge. But he did not stand there. Instead, he began to run. He ran faster and faster, not knowing where he was running, ducking around the trunks of the birch trees, leaping over bushes hazy with the green of buds that would soon open. His eyes were open, but all that he saw was the motion of the world around him as he ran. And though he heard many things stirring in the first light of the new day, he heard no words coming to him from inside his heart.

Rabbit Stick stood to greet the day. Young Hunter was still sleeping, but Rabbit Stick did not wake him as he might have done on another morning. He knew that many things had happened on the bank of the Long River. Sparrow had come to their lodge twice, and then, instead of remaining in the village, had run each time all the way back to the Long River. Truly the young man's spirit was like that of the little bird that will not rest—or perhaps it was only that he was trying to catch up to that elusive spirit of his, not seeing that it was there waiting to be heard, waiting within himself all the time.

Rabbit Stick shook his head. He himself understood what it was to have a restless spirit. But one could never explain such things to the young. The young have to live those things to understand them. Because of all the news that Sparrow brought to them, first of the drowned man and then of the coming of the Bear People with their stories of villages destroyed by a great beast, he and Sweetgrass Woman and Willow Woman had not expected Young Hunter to return at all that night. They knew he would remain by the Long River with the fishing camp party and the newcomers from the north. And then, as they sat by the fire, Rabbit Stick had sensed the presence of his grandson's spirit body watching them, like a small warm light that he felt in the center of his own being. From his own small experience of travel outside his body—when he had been trapped in the rock slide—Rabbit Stick knew how tiring it was to send one's spirit walking without breath. And so he had been certain that Young Hunter would not be back before the new day's light.

But Young Hunter had come home. Rabbit Stick had heard his grandson stumble in just before the time of going-into-the-dawn. And now, lying on his back, with his arms wrapped around Willow Woman and Agwedjiman on the other side, he was sleeping and snoring loudly. Behind his head, Danowa was sitting with his head raised up, and at Young Hunter's feet, Pabesis, still sleeping, was curled up. Although Rabbit Stick could not see them there behind the closed flap of their part of the two linked wigwoms, he could see them all clearly in his mind.

And he knew that Willow Woman was awake. His new granddaughter always woke even earlier than Rabbit Stick. Rabbit Stick smiled. She would stay there by Young Hunter's side, comforting his late sleep, supporting and strengthening him with her presence. She, too, had listened closely to the stories that Sparrow told and knew, as did all the others, that, within a few sunsets, there would be trails to walk and little time for sleep if they wished to continue waking up to more new dawns.

The sun was two hands high when Bear Talker began stirring the coals in the fire before their lodge. Medicine Plant sat behind him, nursing their son. As he stirred the coals, Bear Talker found himself wondering again at the strange words his wife had said. *How could it be true that they would not be the ones to raise their own child? Why must she give their boy to be raised by another?*

But that was a question to be answered later. Now he had to see what the bone would tell him. He held out his hand, and Medicine Plant gave him the shoulder bone taken from the caribou Young Hunter had recently shared among the people. Bear Talker placed it carefully on top of the bed of coals.

"Show us the paths that we must follow, Caribou. Your people travel far and see many things. Help us to see the way to go."

Bear Talker began singing, and as he sang he tapped lightly on his drum. The drum and the deep sound of his voice blended with the crackling sound of the fire, and everything else seemed to grow silent and listen in a great circle around them.

Bear Talker finished the song and hung the drum back up on the outside wall of the lodge. Then, with his bare hands, he brushed the coals away from the scapula and flipped it out of the fire onto the ground next to him. He flicked away the few coals that clung to it, then blew across the surface to clear away the firesand. Medicine Plant leaned over to look at it closely with him. For a long time, the two deep-seers stared at the strange story told by the lines and cracks—the shapes like the flow of rivers and the winding of trails—that had appeared on the flat face of the caribou's shoulder bone.

CHAPTER THIRTY-FIVE
THE STIFF-LEGGED BEAR

Long ago, at the time when the mountains of ice still held the winter land through every season, there was a man named Long Hair. He was strong and quick-minded and afraid of nothing. He lived with his grandmother in a little wigwom apart from all the other people. His grandmother taught him about the medicine plants, and he was a good hunter, always bringing her plenty of game animals. Even though he always shared whatever he hunted with the rest of the village, Long Hair spent much of his time alone in the woods, listening to the sounds of the birds and animals. It was said that he liked to speak with the animal people better than he liked to talk with human beings. He was not very patient with the human people.

One day, a messenger came into their village from downriver.

"The springs are drying up," the messenger said. "Our people go to the headwaters where the springs rise to find out what is wrong, but they never return. Who will help us?"

"I will go," Long Hair said. "There is nothing else to do and I am bored."

Long Hair's grandmother gave him a pouch full of dried meat and berries so that he would have food to eat as he traveled. He picked up his spear and began to walk. But as he walked, he listened to the sounds of the forest around him. For a while, everything seemed to be as it always was, but then he heard a sound he had not heard before. It was a sound like weeping.

Long Hair left the trail and followed that sound. It led him to a little valley with high cliff walls and caves in the cliffs. There, sitting on a very large mushroom, was a little man, one of the Mikumwesu—the Little People who are the friends of the bears. Long Hair was surprised to see Mikumwesu. Everyone knew that the Little People were very shy and hid from the sight of the human beings.

"My small friend," Long Hair said, "why are you weeping?"

Mikumwesu took his hands away from his face and looked at Long Hair.

"My big friend," he said, "I am glad you have greeted me this way. Because you are my friend, I can tell you what is wrong. My wife is very ill. She cannot eat and I am afraid she will die."

"Take me to her and I will do what I can do," Long Hair said.

Mikumwesu led Long Hair to the mouth of one of the caves. It looked too small for him to enter, but as soon as he bent his head down, Long Hair found himself inside the cave. There, on a bed made of rabbitskins, was a little woman who was very sick indeed. Long Hair, though, knew what was wrong.

He went outside and found the plant that was needed, the spotted lily, whose roots settle the stomach when made into a tea. He made that medicine, and the wife of Mikumwesu soon became well.

"My big friend," Mikumwesu said, "great thanks to you. You have saved the life of my wife. Now I must help you, also. I know where you are going, and I know that you will find a great monster waiting for you. The monster is a giant, stiff-legged bear with teeth longer than your body. It is so large it looks like a small grassy hill. This creature and its relatives have been draining the springs, drinking all the water so that your people will come looking. Then it kills them by piercing them with its teeth and crushing them beneath its feet. Even now it knows that you are coming, and it is waiting to kill you as well."

"How will I be able to defeat this great stiff-legged bear?"

"Big friend," Mikumwesu said, "I will come along and help. Now, follow me."

Then Mikumwesu led Long Hair back into his cave to a trail that led deep into the earth. When they came out at the end of the trail, they were on a hill looking down over a wide plain. All that Long Hair could see on that plain was one large brown hill and a number of smaller hills near the trail that led onto that plain.

"Watch carefully," Mikumwesu said.

Then Long Hair saw that some of the small grassy hills were moving. Those hills were moving ever so slightly. The largest of the hills lifted up its head, and Long Hair saw the glint of two huge teeth.

"We cannot go too close," Mikumwesu said. "The stiff-legged bears have long noses and can smell us from very far away. That is why it does no good to try to hunt them. They will hunt you first. So we must stay where the wind blows toward us until we are ready."

Then Mikumwesu reached into his pack and brought out a bundle. He untied it and took from it several long pieces of bone and a rawhide string. He put those pieces together.

"This is a great weapon," Mikumwesu said. "We will use it to destroy the stiff-legged bears. But you must start a long fire across the plain to drive them this way. Then, when they run through the narrow place between the hills, I will be able to strike them."

Long Hair did as Mikumwesu bade him. He circled around and made a series of fires. Soon a line of smoke and flames began to move with the wind across the large plain, driving the animals before it. They all ran until they came to the place between the hills where the way was so narrow that they had to go through one by one. Mikumwesu waited on the other side, and as each of the stiff-legged bears came through, he struck it with his weapon in the one place where a small spear could pierce its thick hair.

Bear Talker finished the story and brushed his hands. He looked around the small circle of listeners who had come as they had been bidden.

"What was that weapon?" asked Sparrow in an eager voice, leaning forward as he spoke.

Bear Talker almost smiled. He had told Medicine Plant that Sparrow would be the first one to speak and that he would surely ask a question. He almost looked back over his shoulder at Medicine Plant, who was rocking the small woven cradle tied between their wigwom and a little ash tree. But to look back would have spoiled the dramatic effect. Instead, Bear Talker looked toward Young Hunter. Young Hunter was careful to look down at the earth. He knew what that weapon was and that the Long Thrower, that weapon which used a sinew string to hurl a small spear farther than even an atlatl could throw it, was a secret of the deep-seeing people, a weapon too terrible for all human beings to know about.

"It was the weapon of the Mikumwesu," Bear Talker growled. "Did you not listen to the story? If you want to know more about that weapon, perhaps you could go and ask the Little People yourself."

Sparrow leaned back with a sour look on his face. Red Hawk and Blue Hawk looked quickly at each other, decided to say nothing, and then looked over toward Young Hunter. But of the five who had been called to hear the story of the stiff-legged bear, a story they had never before heard told, it was not Young Hunter who spoke next. It was Willow Woman.

Willow Woman looked straight into Bear Talker's eyes. "The stiff-legged bear is the Walking Hill which is killing so many of our people now," she said, speaking her words not as a question but as a simple, gently spoken statement.

Before Bear Talker could answer, Medicine Plant leaned over her husband's shoulder and spoke.

"You are right, Granddaughter," Medicine Plant said. "And it was only with the help of the Mikumwesu that Long Hair was able to defeat those great beings. That is why we have been given this message."

Medicine Plant held up the scapula of the caribou and pointed with a long fingernail to the cracks which looked almost like the figures of two people—one large, one very small. She looked slowly around the small circle of faces that watched, those who would have to do the work spoken of by the message bone. She looked at Young Hunter, at Sparrow, at Red Hawk and Blue Hawk, but she said nothing until her eyes reached those of Willow Woman.

"Granddaughter," Medicine Plant said, "you are the one who must now ask the Mikumwesu for help."

CHAPTER THIRTY-SIX
WITHIN THE TREE

The great oak tree stood on the side of a hill at the head of a valley two looks away from the hill of many caves. There were many great trees, but this oak was larger than any of the other big trees around it, so large that twenty men with their arms joined could not have encircled it. The tree was so old that its center had become hollow, and the hollow of that tree had long been used by the bears, who came generation after generation to den up and to sleep there during the season of long nights. The bears had dug into the earth in the center of the tree and back into the hillside. Because it was the place of the bears, the Only People always avoided this tree and kept a look away from the valley, showing the respect that bears needed.

Although the time of winter sleep was now long past, the great hollow tree was not empty of life. But there was no bear within it. Instead, the great, gray-skinned Ancient One hid there in the half-light. It had been afraid to remain out in the bright light of the Day Traveler, and afraid also to go back into the stone caves after being trapped by the fall of boulders over the mouth of the largest cave. Its fear reminded it of how all of its brothers had died in a similar avalanche many seasons ago, and it knew it would never again be comfortable circled by stone.

As it crouched within the tree, it gnawed on the leg of a two-winters-old moose. The Ancient One had found the animal

231

dead, already killed by a long-tail, and driven the cat away with a few hard-thrown stones. Then it had tossed the dead moose over its shoulder as lightly as a human would lift up a rabbit, and gone seeking a place to hide.

This place was good. The Ancient One leaned his back against the inside of the hollow tree. He felt the life in the tree against him, and it seemed as if it were speaking to him, telling him a warmer story than he heard in the voice of the caves. It was a story that touched his great, deep loneliness. It made him feel less like a stone himself. A wind stirred the high branches of the tree far above, and the great oak creaked and moved and the Ancient One felt it. And as the Ancient One felt that life touching him, strange things began to happen within him, and he did not understand what those things were. He lifted his head and began to make a howling cry that was much softer than the hunting call of his lost giant people. It was so long since he or any of his kind had made that cry that he did not know he was mourning.

Mikumwesu sat high in the branches of the cedar tree at the edge of the village. A cat owl sat next to him. Its keen ears had heard him the night before as he came climbing up the trunk, but he had touched it with a friendly thought, and the cat owl had not spoken, even though it was the self-appointed guardian of this village, the one who would call out to the people whenever it saw a strange person coming close at night.

Mikumwesu had settled on a branch near the owl and, leaning close, begun to comb its feathers softly with his long, thin fingers while it made a soft churring sound. The owl was sleeping now, so Mikumwesu was careful not to disturb it. He had learned well from his parents that, although almost all of the animals and birds of the forest loved the presence and the touch of the Mikumwesu, there were times when they wished to be left in peace. It was only right to respect them then.

Mikumwesu watched the people in the village below. He was too shy to approach them. He wished that it were not so, but they were all so big and he was so small. So he only watched and wondered at the many interesting and amusing things they did. Right now he watched that young woman who carried the crow on her shoulder. He liked the look of her, and he felt a gentleness in her spirit which made him think she would be the type who would enjoy playing with him.

Mikumwesu loved to play. He liked the games that he played with the animals, wrestling with the bigger ones such as the wolves and the bears or playing games of chase and run-away with the smaller ones, trying to find them when they hid from him. He had played such a game just the day before with a pine marten, running up the trunk of a dead, leaning birch tree just ahead of the marten and leaping off into the deep, soft leaf litter below as the dead stub broke. Then, as the little red-coated one turned and scampered into a hollow log, Mikum-wesu pretended that he could not find it, until the marten came out and nipped him from behind, chuckling as little animals chuckle.

But as much as Mikumwesu enjoyed playing with the animal people, he greatly missed the other games, the ones that he had played with his parents when they would make shapes with rawhide string and pass them from hand to hand, telling stories with each shape. Perhaps that woman below knew such stories. Now she was picking up sticks and carrying them beyond the edge of the circle of wigwoms that made up the center of the village.

Many in the village now were preparing food for them-selves. Although Mikumwesu and his people never ate the flesh of animals or birds or even fish—living only on the many gifts of nuts and berries and good-tasting bark given to them by the plant people—he found it fascinating to watch how the people skinned the animals they caught, how they dried the fish from the Long River with smoke. He did not disapprove of their hunting and fishing—although he and his parents had, at times, steered away from those hunting and fishing certain birds and animals and big fish the Mikumwesu had grown to know and think of as special friends. To disapprove of the big people hunting and fishing would be like disapproving of the hawk as it dove to catch a rabbit or like disapproving of the wolf pack as they circled a deer. As long as the big people hunted and fished in the right way and showed respect, Mikumwesu and his parents had only watched and made no judgments.

Now, though, a hard thing was going to happen. Unless Mikumwesu helped these big people, they would be wiped out by the Walking Hill. Mikumwesu felt great sympathy for the huge animal. He had touched its mind more than once, trying to bring it calm and peace. But the pain of its wound was too great and even Mikumwesu could do nothing.

Mikumwesu had sometimes pulled a lodged spear head from the heavy muscles of a deer or an elk wounded by human hunters but not badly enough to kill it. He had done this because the animal had been suffering and had come to him for help. An animal would not do this if it had already given its death to the big people, accepted that it would die and have its body used with respect. But the Walking Hill would not come to him for help. And even if it had, Mikumwesu knew that the spear point was lodged too deeply, wedged in between tooth and bone. The force of the great animal's own jaws biting down on that spear point had driven it ever deeper.

Walking Hill was filled with anger that was fed by loneliness and loss, the feeling of being the last of his people. Mikumwesu understood that feeling. He wondered why it was that he could find no others like himself. The bird and animal peoples accepted him. Only the day before he had slept with a family of wolves, curling their warmth around him while he picked the burrs from their fur. But he missed the touch of the minds and the sound of the voices of his parents.

That deeply driven stony pain and loneliness had made Walking Hill a monster. He sought only to kill now, not knowing that he was really seeking for the peace that his own death would finally bring him. Mikumwesu sighed. There was no other way. Somehow, despite his shyness, he would have to speak to them. He would have to help the big people to kill the great animal; otherwise, so many more would die. But he still felt touched by the great animal's loneliness. And as he thought of that loneliness, that feeling of being the last, Mikumwesu felt something, heard something within his mind: a crying sound higher than the sad howl of a lone wolf. He reached out with his own mind, circling to see if he could find it, find that other lonely spirit.

CHAPTER THIRTY-SEVEN
TOUCHING

Willow Woman sat in the small lodge that Medicine Plant had helped her construct beyond the edge of the village, far from the sight of any of the Only People. It was a lodge made of dry fallen branches and sticks woven together, with the leaves of last winter scraped over the top. From a distance, it looked almost like the nest of a squirrel fallen to the ground, especially because of the young crow that sat on top of it, now and then unfolding her wings as if to fly before changing her mind and settling back down again.

Like a squirrel's nest, it was warm inside that little lodge and as Willow Woman sat there, she cradled the baby and sang to it the old song about sleeping in the cradle board hung on the branch of a tree.

Kaawi, Djidjis
Djidjis, kaawi
Wey o wey, Djidjis
Oligawi

Djidjis. That was what Willow Woman called him, this strong child of Medicine Plant and Bear Talker. Baby. It was not that he had no other name. If anything, he had too many names. Bear Talker insisted on calling his son Bright Sky. But

236

to Sweetgrass Woman, who had midwifed him to breath, he was Looks Backward. Medicine Plant, however, who no longer tried to hide the fondness in her gaze as he contentedly suckled at her breast, referred to him sometimes as Big Voice and other times as Old Eyes. It was confusing, especially when all of her three elders spoke at the same time to the child, all using their own chosen names for the boy. For days now, the arguments had gone on.

So Willow Woman, who had been chosen by Medicine Plant as the one to be the second mother of the little one, simply referred to him as Djidjis. She did this remembering the story of how Gluskabe, the Talker, became too proud of himself. The Talker said he was able to defeat anyone. But when he was told to quiet a crying baby, he quickly learned that his power was not that great!

When Willow Woman saw the wisdom glinting behind the bright black eyes of Djidjis whenever the three older people argued about what name they should properly call him, it was easy to believe that he already understood every word and was prepared, indeed, to vanquish even one as great as the One Who Shaped Himself.

Willow Woman reached out a hand to adjust some of the branches of the debris lodge. It was the kind of shelter that would be warm inside when the cool winds blew but cool inside when the heat of the Day Traveler's bright face shone down. She had first learned to make such a survival shelter from her father, Deer Tracker. She remembered his story of how he had made such a shelter when he had an accident one winter far away from the village in his hunting territory.

As Deer Tracker had walked along a ridge covered with snow, the snow beneath him had given way. Instead of stepping onto solid ground, he had stepped onto a thin bridge between two great stones on the edge of the hillside. A branch had fallen between them before the snow began, and then the snow had covered it, making it seem solid. It had been solid enough to hold the weight of the snowshoe hare whose prints Deer Tracker followed, but it could not hold the much heavier body of a man. When he'd crashed through and went tumbling down the slope, his leg had been broken.

Some men might have given up then, but Deer Tracker was stubborn. That was how he had earned his name, for being the one who never would lose a trail or give up when following a wounded deer. Although it was only the Moon of Frost Coming and so the snow was too thin for him to dig it into a shelter cave, there were many fallen branches and a thick layer of fallen maple leaves on that hillslope. Deer Tracker made himself a shelter: first, he propped branches up over a huge maple log, and then, lying on one side and digging like a dog, he heaped up more and more of the leaves. When there were enough of them, held in place by the framework of branches, he wove a door from smaller branches and then crawled into his shelter, secure from the wind and cold. More snow fell that night; but inside his shelter, even without a fire, Deer Tracker was warm.

He straightened his broken leg and wrapped it into place. After that, the pain was not so bad. He bound his leg well, so well that it had already begun to heal when his wife, Near the Sky, and her brothers found him four sunrises later. It was not hard for them to find him, even though snow had fallen twice and obscured his tracks. Deer Tracker had made a fire in front of his little lodge, and the rising smoke and the smell of root tea being cooked in a birch bark cup had drawn them to the place where he was waiting.

And, just as her father had waited to be found, so Willow Woman herself now waited. She had been within the little lodge for a full day and a night, and the Day Traveler had just begun his morning travel. Except for answering the call of nature, she had not left the lodge, and Djidjis had been with her all of this time. He had slept soundly through the night and

238

he had not cried. The babies of the Only People were very good at being quiet when their mothers told them to be silent. They would only cry when they were being teased—as the Talker teased that baby long ago, trying without success to control him—or truly in need of help or very, very hungry. It was important for the little ones to be quiet so as not to frighten away the game or, in the old days, not to let the Ancient Ones that hunted the people know where their human prey was. The loud sound of a crying child, it was said, would attract the dangerous Ancient Ones. If a baby cried too much—and was not suffering from one of those sicknesses that the people knew how to remedy, the colds and pleurisy that a tea made of the root of butterfly weed would quickly cure, for example— then the mother would speak or sing softly to the child while pinching that little one's nose shut: little ones breathing through their mouths had to stop crying.

Willow Woman smiled, remembering the story that Near the Sky had told her about a little frog that sang so often and so loudly without ever listening that it was finally caught and eaten by a heron.

Djidjis had not had the chance to become hungry. As if knowing the exact moment when the child would be hungry, Medicine Plant had come by regularly to breastfeed the baby. The door of the little lodge was open, and Medicine Plant would simply be kneeling there, not appearing suddenly, but just being there where no one had been a mere heartbeat before. It always seemed to happen when Willow Woman was not looking at the door, even though she tried to keep her attention focused there so that she might see, for once, the deep-seeing woman approach and not be surprised. She wished that Talk Talk, her small black friend who even now sat on top of the little debris lodge, would at least give her some warning when Medicine Plant was close. But even though she always would make that small *chuck-chuck* call to alert Willow Woman whenever anyone else drew near, Talk Talk would not do that when the person approaching was the deep-seeing woman. Like the human people, Talk Talk and her bird cousins had too much respect for Medicine Plant.

Djidjis reached up and grasped a handful of Willow Woman's thick, shining black hair. His grip was very strong. All babies have a strong grasp, but Djidjis seemed twice as strong as any other baby that Willow Woman had ever held. When he pulled on her hair it really hurt. But he always did so as if trying to bring her face close to his so that he could look at her better with those amazing eyes of his, those eyes of an old person. Truly this child carried within him the spirit of some elder from long ago, returned to help his people.

Willow Woman stopped her song and looked down at the baby while disentangling his short fingers, one by one, from her hair.

"I know you wish to speak to me," Willow Woman said to the baby. "I see it in your eyes. But even though your spirit knows who you are, this new body of yours has not yet learned enough for it to speak what your spirit understands."

Djidjis looked up at her, as if he did indeed understand every word. Then he slowly turned his head away from her, looking toward the door of the lodge, his eyes appearing to touch someone else's.

It is Medicine Plant, Willow Woman thought. *Once again she has come up on me so silently that I did not know she was close.* But when Willow Woman turned her own eyes toward the door, they did not see what she expected. Instead of the familiar, strong, broad-faced woman who held the secrets of deep-seeing, she saw a person she had never seen before. Not only was this person a stranger, but, although he was a well-formed, strongly muscled man whose narrow face showed his age to be that of an elder, he was no larger than a child of six winters.

Djidjis smiled and then made a small laughing noise. It shocked Willow Woman. Though it was far from the sound of the spoken words for welcome, it was clear that the baby was reaching out to bring the little man into the lodge. Willow Woman said nothing. She could sense that her own words would be too loud, too frightening for this small man to hear. She dropped her own eyes to point with her chin toward the space at her side. Gracefully as an otter, the little man slipped into the lodge and stood very close. He looked at her, as shy as the partridge who will fly up wildly at the first quick move. Then he held out one hand toward Djidjis. The baby grasped the little man's hand with his own small fingers.

Willow Woman looked at the little man's face. He was so close to her that she could hear him breathing. The look on his face was very happy and also very sad. As Djidjis held his hand and tugged at it, Willow Woman saw that the little man's eyes had tears in them, and she felt his overwhelming loneliness. She saw, too, that he was very tired, tired in the way a person becomes when traveling very, very far from home.

He has come to help us, Willow Woman thought, *but we are also going to help him.*

She could feel singing in the lodge, a song she was not sure she had ever heard before. It was coming with her own breath, and she recognized it as a lullaby. She allowed it to grow softly, filling the air around them. When the song finished itself, Djidjis was asleep. His hand still tightly held onto the slightly larger hand of the little man who, with his head leaning against Willow Woman's side and his knees drawn up close to himself, had also given himself to sleep.

CHAPTER THIRTY-EIGHT
STRANDS IN THE WEB

Walking Hill pressed his head against the beech tree, rocking it back and forth until, with a sound like the crashing of thunder, it broke and fell. He split the tree's outer bark with his powerful teeth and used his long nose to pull out the inner bark, stuffing it into his mouth. Although the pain was never gone from him when he ate, he knew that he had to continue to eat to live. And he had to continue to live to be able to wipe out all of the small two-legged ones who had caused him such agony. He was gaunt now and his heavy coat of gray was matted, but he had lost none of his power, none of his speed. His eyes were red, and he seldom slept more than part of the night, not lying down but leaning against the trunk of a tree.

It had been several sleeps since he had found a fresh scent. The trails that he found always either led from the little villages into the Long River, where the dugout canoes of fleeing people had embarked, or—if they were that one familiar scent—back away from the river, up along the narrow valleys before ending at a cliff face or some other place where he could not pass. Those trails were the trails left by the female small being he had not yet been able to catch, trails meant to draw him away from his pursuit and slow him as he came down the Long River. She was like the little biting ones that buzzed in front of his eyes. Always there, always bothering him, yet darting away when he tried to crush them.

242

Walking Hill had grown more cautious following the now-familiar scent of the female small being. Once, as he entered a narrow place between high granite cliffs, an avalanche of great stones had come down toward him. But he had been too quick, had wheeled and run to safety before being crushed. Now he knew that such trails might be a trap, and he would not be caught that way again. He would be cleverer and pretend not to notice her trail, not to notice her trying to get him to follow her into another trap.

Because he had grown more cautious, the female small being had grown bolder. Walking Hill had almost caught her in her boldness. As she came close to the edge of a beaver meadow clearing, where he had concealed himself behind a hill that was once a giant beaver lodge and now was grown high with new grass, she had followed his trail as he had hoped. Then he came thundering out, shaking the earth of the meadow with his heavy feet, cutting her off from the forest and the tall trees. But the small being was too quick for him even then. He had seen her for a time in the tall grass, but her scent had disappeared at the edge of the pond, and though he waited, he had not seen her again or caught her scent. He stood without sleeping at the big pond's edge throughout that day and well into the next morning. Then, accepting at last that he had lost her trail, Walking Hill turned and went back to the river, back to following it south.

As Walking Hill came down the Long River that day, he crossed at a ford in one place and swam the deep water in another, searching on each side for human life that he could destroy. For too many sleeps, all he had found were deserted wigwoms and cold hearths. Now, though, he saw something rising above the trees beyond the next bend. Smoke. Soon he also smelled it and knew that he was close to a place where many of the two-legged ones lived. He moved back from the river, back among the gray-barked trees. He would come upon this place slowly; he would watch and be sure that none of them would escape him. And because his eyes were on that smoke beyond the trees, he did not see the human figure moving quickly upstream, running on the opposite bank of the Long River.

As Sparrow followed the river trail north, he moved with that special swiftness for which he was known. He did not wonder at why Bear Talker had sent him this way. To ask a deep-seeing person how he could see things that were far away or, sometimes, glimpse enough of what was coming toward the people to be able to save them from great troubles, would be like asking an otter how it knew how to swim. It had been clear, looking at the markings on that burned shoulder bone that Bear Talker held before their eyes, shaking it as if it were a rattle, that there was a pattern there to be read. He did not doubt that Bear Talker could read that pattern.

Instead, Sparrow wondered why Bear Talker had sent a useless person such as himself. Until that moment, he had believed that the deep-seeing man had given up long ago on ever making anything of him. Sparrow knew and accepted that he was not like his friend Young Hunter, an important person who had already done something great for the Only People. He did not hold jealousy in his heart, but he did hold disappointment about himself. At times, he would look into his reflection in still water and wonder what it was that was written in his face to make him so uncertain and weak. And, as he looked at that reflection, it seemed as if he saw his own father's face—and that resemblance was reason enough for his failure to be of any good to anyone. The only thing his father had been good at doing was walking away.

Sparrow shook his head to clear it. Why was he standing and looking into this pool of water at the river's edge when he should be running? He looked down at his legs, well covered with leggings made of tough mooseskin and tied on tightly to protect him when he came to thick brush and briars. He looked at his feet, covered by puckered mokasins sewn of the long tubes of skin from a moose's legs. He was ready to run and he would run well.

Running, Sparrow thought as his feet began to move. *That is what I do. I am good at that. I am as quick as a mink on a log, as quick as a trout striking at a fly, as quick as a hummingbird. ...*

That was how Sparrow always made his own feet move faster, by comparing himself with all of the other quick ones around him. He had a long list, and as he ran through it in his mind it was like a song, each line of it carrying him faster and faster along his way. *Quick as the heron striking at the fish, quick as the frog's tongue catching a moth, quick as the flash of the Thunder Beings' lightning spears across the dark sky. ...* And now Sparrow's feet hardly seemed to touch the stones, and he was gliding, his running feet perfectly holding the rhythm of the earth's heartbeat.

At the fishing ledge on the edge of the Long River, Blue Hawk and Red Hawk fed fires that burned higher than they had burned when the racks above them had been covered with drying fish. All of those drying fish were gone now, and no one else was there along the river fishing, even though the shimmer of many fish in the shallows showed that the run was still continuing. Red Hawk and Blue Hawk kept their minds on their task and on each other. Since they had been very small it had been that way, as if the two of them shared one mind and thus could always see in two directions at once, each perfectly aware of the other. That was why Medicine Plant had chosen them for this: to keep the smoke rising, the smoke that would draw the attention of the great and dangerous being that would soon be drawing close.

Rabbit Stick stopped climbing and reached up to grasp the thong around his neck. He smiled at the thought of the way Sweetgrass Woman had stared at him when he came back up from the river, where he had rescued it from the fish-drying rack while all the others were bundling up the dried fish, along with whatever other belongings they would need in their flight. *She thought I had lost this or thrown it away. But I have kept it. After all, it is my own toe.*

Rabbit Stick tapped the dangling dried brown piece of flesh and bone so that it swung back and forth on the end of the thong. *It is mine and ...* Rabbit Stick smiled, *it is important, even at my age, to do some things that will drive my wife crazy. Life is so much more interesting when we have something like this to argue about.*

Rabbit Stick turned and continued the steep climb up the hill. The limp which had bothered him for many days now was gone. It had vanished as soon as he slung the thong around his neck, as if now that it had returned, his severed toe was again doing its duty and restoring health to his stride. He was at the very end of the long line of people making their way up to the Wind Eagle's Place. They could see everything coming toward them in every direction from the Wind Eagle's Place, and if not completely safe there, they would at least be able to see anything dangerous coming toward them from a long way away. There were places, too, where big stones could be rolled down onto the trail, to block the way of anything that pursued.

Few people ever climbed up there unless they were deep-seers or those with a special relationship to the wind. It was said that the great bird that made the wind with its wings liked to come and roost in this spot when it was not in its favorite perch looking out over the big lake to the west. Although the Creator had made that Wind Eagle invisible so that no one could disturb him—as the Talker once did long ago when he was tired of feeling the wind blow and bound the great bird's wings for a time—the presence of the Wind Eagle could be felt up here. But they were following Medicine Plant and Bear Talker, so the Only People and the ones who had survived from the

Bear People villages climbed without question. They might not be comfortable staying on that high place, but with the food and water they brought with them, they could manage to stay there for at least the space of a few days.

Bear Talker, far ahead in the long line of people, stopped and looked back. He waved and Rabbit Stick waved back at him, making the signal that all were accounted for and the deep-seeing man could resume the climb. Instead, Bear Talker waved his arm a second time, making the questioning sign once more. Rabbit Stick smiled. He understood. Bear Talker understood what Rabbit Stick had signaled him, but he was winded from the climb and looking for an excuse to rest a little longer. Rabbit Stick stopped climbing and turned to look around, pretending to see if he could catch sight of anyone who might have straggled behind, even though he knew perfectly well that everyone, from the very young to the very old, was here on the mountainside.

They had been walking for a long time, ever since the first light from the Day Traveler had reddened the Dawn Land sky. Now the Day Traveler was almost to the other horizon. The land stretched out below Rabbit Stick. The Long River was a distant thread from this place, even smaller than from the cliffs on the hills back toward the river, much higher than the slope where Rabbit Stick had fallen. As Rabbit Stick looked back, he thought of how not everyone was there with them. He had listened as Bear Talker and Medicine Plant gave their instructions to the brave young people who remained behind, and he heard echoing in his mind the exact words that Bear Talker had spoken. Rabbit Stick knew he could not be with them, so his worries spoke loudly to him as he heard those words once more.

"If all goes well," Bear Talker said, "we will see all of you again in three dawns. Medicine Plant and I will meet you by the great waterfall."

Tsaga, Bear Talker had said, not *tsiga. If,* not *when.*

247

"It is like the strands of a spider's web that you can see before you on the trail." That was how Bear Talker explained it to him once, explained how a deep-seer could see those things which were coming but had not yet arrived. "You see how all the things on that web are connected, how touching one strand makes all of the others move with it."

The mosquito that had landed on Young Hunter's forehead was starting its meal now. But Young Hunter did not move. It was important for him not to move, to remain as still as stone, to see and not be seen. Only his narrowed eyes and a bit of his forehead were uncovered as he lay there with the elkskin robe over him. He was concealed not only by the robe, but also by the arching canes of the raspberry plants that grew here where the hillside had been burned two seasons before. He could see clearly down to the little shelter made of piled brush where Willow Woman was waiting. His forehead was blackened with charcoal, which stuck to the bear grease rubbed into his skin—enough charcoal to make him hard to see, enough also to keep away the little biting ones. But not enough, it seemed, to keep away this early and very determined mosquito.

Young Hunter sharpened his gaze. Had he seen a small motion near the entrance to the door of the debris shelter? It was hard to say. It was almost as if there had been a rippling in the air, like a wave of heat. But he had seen nothing clearly and Willow Woman did not call to him for help. Even Talk Talk, the young crow that had become Willow Woman's constant companion, did not stir from its place on top of the lodge or call out a warning—as it had already done once earlier when an eagle came swooping low over the beech trees, cocking a head at the strange sight below it of a man's head peering out from a raspberry bush, and then lifting back up into the wind. Young Hunter strained his ears to listen. When he began to hear Willow Woman's voice singing a familiar lullaby, he relaxed again.

"But that which is coming is not set in its pattern, not like the print of an animal's foot which shows the direction where it has passed, a direction that cannot be changed. That web of what is coming is more like a path in front of you," Bear Talker explained, "or like many paths in front of you. Each strand of the web is a path. We, who see deeply, are just able to see farther along those paths. Then, when you come to the places we have already seen, you can decide whether to go that way or not."

The mosquito was now feasting. It seemed as if Young Hunter could hear it sucking his blood. The tickle of its legs and the sharp stab of its bite made it hard for Young Hunter to remain still, but he did not move, aside from wrinkling his forehead. The mosquito shifted its legs and continued to drink.

At least the mosquito was alone and not one of a swarm. Young Hunter remembered the story about Lazy Man, Malkoke, the one who was too lazy to even wave his arms to drive the mosquitoes away. But Lazy Man always could find a reason for his laziness. When someone saw all the mosquitoes on him and asked him why he did not simply shoo them away, Lazy Man had an answer: "These mosquitoes have already finished and they are just resting now. If I drive them away, that will leave space for more mosquitoes to come who are still hungry."

The big elkskin was arched back over Young Hunter in such a way that it made a small tent beneath the raspberry tangle. Behind him, the three dogs were as silent beneath the elkskin as was their master. Even Pabesis was calm. Young Hunter reached one hand back to stroke their heads, letting his hand rest longest on the broad head of the youngest dog. Since saving Rabbit Stick's life, Pabesis had begun behaving in a new way. It was as if the old wisdom he held inside him had finally gained control over the awkwardness of his growing body and over that desire to play, which all dogs share, but which is sometimes intolerable in those still part-puppy.

Only a moon ago, Young Hunter would not have trusted the young dog to have the patience to remain silent this long. But when he had called Agwedjiman and Danowa to him after hearing the words of Bear Talker and Medicine Plant, Pabesis had come up to him, placed one paw in Young Hunter's lap, and looked up into his eyes. *I can help you*—that was the message Pabesis gave him. And Young Hunter had accepted that offer. Now, Pabesis, too, was a strand in the web.

Strands in the web, linking together to make the pattern of that which was coming. Strands that might hold or strands that might be broken.

CHAPTER THIRTY-NINE
TRAILS COMING TOGETHER

Sparrow found them where they crossed the trail and then disappeared into the water, at the fording place where one could wade across waist-deep on the gravel riverbed. They came out of the forest and went right across the riverside trail he had been following. He had been running for a long time; the Day Traveler had moved the width of five hands across the sky, and it was well past the middle of the day. It was only when he stumbled, as his foot fell into a depression pressed deeply into the soft earth at the Long River's edge, that he stopped running. When he saw what they were—tracks, giant tracks—he felt a weakness come into his legs, and he could hardly stand.

He went down on one knee to measure the width of one of the strange tracks. They were almost as round as a bowl, like no other animal prints he had ever seen before. This single footprint was wider than both of his hands with fingers spread out! He stood and looked back at the length of this animal's giant stride. How could any animal be this large? Truly, this must be one of the ancient dangerous ones, one of the ones that hunted the people in the winter stories of that old time when the mountains of ice covered much of the land. This was the one the People of the Bear had spoken of, the one only a few of them had seen in the distance behind them as they fled

251

in their dugouts down the Long River—an angry four-legged being as large as a walking hill.

Sparrow wrinkled his nose. There was a strong, musty smell here, too, so unfamiliar that he knew it, too, came from this creature. The tracks led into the river, and he knew that there would be further tracks on the other side, heading down the Long River. It had crossed not long before he reached this place. The dirt was still loose and crumbled when he touched the edge of the deepest tracks. But he would not follow across the river. That was not what he had been sent to do. His job was to find the one who had warned the Bear People—the person who had come into their villages and filled them with such fear that they fled without taking their possessions with them. That person would be coming toward the river trail, following the tracks of the great beast; of that Sparrow was now certain—unless the great beast had finally caught that person.

But there were no other tracks here—no human tracks, at least. Sparrow looked into the forest. He could see where the great beast had shouldered aside some trees and splintered others. He breathed deeply in and out several times to try to slow the pounding of his heart as he thought of its power. Then he began to follow the tracks back into the forest.

The soft whistle that came from the debris shelter was one of the signals they had agreed upon for calling to each other. It was the signal for him to come. Young Hunter slid from beneath the elkskin, using his motion as an opportunity at last to brush away from his forehead the now fat-bodied mosquito, which flew lazily away. The three dogs came out behind him, heads down, fanning out to circle around the little lodge.

Twelve quick paces and Young Hunter was at the door. He bent down to look in and what he saw took his breath away. It was clear that Willow Woman's lullaby had been a good one. There, sleeping peacefully in her arms, was little Djidjis; while next to her a skinny, large-nosed person, no larger than a child of five or six winters, was also sleeping, his head resting trustingly against Willow Woman's side.

Another head thrust itself next to Young Hunter's: Pabesis'. Danowa and Agwedjiman had held back, watching to either side of the lodge while Young Hunter looked in, but Pabesis could not restrain his curiosity. *Perhaps,* Young Hunter thought, *he has not quite finished being a puppy.* Even as Young Hunter thought that, Pabesis gave a happy whine.

It was not loud, but it was loud enough. The small sleeping man opened his eyes and stared at Young Hunter and Pabesis. At first there was some surprise in the small one's eyes, but it vanished so quickly that Young Hunter himself was surprised. It was as if the little man had looked into Young Hunter's heart and been reassured by what he saw there. A broad smile spread across the little man's angular face, and it grew even broader as he turned his gaze to the dog.

Suddenly, quick as a weasel grabbing a rabbit, the little man leaped at Pabesis, wrapping his arms around the young dog's neck. The two of them went rolling out of the door of the lodge, knocking loose the main supporting limb that held the lodge up. The debris shelter collapsed over Young Hunter and Willow Woman, who bent over Djidjis as the roof caved in. Leaves and twigs went down Young Hunter's neck as he thrust his arms out, pushing the remains of the shelter aside so that he and Willow Woman sat there facing each other in the midst of the wreckage.

He expected the baby to begin crying, but instead, Djidjis woke up making the happy cooing sound of a child who is being amused in the best possible way.

"Look," Willow Woman said, pointing with her lips behind Young Hunter.

Young Hunter pulled a twig out of his ear and brushed the dry remains of maple leaves out of his hair as he turned to look at whatever was so amusing to his wife and the baby.

There, rolling over and over on the ground, were Pabesis and the little man. Both of them were making the yelping play sounds of young dogs. On either side of them, their eyebrows raised in what appeared to be both disapproval and disbelief, Danowa and Agwedjiman were watching.

As Blue Hawk placed more branches on the fire, he saw from the corner of his eyes a motion in the trees. It was a subtle motion and yet it was also as if the whole forest itself were moving. Something gray and massive was there, breathing, moving more silently than something that large should be able to move. The trees were a long spear's throw away from the place where they fed the fires by the river's edge, but now Blue Hawk wondered if the distance was enough. Because he was the older of the twins, having emerged and drawn breath a few heartbeats before his identical brother, he was the one who usually made the decisions for the two of them. Sometimes that was not a hard task, but now, when he knew their lives depended upon his judgment, he was deeply worried, even if he tried not to show it.

"Brother," he said in a low voice to Red Hawk, whose back was turned toward that part of the forest since he was looking upstream in the direction they had thought it would come from, "we are ... "

"Not alone?" Red Hawk said.

"Uh-hunh, Brother," Blue Hawk continued. "Let us move a little closer ... "

"To the river's edge?" Red Hawk said. "I agree, Brother. I feel the eyes of something watching us."

"Do not move too quickly, Brother," Blue Hawk whispered, as he dropped the last of the branches onto the fire and began to edge his way closer to the river.

"Do not move too slowly, Brother," Red Hawk answered.

The tracks led straight to the edge of a meadow formed long before by the dams of beavers. Such places were often good hunting for deer and moose, and although this was clearly a place where there was much game, Sparrow had seen no markings to show that it was anyone's hunting territory. Perhaps someday he might want to come and build a lodge here. It was a beautiful place.

But it would be lonely. It would be a full day's journey away from the fishing village of the Only People on the Long River and even farther away from their winter village back toward the Waters in Between. Now that the Bear People had left the northern stretches of the river, there would be no one close for Sparrow to be with. And he knew that he would have no wife to come to this place with him, to help him start a new village as some young people did when the urge to find a new place came upon them.

Sparrow continued to follow the big animal's prints. They led right to the edge of a big pond where a large beaver lodge, which looked to be twice the height of a tall man, could be seen in the deepest water just off the shore. The tracks went back and forth many times. The ground was pounded flat here and there were trees broken and pulled up. The big animal had waded in deep and then come out again. Had it been hunting for beaver? The mud bottom had probably begun to pull it down, and it knew it might be caught if it did not come out. With all of that weight, despite the width of its huge feet, the great beast might be trapped if it went into a boggy area.

Sparrow leaned over the edge, looking down into the still water to see his own reflection. The waters of the pond were dark and it was hard to see deeply within them, but there seemed to be something moving down there. Was it a large beaver? He leaned closer, and as he did so, something came out of the water, grasped him, and pulled him in headfirst. The water closed around his feet, leaving only a spume of bubbles and a few ripples on the surface of the pond.

Is this what all the Mikumwesu are like? Young Hunter thought. In the short time since the little man had been leading them along the trail that ran south and parallel to the Long River, he had already discovered that, compared to Mikumwesu, the high spirits of Pabesis were like those of a turtle.

Mikumwesu kept running around Young Hunter and the two dogs, jumping up on their backs, tickling them, trying to wrestle with them. It had been hard enough to settle Pabesis down after Mikumwesu had been playing with him, but now even Agwedjiman seemed to have been infected by the little person's spirit of play. In fact, Young Hunter himself could not help but smile. If all of the Mikumwesu were as filled with fun as this little man, then their lives with each other must be filled with as much joy as those of the otters.

Young Hunter stopped walking. It had come to him as clearly as if it had been spoken to him. *Mikumwesu is not with others of his kind now.* Was his joy a result of loneliness?

After separating himself from Pabesis and the game of rolling around, the Mikumwesu had stood up with great dignity, wiped the leaves from his arms and chest, straightened the rabbitskin robe belted around his waist, and then spoken to them. His words were clearly some kind of greeting, but they were in no language either Young Hunter or Willow Woman could speak. The little man had continued speaking, moving his hands as he spoke to try to explain his quick flow of words. But even the language of his hands was so quick, like the motion of a bird's wings, that Young Hunter and Willow Woman found it hard to follow. Finally the little man saw that they could not understand and slowed down.

He placed one hand on his chest. "Mikumwesu," he said, speaking the word used by the Dawn Land People for the little ones that most people only saw in stories or dreams. "Uh-hunh?"

"Uh-hunh," Young Hunter said. "Mikumwesu."

The little man had smiled then and made more signs with his hands. This time, the motions were slow enough to understand. He cupped his hand over his chest and held it out. He was offering his help to them.

He touched Willow Woman and Djidjis and then made walking signs as he raised his hand up and then formed a circle. Willow Woman was to take Djidjis and go join the rest of the people up the mountain.

He placed his hand on Young Hunter and then joined his fingers together and moved his linked hands toward the Always Summer Land. Young Hunter was to come with him and go that way, down the river.

He spread his arms wide and made the motion of something huge walking, then grasped Young Hunter's hand and held up their hands together as if to halt its progress. Together, they would stop the Great Walking One.

With Talk Talk flying ahead and Danowa scouting behind her, Willow Woman set out on the trail to the mountain. With their small new friend, Young Hunter and Agwedjiman turned their faces in the direction of the Always Summer Land. And as they walked, while the Day Traveler crossed the Sky Land above them, Mikumwesu frolicked and played.

Now, though, as the thought crossed Young Hunter's mind that Mikumwesu might be alone, Mikumwesu suddenly stopped playing. He dropped the stick that he had been throwing for Pabesis to fetch. He walked straight to Young Hunter and looked up into his eyes. As Young Hunter looked back, he saw that there were tears in Mikumwesu's eyes, and he read the loneliness that was, indeed, held within the small one's heart.

Young Hunter went down onto one knee and held out his hand, grasping the small man's own hand at the wrist.

"Little Brother," Young Hunter said, "it seems you are able to read my heart. Know this, Little Brother, when we have done what we must do here, if I survive, I will help you to search for your own people."

CHAPTER FORTY
THE BEAVER LODGE

Sparrow had always been a good swimmer. Even as a small child he had enjoyed few things more than slipping into a certain sheltered cove in the waters of the Long River where a family of otters often came. He had heard that those little playful ones would sometimes allow a human child to take part in their sport. So, with patience that Sparrow was never able to show with human beings, he had waited and watched by the shore, until the day came when one of the otters came humping up to him, carrying a small flat stone balanced on its head, and dropped the stone at his feet.

From that day on, Sparrow joined the otters many times in their game of dropping a stone to the bottom and then diving to find it. Thus, he had learned long ago how to take a deep breath and hold it before diving beneath the surface.

He had taken such a deep breath as those strong hands came suddenly out of the water of the beaver pond and pulled him in. He opened his eyes beneath the water and found himself being pushed forward and downward toward the underwater entrance of the large beaver lodge he had noticed just off the shore in the deepest part of the pond. Whoever held his shoulders firmly from behind was larger and stronger than he was, yet he felt no fur on that body which was so close to him. It was not one of the beaver people. It was said that even

258

when they took the form of humans, the beaver people still kept their furry coats. Sparrow kicked his legs and reached his arms out to pull himself into that entrance to the beaver lodge. He had done this before. If a man had narrow shoulders, he could easily squeeze in through the tunnel that led up into the lodge, where there would be a dry shelf on which, in a lodge as large as this one, several human persons could easily fit, though the low roof would prevent them from sitting up.

Sparrow's kick lifted him up in the water to press against the body of his captor, and he realized, with sudden excitement, that the one behind him was clearly a woman. Now, though, he was in the tunnel and could not look back. He pulled himself forward carefully with his hands. If a beaver was in the tunnel, it would not harm him unless he grabbed it hard from behind or ran headfirst into one coming toward him. Beaver were gentle creatures, he knew. In winter, a hunter could walk across the ice, make a hole in the lodge, and reach in with his arm to stroke the backs of the beaver resting in the lodge. They would make no move to bite him as long as he stroked their backs. Then, when his hand found the base of a beaver's tail, he could grab hold of it and pull it quickly out. Sometimes one could catch several beaver that way before the others took fright and dove into the little pond in the center of their lodge to escape beneath the ice. However, once a beaver had been pulled from its lodge, it was more than ready to bite, and if a beaver took hold of a person, it would bite off a big piece of flesh with its wedge-shaped teeth.

Sparrow's head came up in the center of the little pool inside the lodge. There was light in there, filtering down from the breathing hole left in the lodge roof. The ledge was just ahead of him, and he pulled himself halfway up onto it to look around as his eyes grew accustomed to the shadowy light. The ledge had been covered with ferns and other sweet-smelling plants and was almost as soft as a bearskin robe. A large female beaver lying on her side with two small kits at her breasts

259

looked at him from less than an arm's length away. She made a soft chattering sound between her teeth—reminding him that he was welcome as long as he kept his distance—and then turned her attention back to her little ones.

Sparrow pulled himself fully onto the ledge and leaned up on one arm to look around the rest of the lodge. Another, younger beaver was lying on its stomach at the far end. It had not even opened its eyes to see the new visitor. The surface of the little pool boiled with motion as a larger male beaver glided up from the depths and surged onto the ledge. It paid no attention at all to Sparrow, simply shouldering its way past him and crawling over Sparrow's outstretched legs to waddle over and nuzzle against the nursing female. She made sounds that Sparrow thought were surely a warm and happy greeting, and she reached up with her paws to pat the sides of the male beaver's face. He held out in its own paws the stick he had brought to her, a carefully cut piece of alder still covered with sweet-tasting bark. As she took his offering and the male beaver began to play with the two young ones, Sparrow turned his gaze away from them. His eyes were moist with tears, and he knew that he would never again be able to think of hunting beaver in their winter lodges.

For the first time, Sparrow noticed the pouch. It was made of white, smoke-tanned leather and embroidered with porcupine quills. It hung from the roof of the lodge just over the pool. Surely it had been hung there by the person who had pulled him into the water and brought him to this lodge. But where was that woman now? Sparrow looked over the surface of the pool. A single, peeled stick floated on it, going around and around. Then, at the center of the pool, something dark began to rise. Sparrow held his breath as he watched, not moving, not even blinking his eyes. The water parted about it, and he could see that it was the head of a person, not a beaver. It was a woman with thick, dark hair, which was wound around her face so that only her eyes could be seen. Her eyes looked straight into Sparrow's, and it seemed to him as if he had never seen eyes so dark and filled with sorrow as hers. It seemed, too, as if he had never seen eyes so beautiful, as large and beautiful as those of a doe. One hand came up out of the water, a strong-looking, finely shaped hand that grasped the ledge close to Sparrow. Then, with a motion as smooth and quick as that of the beaver itself, she was up on the ledge beside him.

"Have you seen it?" She spoke no louder than a whisper, but her voice was deep and throaty, and it thrilled Sparrow to hear it. Although he still could see no more of her face than her eyes, for she held her long black hair across her face with one hand, he noticed the firmness and fine shape of her body beneath her wet clothing, a soft-tanned robe of deerskin which was belted at the waist and which ended just below her knees. Suddenly, he felt a shyness he had never felt before with a woman. Always before, he had been the quickest-tongued of all the young men, the one always ready with a word to flatter or charm the girls, but here, in this magical place with this strange woman beside him, he could not make his mouth speak a single word.

The woman reached out her other hand and struck him on his shoulder with her open palm. "Answer me," she hissed. "Have you seen the Walking Hill?"

She has touched me, Sparrow thought. *What is wrong with me? My mind is as simple as that of a child of four winters.*

Somehow, though, he managed to speak.

"*Nda,*" he said.

"No? No? Are you certain? It does not give up easily. It could still be waiting for me. While you were standing there by the water like a foolish child, it could have crept up on us and killed us both. Once it waited for me for three sunrises beneath a great tree before it went away."

"Tracks," Sparrow said. He seemed to be unable to say more than a single word at a time.

"Tracks?" Her voice indicated that she was growing disgusted with him, so he took a deeper breath this time.

261

"I did not see it," Sparrow said. "But I found the place, a look away from here, where it crossed the Long River, going downstream."

The woman grabbed his shoulder. "Downstream?" she said. "But the fishing village of the Only People is downstream. I must warn them before it reaches them."

Sparrow reached up and grasped the hand that held his shoulder so tightly that it hurt—even though he did not mind the pain at all.

"It is all right," Sparrow said. "My people know that a great monster, one that hunts the human beings, is coming toward them. They are ready. Our deep-seeing people—and one of them is my best friend—" Sparrow said, letting some pride creep into his voice, "they have seen this. They know about you, as well. That is why I am here; I was sent to find you."

The woman let go of his shoulder but did not pull her hand from his grasp. Sparrow was glad of that.

"What do they know of me?" she asked. She pressed the hand that held her long hair across her face more firmly against her hidden cheek, and for the first time her voice seemed uncertain. Again Sparrow found himself looking deeply into her eyes, and he had to remind himself that a question had been asked and that it was his turn to speak.

"They know ... ," he said, seeking the right words, "they know you have been warning the people. They know you are very brave. So they have sent me to find you so that you can help us to defeat the monster. You can trust our deep-seeing people: Medicine Plant and Bear Talker and Young Hunter."

"Medicine Plant?" the woman said. She pulled her hand away from Sparrow's. She turned away from him and, for a few breaths, her shoulders shook, though Sparrow could not tell if she was laughing or crying. Then, not turning back toward him, she spoke.

"I have heard of Medicine Plant," she said.

CHAPTER FORTY-ONE
TWO ANCIENT ONES

Walking Hill moved through the alders at the edge of the river more silently than it seemed any animal of his size should be able to move. He barely lifted his feet from the earth as he moved, almost gliding. His thick gray coat was the same color as the trees themselves, and he blended in with them the way fog blends into the surface of a stream. The small breeze was blowing toward him from the place where the two small beings were bent over their fires. Soon, it would be close enough to charge at them, to scatter their fires, to lift them and crush them against the folded bedrock that flowed into the Long River like thick frozen syrup.

When he had killed them, then he would follow the trail that he had scented, a trail that surely led to more of their round nests and their fires. None of the four-legged ones were to be seen, the ones that made so much noise when they caught his scent. Walking Hill would not need to lure the four-legged ones away by pretending to run from them and then circling back to catch them, moving more quickly than they expected. Killing the two-legged ones would be easy, for they seemed at times to be deaf and blind. With a few exceptions, they were not hard to catch, not hard to destroy. His huge ears pressed back against the sides of his head, Walking Hill moved a little closer with each breath.

Blue Hawk and Red Hawk had stopped speaking with
their voices as soon as both knew that the monster was close.
Instead, as they fed the fire from either side, they communi-
cated with the small hand signals used by stalking hunters.

"Now?" Red Hawk signaled.

"Not yet," Blue Hawk answered.

"Great being? Where?"

"Behind you."

From the alders behind them came the sound of a single
limb, and not a small one at that, cracking from the weight of
something pressing against it.

"We go?" Red Hawk signaled. He could not see what was
behind him, but he could feel eyes piercing his back. He
looked into Blue Hawk's eyes and saw how wide they were. The
look on his brother's face was that of a field mouse cornered
by a black snake.

Something within Red Hawk told him that if he turned
around, what he saw would be his last sight before beginning
the long walk to the Sky Land. Instead, moving faster than he
had ever moved before, he scooped up a great double handful
of the burning coals and hurled them back over his shoulder.
At the same time, he leaped forward, grabbing his brother's
arm and spinning him away from whatever it was that had
frozen him, whatever it was that now screamed from close
behind as the burning coals struck it.

The scream was so loud and so close that the whole world
seemed to shake and Red Hawk stumbled, but he did not let
go of his brother's arm. He did not stop. He did not look back.
The folded stone of the riverbank slanted steeply down, and
the two of them half-ran and half-slid down it. It was always
moist in this spot from the spray of the rushing water, but they
kept their footing and did not fall. The bedrock shook beneath
them from the incredibly heavy tread of that which now
pursued them, but it could not keep its balance as they did.
They heard it stumble and fall the way a giant stone falls down

a mountainside. Then a great wash of water went over them from the wave thrown up by its body hitting the water.

Again the great beast screamed, but Red Hawk and Blue Hawk did not stop or look back. They reached the small, light dugout hidden beneath the bank, right at the edge of the swift flow of the water, the dugout so perfectly balanced that its stern rested on the stones and its prow moved gently back and forth with the rush of the current.

They did not climb in. Instead, Red Hawk ran into the shallow water on one side of the dugout and Blue Hawk ran on the other side, until they had pushed the dugout into the hip-deep water. Then they rolled into the boat, with Red Hawk in the back, grabbing cedar wood paddles and dipping them into the water, again and again, again and again, still without looking back. Now they were in the strongest part of the current, and the wind behind them pushed them even harder.

Red Hawk took a deep breath, feeling as if knives were being driven into his sides. His palms and fingers were beginning to blister from the burns he had suffered when he scooped up the burning coals. Still, he did not stop paddling. But as he lifted his paddle, he turned his head and looked back. What seemed to be a great snake without a head lifted up from the river no more than four boat lengths behind them!

Young Hunter had come to this place in the oak forest before, but not often. The great hollow oak tree, which only the huge pines of the hilltops bested in height, was regarded by the people as an elder of its people. Sometimes the deep-seeing people would come to leave small offerings near its base—to show respect for the tree and to give thanks for the blessing of the acorns that its relatives gave to the Dawn Land People.

Like the caves sometimes used as shelters by families when they traveled, hollow trees as large as the great oak could also serve as temporary homes, but no humans had ever resided in this tree. This was a place where the bears came to live within the hollow in the oak tree's trunk. No one hunted them here, avoiding the tree out of respect for the bears, but last spring Bear Talker had noted that fresh bear tracks no longer led to and from the great hollow tree. Perhaps even the bears had been made uneasy by the tree's imposing age.

Mikumwesu looked up at Young Hunter and spoke. The two of them had discovered, as they made the long walk to this place, that if the little man spoke only a few words and spoke them very slowly, he could make himself understood.

"Our ... friends ... wait ... here," Mikumwesu said, indicating the two dogs with a lift of his chin.

Young Hunter raised his hand and then lowered it, palm down. Agwedjiman and Pabesis sat down on their haunches, tails wagging. Young Hunter shifted the weight of the three-winters-old buck, which he had hunted at Mikumwesu's request. It was needed, Mikumwesu said, as a present.

It had been easy hunting. The cedar swamp herd of deer had many young ones that had survived the past winter, and Young Hunter knew the places where they would be on their trails at this time of day, when the Day Traveler was only a few hands away from his nightly rest. Young Hunter and Mikumwesu and the dogs had hidden where the small wind blew in their faces from the trail and had watched as the herd went past them in single file. When the young buck with a limp passed, the one Young Hunter had picked out only a few days before, Young Hunter raised his arm that held the atlatl and whipped his spear through the air to cut the lame buck's cord of breath.

As Mikumwesu walked toward the tree, Young Hunter lagged behind. He sensed something familiar here, something as unsettling as the touch of a spider's legs on the raised hairs at the back of his neck. The earth was soft under his feet, cushioned by more generations of leaves from the old oak tree than he could count. Some of those brown leaves rattled underfoot, leaves that had clung to the tree all through the cold season and had only been pushed from the branches by the new swelling buds that made the highest branches of the tree seem to pulsate with green life.

Mikumwesu was in front of the great hollow in the tree, a deep blackness like the mouth of a giant animal. He spoke in that quick, high voice of his, and Young Hunter heard something within the tree move in response.

Mikumwesu held out one small hand toward the hollow, and from within the tree another hand emerged, a hand that seemed to be as large as the small man himself. Mikumwesu grasped the long fingers of that hand with both of his hands and stepped back, pulling—like a robin steps back, drawing a worm from the earth. A long arm followed that hand, an arm gray and knotted with muscles like stone. Then a shoulder and a head, as the great man-shaped being came out on its knees, like a little child being pulled forth by an elder.

Only once before had Young Hunter been this close to what he now saw to be one of the gray giants, the fire hunters who had seemed ready to destroy all that they encountered. Only two winters ago, he had faced the one-eyed leader of those Ancient Ones, and blinded it with a small spear shot from the Long Thrower. He had thought all of those gray giants had perished in the landslide that followed—until he had seen what seemed to be an Ancient One at the top of the cliff the day Rabbit Stick fell from the high cave. Now he knew that his eyes had not deceived him then.

Young Hunter stepped forward, wondering why it was that he felt no fear as the Ancient One turned its head to look at him.

CHAPTER FORTY-TWO
RIVER WOMAN

As they ran along the trail back to the Long River, Sparrow marveled at the long strides the strange woman took. She ran as he did, gliding with the wind, just ahead of him. She would not let him come up to her or go ahead of her, and she turned her face aside each time he tried to look closely at her. But he did not need to see her face to see how strong she was, how graceful.

Is this woman Mannigebeskwas? Is she the Woman Who Walks Alone, the one who lives in the forest? People had joked that only that woman-being out of the old stories would ever satisfy Sparrow, that he was like his father, always seeking something that was as insubstantial as the mists over the Long River when the Day Traveler began his morning travel. *Or is she one of the old dangerous ones who disguises herself as human to lead a person into danger?*

Sparrow pondered as he ran, dismissing his other questions. No, this was a real woman, a woman of the people. Her desire was to help him and help the people. Still, he did not understand why he had never heard of her before. She was probably from one of the upriver villages—one of the People of the Bear. Even though those villages were very far upriver, the word always passed eventually from one village to another about special people and unusual happenings until it came to the Only People. Yet Sparrow had heard nothing about a tall, strong young woman such as this.

They reached the river even more quickly than he had expected, coming to it upstream from the crossing place where he had seen the tracks of the Walking Hill.

"Stay back," the woman said, motioning at him with her hands as she vaulted down the bank, lightly as a doe leaping over a log. Sparrow did as she said. It was strange how good it felt to do as she said, to have her tell him what to do.

The woman vanished in the brush, then came out, dragging one end of a dugout canoe which had a long coil of rope in the back of it. She stepped into the canoe and moved to the bow. Taking a paddle in her hand, she crouched on one knee.

"Hurry now," she said without looking back at him, "push us off."

Her long hair still covered the whole side of her face that was closest to him, but Sparrow knew that she saw him out of the corner of her eye. He dove off the bank, doing a flip in midair as he did so and landing on his feet in the sand right at the back of the canoe.

"Stop playing," the woman said. Her voice was gruff, but Sparrow could tell she was impressed. He pushed hard and jumped in as the canoe slipped into the current. There was a second paddle in the bottom of the canoe, along with a pole that could be used to push off against the bottom. Sparrow took the pole and used it to thrust them forward even faster toward the place where the current ran smoothly and swiftly. As he did so, he remembered one of the wintertime stories Young Hunter's grandmother had told when he was a little child.

"In the old days," Sweetgrass Woman said, "the Owner Creator made the rivers so that they flowed upstream on one bank and downstream on the other. To get anywhere, all the people had to do was pole their dugouts over to the correct side of the river. There were no waterfalls and no rapids in all the rivers."

"Why is it not that way today, Grandmother?" Sparrow was the one who spoke. Even back then he was always the one to ask questions first.

"Laziness," Sweetgrass Woman said. "The people got too lazy. That was back when the maple syrup flowed out of the trees all the time and when there were no thorns on the bushes and the berries were always ripe. People became so fat and lazy that they did not even brush their hair or wash themselves. They smelled bad!

"The Owner Creator wondered what it was that smelled so bad. The Owner Creator looked and saw that it was the Only People. Then the Owner Creator sent the One Who Shaped Himself to change things, to make things harder for the people so they would appreciate things and not be lazy. That was when rapids and waterfalls were put into the rivers and the rivers were all made so they only flow downstream."

They were floating downstream rapidly now, and Sparrow used his paddle more to guide the dugout than to speed its way. In places, it was hard not to graze the backs or sides of fish as he dipped his paddle. The river was filled with fish swimming upstream in great numbers, as always in this season when so much life returned. It was as if the river of water were filled with another river, a river of shimmering finned life flowing in the opposite direction. A huge flock of pigeons passed low over them, heading for one of their roosting spots in the chestnut woods that covered the slope of the sunset side of the Long River, and for a time, all that Sparrow could hear was the beating of countless wings. Then they rounded a bend where a hill cut off sight of the pigeon flock and the water was deeper and smoother. Sparrow took a deep breath. He would speak to her now.

"I have something of yours," Sparrow said. "You forgot it when we left the beaver lodge."

He untied from his belt the embroidered pouch that had hung from the top of the lodge and held it forward. Without looking back, the woman reached one hand back and took the pouch, brushing Sparrow's fingers as she did so. She brought it forward to look at it and then reached back again behind her to drop the pouch by Sparrow's knees.

"It is not mine," she said. "I never saw it before."

Sparrow picked up the pouch and studied it, wondering what was inside it. But he did not have time now to look. He could tell from the woman's voice that this was not her pouch. But whose had it been? Was it meant to be a gift to him from the beaver people? Sparrow had heard of such things happening, of people entering the homes of animals, places where the animals took on the shapes of human beings when they were alone. Sometimes a person who was a welcome guest in the home of an animal would be given something. Sparrow vowed that he would make a trip back to that beaver lodge and leave something for the beavers by the side of the pond to show his gratitude.

"We are turning," the woman said, her voice once again gruff.

Sparrow quickly tied the pouch back to his belt and picked up the paddle from the bottom of the dugout, straightening the boat with a few strokes.

"I am Sparrow," he said. "I do not know your name."

His only answer for a time was the rhythm of her paddle entering the water and the sound of her breathing. His eyes were on the muscles of her shoulders and upper arms as she paddled.

"Are you the Woman Who Walks Alone?" Sparrow tried to make his voice playful, but his words almost choked him as he spoke them and he was barely able to get them out.

"Perhaps," the woman said. Her voice was not gruff now, but sad.

"Shall I call you that name?"

"*Nda,*" the woman said. Her voice was almost as hesitant now as Sparrow's. She stopped paddling for a breath and hunched her shoulders as if listening to the river's waves, which slapped against the side of the boat almost like an insistent voice. Her left hand grasped the side of the boat and held it so tightly that the wood creaked and her knuckles grew pale. For a moment, Sparrow thought she was about to turn and face him. Instead, in a soft voice, she spoke.

"Call me ... River Woman," she said.

Then, lifting her paddle, she began to stroke harder than before.

CHAPTER FORTY-THREE
TWO FIRES

Young Hunter's face showed no expression as the gray giant tore one of the front legs from the deer, stripped away the skin with its long fingernails, and then, after glancing sideways at him, began to tear off the raw flesh with its large teeth.

The strange part of all this, Young Hunter thought, *is not my own lack of fear. The strange thing is that this Ancient One seems to be afraid of me.*

It had been that way ever since Mikumwesu had drawn the giant man out of his hiding place in the hollow tree. The Ancient One had stared at Young Hunter in a way that indicated both familiarity and something close to panic. He had looked with alarm at Young Hunter; then, with the same alarm, up at the Day Traveler, who had not yet dipped beneath the horizon; then back at Young Hunter again. Mikumwesu had patted the giant's arm, then motioned for Young Hunter to come forward—not too fast, slowly—and place the deer's body on the earth by the giant's feet.

It was almost dark now. Young Hunter turned back to laying the bed for his fire, leaning small twigs together and making another leaning pile of large sticks above them. He had carried a coal with him, kept alive in its bed of punk in the clamshell fire carrier hung from his belt, so he did not have to

273

use a fire drill but had only to tip the coal out into the tinder and blow it into life. The fire was reflected by the large eyes of the Ancient One as he stood and walked slowly toward it, bringing the remains of the deer carcass with him like a great bear carrying a rabbit.

Mikumwesu was with the Ancient One, had never left his side. The little man pointed to a spot on the ground across the fire from Young Hunter, and the giant man sat there. There was another look in the Ancient One's eyes as he leaned toward the fire. It was, Young Hunter realized, a look of grateful relief. It was like the look in the eyes of a small child who, left alone in the lodge, has wakened from a dream of monsters and found his mother leaning over him. The Ancient One put the deer carcass down, lifted one long hand, then paused and looked again at Young Hunter. It was the look of one asking permission to continue.

Young Hunter made the sign for yes, moving his index finger up and down.

The Ancient One drove the long fingernails of both hands into the deer's throat. He pulled, and with a *crack* like the branch of a green tree breaking, the carcass split open. The gray giant reached in with two fingers, delicately scooped out the heart and liver, and placed them at the edge of the fire so that they would be seared by the flames.

Young Hunter shook his head. This was as confusing as walking next to himself on a trail, not knowing where his spirit was taking his body. He put more wood on the fire from the tall pile of dried sticks he had gathered to keep the blaze burning throughout the night.

Young Hunter looked at Mikumwesu, trying to understand, to see within the things that were happening and not have his eyes stop at the outward appearance. Bear Talker had told him that he could do this, and Medicine Plant had agreed that it was a gift that he had been given. A gift that he had to learn to accept, even if it was a gift he had never requested.

Young Hunter realized that he was breathing very fast, so he tried to make his breaths slower and deeper. He put more sticks on the fire, and as he did so, as the sparks flew up, he saw.

He saw that, large as the Ancient One was, he was not merely the last of the gray giants, but also the youngest. He saw that, small as Mikumwesu was, he was much older—not only older than Young Hunter, but older than the Ancient One, older than the great hollow oak behind him. Seeing this, Young Hunter began to understand.

"The Walking Hill ... is in ... pain," Mikumwesu said. He used his hands as he spoke, making the signs for the words. "I ... feel the pain. We all ... go to the great falls. There ... we all ... help."

Red Hawk did not know how long he had been paddling and feeling the breath of the great monster close behind him. But when at last, far, far down the Long River, he looked back, he saw that it was no longer in the water behind them. It was climbing out onto the bank, the water streaming from its long hair, shaking itself, and then following, running on the shore, its determined angry eyes still upon them. But it could not move as fast as the dugout and the river was wider here.

Red Hawk touched his brother's shoulder.

Blue Hawk spoke without turning. "It is ... ?"

"Not gone," Red Hawk said. "But we can rest now."

Even without paddling they were leaving farther behind the beast that was as large as a walking hill. Red Hawk knew, though, that this would not last. They would soon come to another place where the river washed over a sandbar and was shallow enough to slow them. But the place they wanted was upstream from that sandbar, although on the same side of the river as the bank on which the great beast was now running.

In fact, for they had traveled farther and faster than Red Hawk realized, the place they were aiming for was suddenly before them at the bend just ahead. There the flow of the stream had cut into the bank between two huge boulders, each ten times the size of a wigwom. The river was not as high as at the beginning of the thaw; its waters had receded from between and beneath the two overhanging boulders, which angled to form a great lean-to. The two brothers aimed the dugout at that spot, splitting a silver line of fish that surged along through the current close to the shore. Fish leaped from the water and the brothers ducked their heads as the prow of the boat grounded itself in the rough gravel and lurched to a stop beneath the overhang of stone. They crawled out, too weak to stand—even if there had been room enough beneath the great boulders.

"We must pull ... " Blue Hawk gasped, trying to take the lead as he had always done in the past.

" ... our boat under the rocks," Red Hawk said.

They grabbed each side, trying to drag the dugout farther under the leaning boulders, but it was wedged between a buried piece of driftwood and another rock. Red Hawk tried to pry it free with his canoe paddle. The tough shaft bent and then the blade snapped, leaving him holding only the long handle of the paddle.

Suddenly there was a loud splashing of water, almost as deafening as a great clap of thunder. There was not enough time to save the boat and their own lives. Red Hawk scrambled back on his hands and knees, deeper under the overhang, trying to pull Blue Hawk with one hand and still holding the useless sharp-splintered shaft of the paddle with the other. But Blue Hawk tripped and his legs sprawled back behind him just as the forehead of the Walking Hill struck the overhanging rock, making it tremble. The long, snakelike nose of the great beast reached beneath the overhang and caught hold of one of Blue Hawk's ankles.

As Angry Face worked her paddle, it was hard for her to keep her eyes and her mind forward. No man had ever spoken to her with such warmth as this one called Sparrow. It had been hard for her not to laugh at his antics, too. He was just like a squirrel, as quick and as charming as that small, agile animal. It was clear to her that, for some reason, he was showing her the kind of interest that she had seen other young men show the girls of her village, but never her. Never before her. And the way he said the name she had given him, the first name that had come into her mouth. River Woman. The way he said it was so pleasant. ...

But, she thought, a thought as bitter to her mind as the taste of a raw acorn, *one clear look at my own scarred face will be enough to make the smile on his face fade away and the tone of his voice change.*

So she kept her eyes and her mind forward. She would think only of what they would do when they reached the Great Falls. What Sparrow had told her—as hard as it was to be-lieve—had given her hope for the first time that the great beast, the hill that walked, might indeed be defeated. But so many things would have to happen in the way the deep-seers had envisioned. And even those who see deeply cannot say what will happen with any more certainty than one can point to the exact spot where a maple seed will land as it spins toward the ground.

"River Woman," Sparrow said, "look ahead toward the sunrise side of the river. See the smoke? That is our fishing place."

Angry Face squinted her eyes against the reflection off the water of the bright light from the Day Traveler, already moving down toward the tops of the trees. She listened hard with her keen ears, but could hear nothing more than the sounds of the river, the calls of a few birds, the thin crackling of the still-distant fires. She lifted one hand to shade her vision and made out, just below the rising column of smoke, what looked to be drying racks for fish on the shore, just above the slant of dark stone that flowed into and cradled the rippling small waterfalls of the Long River's best fishing spot. She drew in a quick whistling breath.

"It has been here," she said, her voice heavy as a stone. "Its marks are on the land."

Cautiously, they brought the dugout in toward the shore. They saw the ruined fish racks and the scattered fires, a thin plume of smoke still rising from one of them.

"Wait," Sparrow said. "I will see what has happened."

Angry Face put out a hand to stop him. Her own heart was beating so hard in her ears that she thought she would go deaf.

But Sparrow was too quick. He flipped out into the water and dove like an otter, coming up onshore with a little leap. He began to run back and forth—stopping, kneeling, rising again, going down the bank to the water's edge, then up again onto the rocks and the soft earth farther up on the shore toward the gray alder trees. Then, just as quickly, he was back at the water's edge, diving in, coming back up into the boat where Angry Face looked at him, one hand holding her long hair across her face, the other still grasping the paddle. It seemed as if he had done it all in less than a handful of heartbeats.

"This is what the tracks say to me," he said, using his hands to help his voice tell the story. "My friends were there and there, feeding the fire. The big animal crept as close as it could through the alders, then it charged at them. But they leaped aside—there! They reached their boat and went down the Long River. I do not think it caught them because it followed into the river, and its tracks do not come out anywhere near here. It followed them in the river."

"And now," Sparrow said, his tone of voice showing how pleased he was with himself, "now we follow, too, to the Great Falls."

CHAPTER FORTY-FOUR
ABOVE THE GREAT FALLS

Young Hunter watched from the top of the cliff above the Great Falls as the Ancient One and Mikumwesu made their way to the place they had chosen. He had been to this place before. Yet he had never been here. He had done this before. Yet he had never done this. Once again he was walking in the footsteps of a legend; yet when he looked ahead, he saw no clear trail ahead of him. It was as before, when he traveled far to meet the Ancient Ones and keep them from coming to the Dawn Land. Yet this was not happening in a faraway place, but in the places where he had grown up, close to the villages and the trails he had walked as a small child. Instead of his going out to meet the danger, it had come to him.

According to Bear Talker and Medicine Plant, he had learned much during the seasons that had passed since his return to the Dawn Land. Yet he felt no wiser, no more certain of himself. Was it always this way? Even when he truly became a deep-seeing person, would he still be so uncertain so often?

Then he smiled. He recognized the voice speaking within his mind. It was the voice of the little boy who wanted simple and clear answers and expected his grandfather and grandmother always to be there to give them to him. Young Hunter picked up a single leaf from the ground. It was an oak leaf, but there were no oak trees close to this place that looked down over the high falls, white and churning as boiling fat. So this oak leaf had traveled with him, caught in his hair or on his leggings, to fall again in this place. Everywhere he went he brought something of the past with him and yet every place was always new. *Everything is connected in some way. Everything is part of the circle of life.*

That was what Medicine Plant had told him. "When you see as we see, you will understand that you cannot understand everything. Then you will understand."

Agwedjiman whimpered softly. Young Hunter turned his head very slowly and found himself facing Medicine Plant's face, no more than a hand's width from his own. Willow Woman stood with her, a smile on her face at having managed to creep up this close without being heard.

"It is time," Medicine Plant said, "to make the fires."

River Woman held a hand up and Sparrow stopped paddling. He listened, but heard nothing. River Woman, though, lifted up one hand and pushed the hair back from around her ear. Sparrow saw with relief that her ear was a beautiful ear, the perfectly formed ear of a human being. With all that had happened he had found himself wondering if she was truly a human woman or only one of the animal people disguising herself.

The fact that she had taken such care to keep everything but her eyes hidden beneath her thick dark hair had begun to remind him of the old story of the girl who would not marry any of the young men in her village; even the men who came to court her from other villages were not good enough. At last, a big, very good-looking stranger came. He was so good-looking, with thick black hair, that she almost married him.

But the stranger always kept his ears hidden below his hair, and she became suspicious. When he came to sit beside her when all of the people were around the fire, she asked him to lean close so that she could whisper to him. As he leaned close, she asked him to push his hair back from his ears. He was reluctant to do as she asked, but she kept insisting. It was well that she did. When he finally pushed his hair back from his ear, she saw that his ear was not a human ear at all. It was black and covered with fur. Thus, she realized that he was a bear pretending to be a person.

River Woman cupped her hand around her ear, focusing her hearing ahead of her, and leaned toward the water, trying to hear around the bend in the river ahead where the two great rocks slanted out over the near bank.

"I hear it," she said very softly. "It is angry."

Sparrow listened. He could hear something now, too. The sound of water splashing, like the sound of great rocks falling into the water—or heavy feet striking the surface of the river.

Sparrow slowed the dugout with his paddle, guiding it so that they veered into the very middle of the river, where it was deepest, as they rounded the bend. From the stories River Woman had told him of the Walking Hill, the great stiff-legged bear, he had thought himself prepared for what he would see, but what he saw—no more than two spear casts away—frightened him.

The great beast was there and it was larger than he had imagined it to be. Heavy-shouldered, it stood on four long legs and was tall as a tree and massive as a hill. As it moved back and forth, half in and half out of the river, the thick hair that hung about its body shook like sheets of gray moss. As big as it was, it moved as quickly as an angry bear. Its two long teeth looked to be three times the length of a man's body, and below them its long nose moved with the suppleness of a snake, reaching now like an arm under the slanting rocks at the river's edge. Sparrow felt a lump in his throat like a piece of bone. Behind the monster, broken like a birch bark basket stepped on by a careless child, floating upside down, was half of a dugout canoe. Sparrow recognized it from the design burned into its prow. It was the canoe of Red Hawk and Blue Hawk.

Suddenly the huge animal pulled its long nose back from under the rock and reared up on its hind legs. It screamed with anger and pain as it shook something free—a tiny stick that had been stabbed into the very end of that long nose. The stick flew, spinning through the air and landing next to the dugout in which Sparrow and River Woman sat. It was the broken-off shaft of a cedar wood canoe paddle, its splintered end red with the blood of the great beast.

River Woman stood up in the front of the dugout and shouted. Her shout was so loud that it could be heard even above the Walking Hill's long, terrible cry.

Sparrow shook his head. He had been wondering if they might be able to float unnoticed down the river before the monster saw them. That would not happen now. The great beast had heard what River Woman shouted.

"My enemy! I am here!"

And it turned, its feet throwing up great plumes of water, giant feathers of water on every side, so that it disappeared for a moment in the water which rose all around it like a wall. Sparrow took another deep breath. It moved so quickly! And the way it moved, with such anger and purpose, told him that it had recognized River Woman's voice. Sparrow was not a deep-seer, but he felt the red wave of the animal's hatred wash over him. It intended to allow nothing to prevent it from crushing them. It would never stop until it had done so. Its hatred made Sparrow feel weak in the center of his being.

The great creature came charging at them, its long nose raised up, splashing through the river. It screamed, a scream like a blending of the cry of the eagle and the howl of the storm wind. It would soon be upon them. But River Woman still stood in the canoe, shouting at it as it came closer, through water that would have been over a man's head but barely came to the creature's belly.

How deep is the river here? Sparrow thought frantically, trying to remember if he ever dove into the place to test its depth. If the river did not grow very deep soon, the creature would not be slowed. They were not moving away from the huge animal but drifting with the current toward it. He began to paddle backward, and as he did so, River Woman seemed to realize what was happening. She sat and began to work her own paddle, turning them away from the oncoming monster as they began to move.

But the Walking Hill was almost upon them now, even though it was slowing down in the deeper water, having finally reached the place where the depth was greater than even its long legs. It was almost close enough to touch them with one final surging stride in the water. It reached out its long nose in a motion that seemed to Sparrow to come down toward them as slowly as a step taken in a dream. It struck—and just missed the stern of the dugout canoe, and the resulting wave of water pushed them forward. Then they were clear of it, leaving the great creature behind.

Sparrow paddled harder than he had ever paddled before, but as he did so, his memory showed him what was ahead. Their passage would soon be slowed by the sandbar and the rocks just above the Great Falls—and the falls themselves were impassable by dugout.

CHAPTER FORTY-FIVE
AT THE FALLS

As Young Hunter crouched to start the first fire, he felt something brush gently against his knee. He looked down. It was one of the front paws of Pabesis. The big young dog was looking at him in that way which made Young Hunter feel he was looking again into the eyes of the dog this young one had been named for, the dog that gave its life to save the strange man called Holds the Stone.

"My friend," Young Hunter said, "you know what is coming to us?"

Pabesis continued to look at him with the knowing a dog can hold in its eyes, a look that speaks at least as much as words. Then he looked up the river and whined.

Young Hunter understood. "Go, my friend," he said. "But do not give your life away again."

Pabesis wheeled, leaped over the long pile of dry brush that would soon make a wall of fire, and disappeared along the upriver trail.

Sparrow looked back. The great animal was following them along the bank of the river, on the sunset side. On either side the hills had risen as the Long River cut down into the valley, growing swifter in its deep main channel but shallower in the rest of its rocky bed. All too soon they would either reach

284

the place where their dugout could go no farther or they would have to stay in the swift-flowing channel that would carry them over the falls to be smashed on the rocks below. He did not need River Woman's keen ears to hear the roar of the Great Falls ahead of them.

The plan had been for them to lead the monster to this place, but Sparrow had not expected its speed to be so great that it would be this close to them.

"Now," Sparrow said, "we must pull for the opposite bank. Perhaps it will decide not to try to cross, or perhaps it will be swept over the falls by the current if it does try."

The boat grounded on the gravel before it reached the shore. Sparrow did not try to push it farther in. He leaped out of the boat. Lightened, it bobbed up and floated back. River Woman was ahead of him. She did not look back as the current pulled the empty dugout backward into the strong flow of the river, toward the falls; yet Sparrow could feel the hesitancy in her. The dugout was a living thing. It had carried and saved them, and to leave it this way, to allow it to go to its destruction, was a hard thing. Sparrow slipped the beaver lodge pouch from his belt and tossed it into the canoe.

"Take this with you, my friend," he said to the canoe. "*Wliwini.* We thank you."

He turned back toward River Woman, and as he did so he saw her face for the first time. The look on it was so caring—so moved was she as she saw what he did to thank the canoe—that it brought a catch to his throat. But as quickly as he saw her face—and thought how fine a face it was, despite what seemed to be a scar to one side of her mouth—she pulled her long hair across it, leaving him with only the memory.

The bank was steep and rocky, and the place where the brush had been piled to make a line of fire was uphill from them where the ground leveled off again. Sparrow could smell the first smoke, and as he smelled it, he saw it begin to rise in several places, all the way from the lip of the falls back along the upriver trail to the place where the river arced and disappeared. He looked toward the opposite bank. He could see not only smoke, but also the fires burning there. But what he saw that made him turn and push River Woman ahead of him up the bank was that the great beast, the Walking Hill, was more than halfway across the deep, swift-flowing channel and was not being swept away.

Mikumwesu and the Ancient One waited quietly in the place the little man had chosen just below the lip of the cliff above the Great Falls. The Ancient One held in his hand the long spear he had fashioned from the tough trunk of a tall dead cedar. It was three times the length of a tall man, but he held it between two fingers as if it were no heavier than a hollow reed.

The little man remembered the night before around the fire with Young Hunter. The roaring fire's heat had begun to melt the cold in the gray giant's heart. As they sat there, Young Hunter had begun to speak in the clear, soft voice of a storyteller. He told a story that had been given to him by his grandmother, a story of a terrible being shaped like a man with a skin as hard and cold as ice. That being had caught humans and eaten them. So it went until the ice-hearted being came to a lonely lodge where a wise woman sat alone. It looked inside, but the woman did not scream or show fear. Instead, she invited the monster into her lodge and called him Grandfather. "Sit by my fire," the woman said, and the monster did so. She piled more and more wood on the fire and the wigwom grew very hot. Then, in the heat of the lodge, the cold began to melt from the monster, and it turned back into a tall old man, a grandfather who would never again harm the people.

When Young Hunter finished his story, the eyes of the gray giant had changed. The fear and the awful hungers of loneliness had melted from the gray giant. Some of Mikumwesu's own loneliness had been lessened as well. He held in his heart the memory of the words Young Hunter had spoken to him again.

"I will help you look for your own people."

The Ancient One lifted his head and sniffed the air. Mikumwesu had smelled it, too: smoke. It had begun to happen, but it was not yet the moment for them to act. Mikumwesu placed a small hand on the gray giant's arm and patted it twice. Not yet. Not yet.

Walking Hill struggled against the pull of the current in the Long River's heart. It pushed against him with a force he had never felt before, and each step he took was harder than the one before. There was a weakness in him now that he had not felt before. Though his pain was not less from the spear head lodged in his jaw, he did not notice it with the same sharpness.

But he did not give up. The hated female being was there ahead of him, and it seemed as if all the pain, all the agony he carried with each breath, was concentrated in her, and he knew that to crush her would be to crush all those things that brought the waves of pain. He was out of the deep water now, and the bed of the river was firm beneath him. Another stride and he was free of the water's embrace. There were two of them climbing ahead of him, crawling between the stones. The stones were of many sizes, some as large as the nests of the small beings, but he began to climb, brushing aside some of the larger stones with his long nose, levering others away with his great teeth, making a path for himself, his wide feet finding their way up on the treacherous footing of the rocks.

River Woman began to turn toward the upriver trail when they reached the top of the slope, but Sparrow grasped her arm, guiding her through the smoke that was billowing down toward them, knowing the way to go.

"This way," he said. "We must go above the falls."

The Walking Hill had been slowed by the rock-strewn slope, but it was still close enough to catch them if they did not move even faster now. The fires were burning all along the slope above the trail, moving down toward them. Somewhere behind those fires was Young Hunter, closing the trap with smoke and flame. So they ran together toward the high place above the falls, and even though red-eyed death was not far behind them, Sparrow thrilled at the thought of running with River Woman's hand in his.

Sparrow looked up, his eyes smarting from the swirling smoke. There was a place ahead, just beyond the high point above the Great Falls, where they could scramble down a trail that cut across the cliff, a trail so difficult, so steep and narrow that the monster could not follow them. As he looked, his ankle turned on a loose rock and he fell, letting go of River Woman's hand.

"Run," he shouted to her. His foot was twisted and caught now in a fold in the stone. "Do not stop."

But she did not run. She turned back and leaned over him, her face next to his, her arms around him as she lifted him. His foot came free and he found himself upright in her embrace. Sparrow tried to break free, to push her on ahead of him, but she would not let go. His ankle was weak, but if he leaned against her he could still climb. Smoke was all around them as they struggled the remaining distance up to the trailhead. There, Sparrow turned his head to look back.

The gray smoke just below them solidified into a looming wall. Huge white teeth glistened and two small red eyes stared down with hate. River Woman shoved Sparrow aside, and as he fell back to the rocky earth he saw the long nose of the great beast strike her in the face, driving her over the edge of the cliff. The Walking Hill screamed, a terrible cry that froze Sparrow as he lay there. A huge foot, a foot that seemed as large as a lodge, lifted over him, and he knew he was about to be crushed like an ant that has strayed into the path of a moose.

Suddenly a big dog was next to him, growling and then leaping toward the great animal's side, drawing its attention away from Sparrow.

"Pabesis," Sparrow shouted. "Get back."

But the dog did not get back. It circled and growled; it darted in, snapping at the great animal's legs like a deerfly buzzing at a moose. The dog's eyes were on the long teeth of the monster as Pabesis ran in and then out again, dodging the killing blow that those great white spears could deliver. The great beast shuffled back, shaking the stones beneath it as it circled to strike at the dog now barking at its flanks.

Sparrow edged his way toward the cliff where River Woman had fallen. It was the very place where the small trail he had planned for them to take led down to the water. He looked down. River Woman had fallen onto that trail. She had been stunned by the blow, but she had not fallen far. Perhaps she had slowed her fall with her hands as she slid down the slope. Now she was partway down, on her knees on a lip of stone above the boiling waters at the base of the falls.

Limping, Sparrow began to climb down the trail. He heard a thud, something hard hitting flesh and bone, and a yelp that was suddenly cut off. He did not look back. He had to reach River Woman before she fell. She turned her head up toward him and her hair fell back from her face. But he could not see any part of her face. All that he could see was blood.

"River Woman," he shouted, trying to make his voice heard above the roaring of the falls. "Do not move."

She reached a hand up—he was almost to her. And then, so slowly that Sparrow could not believe what he was seeing, she began to fall backward, back over the lip of the ledge, then vanished into the water below.

"*Nda!*" Sparrow shouted. "No!" Then, like a bird launching itself into flight, he leaped after her and disappeared into the foaming water. His last thought was a prayer that *Kwanitewk*, the Long River, would show them mercy.

Walking Hill looked down over the edge. He did not see either of the small beings. The snarling four-legged one had gone silent when he struck it aside, hurling it into the air with one blow of his long teeth. The smoke was all around him now, and he did not know which way to turn; he knew only that he must not go over the edge of the cliff, his memory still holding the image of his mother falling.

He turned just as the great spear was thrust against him. His thick hair turned it aside and it did not pierce deeply, but it was a blow stronger than any he had felt before. In the smoke, he made out the shape of a two-legged being, a gray being almost as large as he was. The gray giant stepped back and raised the spear again as Walking Hill screamed and charged.

CHAPTER FORTY-SIX
BELOW THE FALLS

From his vantage point on the hill above the river, Young Hunter had seen the beginning of the fight between the Ancient One and the beast as large as a walking hill, but he had seen it only dimly, through the smoke from a distance. He had seen the gray giant strike the beast with his long spear, and then he had seen it rush at him with such speed that nothing could turn it aside. The two had seemed to become a single many-legged giant animal, twisting and falling, and then they had been lost from his sight.

Medicine Plant and Willow Woman had joined him as he stood there, looking down and waiting for the smoke to clear. He could not see what had happened to Sparrow and the woman who had climbed up the slope with him from the river, just ahead of the Walking Hill. He would not be able to tell if they had succeeded in reaching the narrow trail down the cliff, as they had planned, until he reached the spot where the battle had taken place. He was afraid they had not escaped. The great beast had been so close to them. It had moved with such power that it had been both terrible and beautiful to his eyes.

Now, as the three of them neared that place, Young Hunter felt a fist clench in his stomach. There, lying sprawled among torn bushes, was the body of Pabesis. He started toward the dog, but Medicine Plant put a hand on his shoulder.

"I will see if anything can be done," she said. "Look for the others."

Young Hunter took Willow Woman's hand. He felt that he needed her strength if he was going to continue to stand. How could this happen again?

"My husband," she said, in a voice firmer than he knew his would be if he tried to speak, "let us see what has happened."

They walked to the edge of the cliff and looked down. There, on the rocks below them at the edge of the white water of the falls, was the body of the huge animal. A great spear was thrust into its throat and one of its long teeth lay broken by its side. In death it no longer looked so large or so terrible. The mist from the falls circled its body and its thick gray fur sparkled with a hundred rainbows.

Young Hunter shaded his eyes with one hand and looked hard. There was nothing to be seen of the Ancient One. Nothing to be seen of Sparrow or the woman.

"Look," Willow Woman said. She pointed with her lips down the river. Where the water below the falls grew calm and formed a pool, a dugout canoe was drawn up on the shore. A man knelt beside it, cradling the body of a woman in his arms.

CHAPTER FORTY-SEVEN
FACES

Medicine Plant crawled out of the small sweat lodge that she and Bear Talker had built next to the pool below the Great Falls of the Long River. Her face lit by the fire that burned brightly in front of the lodge, she was surrounded by billowing steam and the smell of the strong herbal tea that had been poured onto the stones. The tea had been made not of one single plant, but of several kinds, each adding its own power to help with the healing that was needed. At one point, Sparrow thought he caught the scent of strawberries; at another, the familiar odor of gold thread—the mouth medicine. The little lodge had shaken many times while they were within it, and the voices that spoke did not seem to have been either Medicine Plant's or River Woman's. Sparrow had waited anxiously, caring for the fire as the dusk turned into darkness.

Now, as Medicine Plant turned and reached back within the lodge, he was even more anxious. More than a moon had passed since Medicine Plant had begun to treat River Woman's wounds, but he was not sure how the healing had gone. And he was worried. Although the wounds were on her face, it did not matter to him if there were scars. What he had seen and felt in River Woman had been deeper than the surface of her skin. He had heard it in her voice and seen it in her eyes. He had felt it in the strength of her hands as she had pushed him aside, saving his life. He had understood then that they had been chosen to be with each other and that his searching was over.

But what if the scars on her face made her feel the anger and confusion that he now realized had been hers for many winters before he had met her? Medicine Plant had told him the story of how badly River Woman had been treated when she was burned as a child. Even after hearing that story, he could not imagine that the name Angry Face had ever been hers. He wanted to run forward and help bring River Woman out of the healing lodge, but Medicine Plant had told him to wait, wait until River Woman spoke to him. He fluttered his hands as if they were the wings of a small bird.

Medicine Plant crawled backward, the strong hands of River Woman held firmly in her own. It was, indeed, like a child being born, brought out of the old womb of the earth from the healing lodge. Now, her face covered by her long black hair, River Woman's head came out, and her shoulders. She was weak from the medicine and the heat and she could not stand. Sparrow trembled, but did not move. He clutched the beaver medicine bundle more tightly in his hands. It was a gift that had carried the dugout through the Great Falls and left it there to rescue them both from the foaming water. If he held out his hand and closed his eyes, he could still feel the smoothness of the wooden dugout against his hand as his head broke the surface of the foaming pool while he clutched River Woman's limp body.

Medicine Plant stood slowly and walked away into the forest, leaving them alone in the small clearing. Somewhere from deep in the trees, even though it was long after the time when the birds sing for the end of the day, a hermit thrush warbled its long, lilting song.

Then, sitting back against the lodge, River Woman lifted up both her hands and pushed back her hair. Sparrow looked at her. The scars left on her face were not large; perhaps they had never been large. But Sparrow did not see scars. He saw only the smile on River Woman's face, that and her arms held out to gesture him into her embrace.

Mikumwesu sat on a boulder below the great falls, his bare feet in the water of the Long River. The distant ones far overhead, the little stars, reflected in the clear pool in front of him. Behind him, a great pile of stones covered all that remained of the body of the Walking Hill. Many of those stones were too large for one man—or even several men—to lift. Mikumwesu remembered how he had watched from his hiding place in the cedar trees near the top of the Great Falls as all of the tall people came to marvel at the Walking Hill where it lay below the falls. They marveled, too, at the great spear which was still thrust so deeply into the giant animal that no one could dislodge it. The deep-seeing people had spoken words as they stood next to the great beast, placed an offering beside the river, and then carefully lifted and carried off the broken-off part of one of the Walking Hill's teeth.

Some of the People of the Bear had spoken of how the next morning they would return to start skinning it. Mikumwesu smiled as he remembered how, when the tall people came back the next day, they found that the great spear had been removed and the Walking Hill buried so deeply beneath the boulders that it could no longer even be seen. Those Bear Village People had then listened very closely to the words that Bear Talker spoke to them as they stood uneasily by that stone cairn. Then they had begun their journey back up the Long River to rebuild their villages, and, this time, they would remember to give thanks to the animals.

Mikumwesu swung his feet back and forth in the water. Soon his nighttime friends would arrive and they would play. He looked at the river and then he looked across it, toward the mountains. Beyond them was *Petonbowk*, the Waters in Between. His new friend, the tall one called Young Hunter, had told him of that lake. Young Hunter had traveled across it before, and he thought that in the lands beyond they might find more of Mikumwesu's people. "Sometime, in the coming season, when the days are long," Young Hunter had told him, "we will travel there to look for your people."

Mikumwesu closed his eyes and thought of that journey to come. He pictured those wide waters in his thoughts, and as he did so, another thought came to him. Something moved deep within the waters of that lake. It would mean danger for them.

Small feet rattled the pebbles of the bank of the river. His friends had arrived. Mikumwesu opened his eyes with delight as a family of raccoons greeted him with soft, chirring cries and then, swarming over the little man, happily began to wrestle with him.

Young Hunter looked at the log. He could see the face of the Ancient One in its grain. It had come to him the night before as he slept, not voiceless, as the Ancient One had been, but speaking in a way he could understand.

It was quiet as Young Hunter sat there, looking into the shape that looked back at him from the wood. In the lodge behind him, his grandparents and Willow Woman were sleeping. He could hear their breathing. Two dogs were curled at Willow Woman's feet. Agwedjiman was in his usual place, close to the door, with Danowa beside him in the doorway, but Pabesis was not with them. The young dog, who had been thrown aside by the blow from one of the Walking Hill's long teeth, was sleeping in his new favored spot. His wounds almost healed, Pabesis slept right between Sweetgrass Woman and Rabbit Stick, with one of the old man's arms around him.

Next to Rabbit Stick, as tall as a man and leaning against
the wall of the lodge, was the broken tooth of the Walking
Hill. Although they could not be seen in the darkness, the
storytelling shapes that Rabbit Stick had begun to etch into
its ivory surface with his stone blade told of all that had
happened. The Walking Hill's path of destruction, the
flight of the Bear People and their return to rebuild their
villages back up the Long River, the coming of Mikumwesu
and the courage of the young people who faced the terrible
being, and the last battle between the gray giant and the
Walking Hill—they were all there, a spiral of story about the
great tooth.

Djidjis, the baby whose eyes showed that he knew more
than his mouth could yet speak, was not in their lodge.
Medicine Plant and Bear Talker had taken back their child.
The day might come when, as the deep-seeing woman said,
Young Hunter and Willow Woman would take the little one to
raise him as their son, but that time was not yet. The way
Medicine Plant held their baby close and talked softly to him—
when she thought no one else was listening—made it clear that
the day for that would not be soon.

Tonight Young Hunter had talked long with Red Hawk
and Blue Hawk until they, too, had finally grown tired and
returned to their small wigwom close to the fish racks, which
were now heavy with salmon. Above Young Hunter's head the
small stars circled, dancing in the great sky. On a branch near
the lodge, Talk Talk, the crow, perched with his head under
one wing. It was quiet, so quiet that the only sounds to be heard
were the soft hiss of the fire and the distant reassuring voice of
Kwanitewk, the Long River.

And in that quiet, Young Hunter also heard that voice
speaking—not from the woods around him, not from the
earth or the sky, not even from the Long River, which kept
moving through the night as faithful to its task as the stars and
the Grandmother Moon in the Sky Land. The voice that spoke

to him came from all those directions and also from within himself, from the center of his dreams.

You will see me again, the voice said. It was the voice of the last of the Ancient Ones, the last of the gray giants. *I will watch over your people. I will help you to guard them.*

Young Hunter sat listening for a long time before he began to carve, bringing the face from his dream out of the wood, toward the light of another new day.